BOOKS BY

Brenda Adcock
=====================

Pipeline

Reiko's Garden

Redress of Grievances

The Sea Hawk

Tunnel Vision

Soiled Dove

The Other Mrs. Champion

The Chameleon

Brenda Adcock

Quest Books by Regal Crest

Texas

ISBN 978-1-61929-102-7

First Printing 2013

9 8 7 6 5 4 3 2 1

Cover design by Donna Pawlowski

Published by:

Regal Crest Enterprises, LLC
229 Sheridan Loop
Belton, TX 76513

Find us on the World Wide Web at
http://www.regalcrest.biz

Printed in the United States of America

Acknowledgments

This story began in the middle of the night over sixteen years ago and languished in the bottom of a file cabinet for years, gathering dust bunnies and largely forgotten. In one of my exceedingly rare moments of intensive housekeeping combined with an annual need to dispose of possessions I haven't seen or touched for an extended period of time, I finally re-discovered this incomplete manuscript. Unfortunately, I suffered a stroke three or four years ago. By the time I found my way back to *The Chameleon* I'd forgotten much of what I intended to do to finish the manuscript. With the encouragement of friends and a supportive partner, I was finally able to finish the long journey.

I would like to thank my beta readers, Carol, Chris, and Patty. I have to give a special thanks to my editor, Patty Schramm for her patience. Without the support of my publisher, Cathy Bryerose, none of my stories would see the light of day. I am grateful every day for her friendship. Thank you to the readers for their support over the years. Last, but never least I would like to thank my partner, Cheryl. She has been very patient with me and understands my compulsion to be alone and visit the worlds my characters inhabit.

To Cheryl —
for always giving me what I need.

Chapter One

CHRISTINE SHAW WAS tired of being awakened in the middle of the damn night. Why couldn't criminals fucking kill one another after the sun was up and sleep like regular people at night? But, no, there was always some asshole that just couldn't wait for the sun to rise before doing the dastardly deed. And on the day after Christmas to boot. Wasn't that sacrilegious or something? But most criminals weren't particularly religious, let alone considerate. She rubbed her eyes to clear her vision as she drove down the late December rain-slicked streets between her apartment in the Village and Midtown. Any other time she might have enjoyed watching the lights reflect off the wet streets, an Impressionistic painting come to life. But life wasn't Chris Shaw's job. Investigating how it ended was.

Chris parked her black Trans-Am in front of the upscale Montclair Hotel in the theater district of Midtown Manhattan. She pulled her overcoat closer around her neck as she stepped from her vehicle. She didn't know why she bothered. She was already cold and wet and in a foul mood that further wetness wasn't likely to improve. She blinked against the pellets of sleet, not surprised to see people still walking quickly up and down the sidewalks and ducking into businesses catering to late night customers. The flashing lights that lined Times Square lit up the busy area a block away.

She hadn't been asleep for more than an hour when the call came in. She'd found someone just as lonely as she was who hadn't wanted to spend the day after Christmas alone. Jill had picked a great time to leave her. Happy fuckin' Holidays. Chris needed to feel something, even if it was superficial and only lasted for a few hours. There were times she would have settled for a few minutes. It had taken her longer than expected to get her overnight companion dressed and poured into a cab. She probably should have gotten the woman's name, but didn't expect to see her again. She had turned out to be one of those gifts that was beautifully wrapped and looked tempting on the outside, but after you opened it you could see yourself in the return line. Chris' old job back in Dallas was looking better and better every damn day.

She nodded at the uniformed officer huddled under the lighted entry of the hotel and wiped her black Ropers on the mat before signing in. It didn't look like the scene of a crime. Deep red

Oriental carpeting covered the floor and was plush enough for an elephant to stomp across without being heard. At least someone had died in a classier place than an alley that reeked of urine and used diapers. Chris approached a second officer near the elevator who appeared to be engaged in an animated discussion with a dapper-looking older man. The officer looked relieved when he saw her approaching. The man he had been speaking to was tall, on the skinny side, and had a hawkish nose. His gray hair was slicked back away from his long forehead. Chris would have been worried if it were Halloween instead of Christmas. The guy was a dead ringer for Basil Rathbone. A shiver ran through her when the man turned his light brown eyes toward her.

"I'm sure Detective Shaw will be able to help you with your problem, Mr. Rayburn," the officer said.

"What problem?" Chris asked as the officer slid a key card into the slot next to the elevator.

"The Montclair is concerned about the negative publicity this—incident—might create," Rayburn said in a subdued voice.

Chris looked around the lobby. Despite the fact that it was after three in the morning, there were a few couples meandering around the lobby area.

"Well, I doubt the Montclair itself is too concerned, but the management might be a little worked up," Chris said in a soft Texas drawl as she looked up to see where the hell the elevator was.

Rayburn pursed his lips like he had just sucked a lemon and leaned toward her. His aftershave filled her nose, causing a stinging sensation. It reminded her of her father. She hated her father.

"I'm sure you understand how something of this nature might upset our guests, Detective."

"Well, Mr....uh..." Chris looked questioningly at the officer, rubbing her nose to drive the offensive fragrance away.

"Rayburn," the officer repeated.

Rayburn, Rathbone, not much difference, Chris thought with a half grin. "Well, Mr. Rayburn, murder should upset everyone, doncha think?" she said more loudly than necessary as the elevator finally opened. "Which floor again?"

"Penthouse," the officer said.

The elevator door had begun closing when Chris stopped it with her hand and said, "When the medical examiner gets here tell him to make sure the sight of his gurney doesn't upset anyone. And I'll need to speak to the hotel security people. This the only elevator to the top?"

The officer nodded and Chris stepped back allowing the door to slide shut. She leaned against the back of the elevator as soft canned music poured over her. *Damn! Were Steve Lawrence and Edie Gorme still alive?* She peeled off her tan overcoat and tossed it over her shoulder, frowning at her reflection in the shiny stainless steel of the elevator doors. She tried to make herself a little more presentable in the black, pleated-front Dockers, white turtleneck, and gray wool jacket that covered her rangy five-eleven frame. The rain had flattened her short black hair that usually swept rakishly across her forehead and she half-heartedly attempted to fluff it up with her fingers. Damn it all, at least try to look like a detective, she fussed at herself.

She was still adjusting her clothing when the elevator opened. The door to the penthouse suite, directly across from the elevator, stood open and Chris saw her partner, Carmen Sandoval, standing a few feet inside. She was talking to someone hidden from Chris' sight by the doorframe and taking notes that Chris was certain would be nearly verbatim and neatly written. Sandoval glanced toward Chris as she left the elevator and looked around the space between the elevator and the suite while she pulled a pair of latex gloves from her coat pocket and worked her fingers into them. Chris released the last glove with a snap and pulled a small notebook from the inside pocket of her jacket, flipping it open to a blank page. She drew a diagram of the entry area and wrote down what she saw. To her right was a door marked Fire Exit. She walked to it and pushed it open, taking note of the key card slot near the handle on the stairwell. To the right of the door was an alcove that held the fire alarm, fire extinguisher and a glass encased hose. Chris shivered. If there was one place she never wanted to be it was on the top floor of a burning building. By the time anyone was able to reach the damn hose she'd either be toast or a bloody grease spot on the sidewalk below. She shook her head. The collection of fire equipment was partially covered by two large pots holding healthy-looking ficus plants. Chris turned to face the door of the suite again. To her left was a huge window that allowed a breathtaking view of Times Square and part of the theater district. Two additional plants prevented anyone from wandering too close to the windows.

Chris looked into the plush suite and saw Sandoval looking at her. For some reason she couldn't help thinking that Carmen was surveying her attire. She let her eyes drift over Sandoval in return and shook her head. How the woman could be impeccably dressed at three in the damn morning had always been a mystery to Chris. As she entered the suite, Sandoval held a finger up toward the person she was questioning. "*Momentito, por favor,*" she said softly.

"Whatcha got, Carmen?" Chris asked as she shot a brief smile toward the plump fifty-ish Hispanic woman Sandoval had been questioning. The woman appeared nervous and beads of sweat had popped out on her forehead despite the cold weather outside.

"A female, approximately thirty-five to forty. Looks like the victim of a blow to the head by a blunt object," Sandoval reported.

"You a forensic expert now?" Chris asked as she unwrapped a stick of gum and shoved it in her mouth. She noticed a blackish-brown greasy spot on her glove covering her right hand. She rubbed her fingers together before stepping back into the penthouse entryway. She walked to the stairwell door and squatted down, pulled a penlight from her pocket, and looked at the underside of the bar used to push the door open. She peeled her latex glove off inside out and shoved it in her jacket pocket as she drew out a replacement.

"She find the victim?" Chris asked as she returned to the apartment and motioned toward the older woman. She stuck her notebook between her teeth as she pulled the new glove over her hand. She motioned to a technician standing a few feet away.

"There's an unidentified substance on the stairwell door," she said when the man joined her. "Have it tested." She took the latex glove from her jacket pocket and handed it to him. "Same shit's on this glove."

"I'll mark it and send it to the lab," the man said.

"Have the photographer take a picture, too." She patted him on the shoulder before turning back to Carmen. "Sorry. So she found the victim?"

"Yeah. About an hour or so ago. Name's Angelina de los Angeles."

"You're shittin' me, right?"

"Not this time."

Chris looked around the opulent suite and blew out a long breath. "A little late for housekeepin', isn't it?" she asked.

"Says she came up and was gonna leave towels and stuff outside the door for the morning shift so they wouldn't have to lug them up here. Door was open so she came in."

"Where's the body?"

"About halfway down the hall leading to the bedroom."

"You get an I.D. yet?"

"Oh, yeah."

"Next of kin been notified?"

"Nope."

Chris knew Sandoval had already done all the preliminaries, but she still didn't feel fully awake. "How come you look so good this early in the mornin'?" she asked Carmen. "You sleep dressed or somethin'?"

"How come you look like shit? Why don't you let me take you

to see my uncle? He can fix you up with some real nice clothes. Not that home-on-the-range shit you call a wardrobe."

"Next time I feel the need to disguise myself as a Puerto Rican princess, maybe I'll take you up on that," Chris quipped.

"You definitely need a new woman."

"Just had one. Didn't help."

Sandoval laughed and turned back to her witness. Chris followed the sound of voices through the suite until she found where the body was lying. A police photographer was shooting crime scene photos as she entered the hallway. *Yes indeedy.* The victim was definitely a woman. She was naked and lying on her stomach, her body sprawled across the hallway. Blood spatter dotted the walls on either side of the short corridor. Her face was obscured by shoulder-length dark chestnut hair. While she waited for the photographer to finish, Chris jotted down anything else she noticed, and sketched a crude diagram of the apartment and position of the body.

The only thing on the woman's body was a ring that, Chris supposed, could be a wedding ring. The diamond looked pricey enough to pay Chris' rent for the rest of her life. Apparently robbery hadn't been a motive. The victim's French nails were well-manicured and elegant looking. One arm was extended above her head and the other level with her shoulder. She noted bruises on the woman's back and near her neckline. Sandoval had probably been right about a blow to the head. Thick, drying blood matted the woman's hair behind her right ear and formed a large sticky-looking pool on the carpet beneath her head. Chris squatted down for a closer look at the head wound.

She glanced down the hallway and noticed two or three of the pictures on the wall weren't hanging straight. She stepped carefully over the body, followed the hallway toward the only door between the body and the end of the hall, and wasn't surprised to find herself in a bedroom. The bed didn't look like it had been slept in, but the covers were bunched up in a couple of places, as if someone had been on it. Probably some big bucks call girl who pissed off her john, Chris thought. A silk robe was on the floor near the foot of the bed and an alarm clock was on the floor between the bed and nightstand. There might have been a struggle in the room, but it was hard to tell what might have been caused by a struggle and what might have been the result of overly-exuberant passion. Chris had been overly-exuberant a time or two, but didn't remember knocking anything over. Well, there was that glass of water once, but that had been the cat's fault. As Chris continued looking around, her thoughts were interrupted by a familiar voice behind her.

"You didn't touch anything, did ya, Tex?"

"No, Arthur," Chris said as she continued jotting down notes to herself.

Arthur Featherstone was a deputy medical examiner Chris had worked with many times. He was strictly no-nonsense about his work and Chris doubted that he regarded victims as people any more, which seemed appropriate since, technically, they no longer were.

"You check the vic yet?" Featherstone asked.

"I didn't touch her, Artie. Swear to God," Chris said, holding up the first three fingers of her right hand.

"I'm going to examine her first. Thought you might want to observe. After all, how many high profile cases do you get?"

"Just got here myself. Don't even know the victim's name yet."

"Well, come on. Let's see if she's who everybody thinks she is."

Chris followed him back into the hallway where Featherstone squatted down next to the body. His assistant was already in the process of bagging the woman's hands and feet and securing them with rubber bands.

"Looks like blunt force trauma to the right temporal area. The injury may have penetrated the skull," Featherstone observed as he looked at the wound on the lower right side of the woman's head. "You got all the photos you need?" he asked the photo tech over his shoulder.

"Yeah, I'm done for now," the man answered.

"Then let's roll her over, Joe," he said to his assistant

As Featherstone and his assistant repositioned the woman's arms and rolled her over, Chris noticed her body first. She appeared to have been in good physical shape and Chris' eyes involuntarily took in the smooth contours of flawless breasts, making her feel like a ghoulish voyeur. Featherstone brushed hair away from the victim's face.

"Recognize her?" he asked without looking up.

Chris pulled her eyes away from the woman's body long enough to look down at a face she knew well. Open, lifeless hazel-green eyes were turned toward her.

"Elaine Barrie," Chris said quietly.

"The great lady herself. Shame. I had tickets for her show next week," Featherstone groused. "Hope I can get a refund."

"What's that on her arm?" Chris asked, using her pen to point at a brownish-black substance on the victim's upper right arm.

"Can't tell for sure until I take a sample for the lab," Arthur answered.

While the deputy medical examiner performed a cursory

examination of Elaine Barrie's body, Chris remembered the last time she'd seen the beautiful, vibrant woman floating across the stage, enthralling the audience with the lyrics of a song that seemed to come from her very soul. Elaine Barrie was only a year or two older than Chris and as a teenager Chris had followed the woman's career. They had practically grown up together even though their lives couldn't have been more different. Chris blinked her brain back to the present as she stepped aside to make room for the gurney that would take the body away. It wasn't the type of transportation the victim had been accustomed to in life. Featherstone stood up and pulled off his gloves while his assistant and two other men deposited the body on the gurney and zipped the black body bag closed.

"Anything you can tell me, Arthur?" Chris asked.

"Besides the obvious? Apparently blunt force trauma. Unlikely she tripped and did that damage to herself, so possibly a homicide," Featherstone said. "I won't be sure until I get her on the table."

"Any sign of sexual assault?"

"Doesn't look like it, but you never know until—"

"You get her on the table," Chris finished for him. "How long you think she's been dead?"

"Based on the body temp maybe two or three hours. TOD was probably between eleven last night and two this morning, but don't quote me."

In less than thirty minutes, the penthouse suite was crawling with more forensic personnel. Chris knew they would cover every inch of the suite thoroughly and there wasn't much she could do except get out of the way and let them work. Re-entering the living room she found Carmen, who looked up from her notebook when Chris reached her.

"Do we have a next of kin?" Chris asked.

"A husband. Carl Janus. The suite is leased in his name."

"Where is he?"

"Probably at home."

"What's this place?"

"Looks like a love nest to me. The maid said the vic stayed here several nights a week. Usually, but not always, alone. All men."

"She know any names?"

"Wasn't introduced, but did mention that the victim was always nice to her."

A uniformed officer interrupted their conversation. "There's a security guard at the door, Detective. Said he was sent up by the manager."

"Tell him to meet us in the security office," Chris said.

Half an hour later, satisfied there was nothing else of interest in the victim's apartment, Chris and Carmen leaned against the wall of the penthouse elevator and watched the numbers slowly decrease until the doors opened into the main lobby. The uniformed officer guarding the penthouse elevator told them where the security office was located. Successfully avoiding the manager, they stepped into a public elevator and pushed the button for the second floor. An engraved metal sign guided them down a short carpeted corridor to another metal sign announcing they had located the "Hotel Security Office". Chris followed Carmen inside. The lighting in the front part of the office was dim, but brighter lights poured through another door into a larger room near the rear. "Hello," Chris called out. "NYPD."

An older man with a military buzz-cut limped into the doorway. He extended his hand with a frown. "Ray Haggarty, Chief of Security," he said. He seemed to be in relatively good physical condition, despite his noticeably gimpy leg.

"Detectives Shaw and Sandoval, Midtown," Chris replied. "We need to see the hotel security tapes from last night and early this mornin'." Haggarty motioned them to follow when he turned and made his way across a large room. Two bored-looking uniformed men sat at consoles on the far side of the room, gazing at a series of monitors in front of them. Each monitor's screen was divided into four sections.

"What areas do your cameras cover?" Carmen asked.

"Two cameras sweep the main lobby and counter at overlapping one minute intervals. A stationary camera covers the elevators, including the one to the penthouse. Those are the ones Jared over there is watching. Samuel is keeping an eye on the cameras that sweep the kitchen, laundry, and maintenance areas."

"Are there cameras in the hallways and elevators?" Chris asked.

"Not yet. Those will be included in phase two of the hotel's security upgrade. Sorry," Haggarty answered with a shrug. "By the time the whole system is on line a mouse won't be able to fart and get away with it."

"So for now we'll have to hope the parts already in place will help us out," Chris said as she squinted at the shifting scenes on the monitors.

"I had the guys make a copy of everything from about ten last night until you guys arrived," Haggarty said, picking up two CD cases and handing them to Chris. "One is the main lobby area and elevators and the other is the kitchen, laundry, and maintenance areas."

Chris took the plastic cases and passed them to Carmen.

"I know you have equipment that can handle those," Haggarty said. "When I asked for this equipment I made sure it would coordinate with police equipment."

Chris looked at him and asked, "Cop?"

Haggarty nodded. "Injured in the line of duty and took an early medical retirement. Took one in the lower back that didn't work out as well as the docs expected," he said with a smile. "But, hell, at least I'm still walking, even if I do resemble your basic penguin."

"Do you miss the streets?" Carmen asked.

"I used to, but my wife sure as shit don't. And it gives me a little extra time with the grandkids, ya know," he said over his shoulder.

"Did your people report anything unusual during the night?" Chris asked, getting back to her investigation.

"Just the normal stuff." Haggarty shrugged as he picked up a clip board. "A couple of vagrants looking for a warm place to curl up for the night."

"Had any problems with hotel thieves? Employees with sticky fingers? Anything like that?" Chris asked.

"We've had our eyes out for that. A couple of hotels in the area have reported some rooms broken into," Haggarty replied. "So far we've been pretty lucky."

"Any special security for the penthouse?"

"Just the elevator. It requires a key card."

"How does that work?"

"That elevator only goes to the penthouse. When it goes down to the lobby, it closes and automatically returns to the top. Only a key card for the penthouse can call it down again."

"Who had key cards to that suite?"

"We issued three cards to Miss Barrie, but I don't know who she might have given them to."

"What about former tenants?" Carmen asked.

Haggarty shook his head. "We change the key code every time there's a change in tenancy and, according to the manufacturer, the cards can't be duplicated."

"What about housekeeping?"

"There's a master key for housekeeping, maintenance, and security. There's a sign-out/sign-in log if anyone uses it."

"Where is that key located?"

"It's in a locked safe at the front desk."

"Were there ever any security problems that concerned Miss Barrie?"

"Well, once there was an obsessed fan who managed to get into her suite. Didn't turn out to be much. Almost felt sorry for the guy." Haggarty laughed.

"Why's that?" Chris asked.

"The guy was so awe-struck about meeting her up close and personal he just stood there with his mouth hanging open and couldn't get a word out. Miss Barrie refused to press charges against him so a security guard and I removed him peacefully and put him in a cab. She even gave him an autograph."

"He was *inside* the penthouse?"

"Yeah," Haggarty answered.

"How'd he get in?" Carmen asked.

"When we investigated we found out he was screwing one of our maids. Got a card from her. Used it to get in through the stairwell and into the apartment as well. Miss Barrie said nothing was missing, but I filed a report anyway. You never know."

"We'll need a copy of that," Chris said. She pulled a business card from her wallet and wrote a number on the back. "If you could fax that to us, I'd appreciate it. What about the housekeeper?"

"She's no longer with us."

"Any other access to that floor?"

"There's a door into the stairwell in case of fire. It can be pushed open for evacuation, but requires the key card to enter from the stairwell."

"Do the suite, elevator, and stairwell door record when the key card has been used?"

"Every time a key card is used it's recorded."

"I'll need a copy of the times any of those areas were accessed between ten last night and two this morning. So far it sounds like a secure floor," Chris said, blowing out a long breath. "Thanks." She extended her hand as she and Carmen prepared to leave the security office.

"Too bad about Miss Barrie," Haggarty said as he shook Chris's hand. "She was a real nice lady."

"You talk to her often?" Chris asked.

"A couple of times, but she was usually a late arriver and I leave about six. Sometimes I'd run into her when she was leaving to prepare for an evening performance."

"We got an address on the husband?" Chris asked as she and Carmen stepped into the corridor again.

"It's a Central Park West address. Uptown and upscale," Carmen answered.

"Well, let's wake him up and see how shook up he is."

Chapter Two

"YOU'RE PRETTY QUIET. You feeling okay?" Sandoval asked as Chris guided her car along Broadway between Midtown and Central Park West.

"Feelin' finer than peach fuzz," Chris answered.

Sandoval laughed out loud. "Where the hell do you get that shit?"

"What?"

"Finer than *peach fuzz*? Jeezus, Shaw!"

"Didn't get much sleep last night or this mornin' or whatever it is. Feelin' kinda blah."

"Probably the holiday blues," Carmen said. "Happens every year around this time."

"I moved here because Jilly convinced me I needed more excitement in my life and different scenery. Now the excitement is wearing thin, I have to dodge muggers in Central Park just to see a fuckin' tree, and Jill's flown off into the wild blue yonder with Captain Hot Pants."

"So go home. Ain't like we'd miss one lost little Texan," Carmen snickered.

Chris had to admit there were times when she was seriously homesick for the state she'd lived in most of her life. She had been perfectly content with the life she and Jill had made in Dallas. When Jill announced American Airlines was transferring her to New York for trans-Atlantic flights, Chris almost let her go alone. Probably should have considering how everything worked out between them. That had been nearly six years ago and the glamour and glitz of the "city that never sleeps" had worn off for Chris about five years earlier. She only stayed so she wouldn't have to hear her former partner at the Dallas PD say 'I told you so'. She was only forty, but living in New York made her feel much older.

IT TOOK CHRIS and Sandoval twenty minutes to gain admittance to the building listed as the home of Carl Janus and his wife, Elaine Barrie. The heavy security in the building made Chris long for the good old days when her parents thought nothing of leaving their doors unlocked and their windows open at night. The final door to Carl Janus's inner sanctum was opened by a man dressed in solid white, who appeared to be either a bouncer or a bodyguard. That, accompanied by platinum hair, cut in a Marine Corps crew cut, reminded Chris of a picture of an albino she had seen once on television.

"Can I help you?" the man asked suspiciously.

"I'm Detective Christine Shaw, NYPD, Midtown Homicide, and this is my partner, Detective Carmen Sandoval," Chris said, shoving her badge into the man's face. "We need to speak to Carl Janus."

"Mr. Janus is asleep."

"Well, wake him up," Chris insisted.

"Can't this wait until morning? Mr. Janus is quite ill."

"I'm afraid this can't wait," Sandoval said.

"Maybe I should call Mr. Janus's doctor first," the man said.

"And who, exactly, are you?" Shaw inquired.

"Mr. Janus's nurse, Ted Warner."

"What seems to be Mr. Janus's problem?" Sandoval asked.

"He has amyotrophic lateral sclerosis."

Chris looked at Sandoval and shrugged.

"You know, Lou Gehrig's Disease," Ted offered.

"Well, we have some bad news for him. Call his doctor if you need to, but one way or the other we're gonna speak with Mr. Janus...tonight," Chris stated forcefully.

Forty minutes later, while Chris and Sandoval cooled their heels on a couch in a room Warner identified as a study, a tall man with stylish salt-and-pepper hair entered the room. He was dressed in a three-piece suit and handed his overcoat to Ted as he approached them. Chris and Carmen rose to greet him.

"I'm sorry to keep you waiting. I'm Carl's personal physician, Robert Blankenship. What seems to be the problem, officers?"

"Mr. Janus's wife has been killed. We're here to notify him of that and find out if he can tell us anything that might help our investigation," Chris said.

"My God! Elaine has been killed? Was it a traffic accident?" Blankenship asked.

"NYPD doesn't assign detectives to traffic accidents, Doctor," Chris said.

"I can't believe this," Blankenship said, obviously stunned by the news. "I know Carl will be willing to help if he can, but I can assure you he won't be able to help much. He hasn't been out of this apartment in nearly six months."

"If you'd prefer," Sandoval said, "you can break the news to him. But we'll still need to ask him a few questions."

"He takes a sedative at night. It may take me a few minutes to wake him completely. Where was Elaine killed?"

"The Montclair," Chris said. "Do you know why she was there?"

"Carl took that suite for her about a year and a half ago. She rested there between shows and sometimes stayed overnight, I think," Blankenship offered.

Blankenship disappear down a hallway, followed closely by Ted Warner. Fifteen minutes later Chris was pacing restlessly around the study when Blankenship reappeared.

"You can come in now, Detectives," he said in a subdued voice.

The overhead light in Carl Janus's room was on and he had been propped up against pillows on his bed. Ted was combing Janus's hair in an attempt to make him more presentable. It was obvious to Chris from looking at the man's face that he had not taken the news of his wife's death well. She leaned over to Carmen.

"Why don't you interview the doctor and the nurse? I'll speak to Janus."

"Works for me," Sandoval said with a shrug.

She, Warner, and Blankenship left the room as Chris went to the side of Janus's bed.

"I'm very sorry for your loss, Mr. Janus," she began.

Tears formed in Janus's eyes and ran slowly down his face. "Thank you," he finally managed to get out through trembling lips. "Do you know who..."

"Not yet, but we'll find whoever was responsible. When was the last time you saw or spoke to Mrs. Janus?"

Janus smiled slightly. "No one calls her that, you know."

"I'm never sure what to call people with both a professional and a personal name, I'm afraid."

"It doesn't really matter now, I guess," Janus said, taking a shaky deep breath and exhaling slowly. "I saw her yesterday before she left for the theater. She called late last evening before I went to sleep."

"Do you know what time she called?"

"I'm not sure. Ted will know."

"Did she say why she was stayin' at the Montclair last night instead of comin' home?"

"No, but it's not unusual for her to stay there. She's always home by the time I wake up in the morning." Janus looked down at his hands.

"Other than personal things, what did you talk about?"

"She said the show went well, but she was getting tired of it. That's the problem with live stage work. Sometimes it's a blessing not to have a long run."

"Her show's been quite a hit."

"You've seen it?" Janus asked, looking up at Chris.

"Actually, sir, I've seen it a couple of times."

"She's phenomenal, isn't...wasn't she?"

"Yes, sir. Was there anything else?"

"She didn't say anything in particular, but I got the feeling there was something else on her mind. Just something in her voice, as if she was excited about something. When I asked her why, she said she had a surprise and would tell me when she got home this morning. She said she was tired after the last show. That was about it. We never talked long."

"Did she always call when she wasn't comin' home?"

"Yes. She didn't want me to worry about her."

"I hate to ask this, but were there any personal problems here at home?"

Janus smiled slightly. "You should be able to tell by looking at me, Detective, that we had at least one problem."

"Other than your medical condition, how was your relationship?"

Janus looked at Chris, his eyes misting over again. "I loved Elaine more than I knew it was possible for one human being to love another. She taught me what love was and I would have done anything to make her happy." Janus paused and looked at his hands again. "Every couple has bumps in their relationship, Detective. We certainly did. But despite that, she knew I loved her and I never had a reason to doubt that she loved me."

"How long were you and Mrs. Janus married?"

"Fifteen years. We celebrated our anniversary the week before Christmas."

"Do you know anyone she was havin' trouble with? Anyone with a grudge of some kind?"

"No. Everyone liked Elaine. She was one of those rare people who simply didn't make enemies."

"Can you give me the names of her closest associates? We'll need to speak to them."

"Elaine's closest friend is a woman named Della Summers. She's known Elaine longer than anyone I can think of. Her manager is Malcolm Gallagher, but the only tears he'll shed will be for the loss of his fifteen percent. I'm sure you'll interview the cast members in her show. I don't know all their names."

"Anyone else?"

"No. Before my illness we socialized quite a lot, but in the past year or so we've fallen out of touch with most of our casual friends."

"Hotel security said there were three key cards issued for Mrs. Janus's suite. We found one in the apartment. Do you know who might have the other two?"

"They're both here. Ted would only use one if it was an

emergency and I couldn't contact her."

Chris closed her notepad and slid it into her coat pocket. There was a light knock on the bedroom door and Blankenship stuck his head in the door.

"Come in, Rob," Janus said.

"I appreciate your help, Mr. Janus," Chris said.

"Will you let me know when you find who killed Elaine?" Janus asked.

"Yes, sir. I surely will."

"You must be from the Southwest. Maybe Texas," Janus said.

"How'd you know that?" Chris asked.

"I used to study dialects when I was acting. Texans have a habit of dropping the g from the end of their words."

Chris smiled. "Just lazy talkers, I suppose."

"FIND OUT ANYTHING interestin'?" Chris asked as she pulled away from the curb and settled into her seat.

"Blankenship said Janus will probably be dead in less than a year," Carmen said looking at her notes. "Was diagnosed with ALS a couple of years ago. It's not likely he killed his wife. According to the good doctor, Janus has virtually no use of his legs and minimal use of his left arm. Right arm is pretty much a decoration."

"Doesn't mean he couldn't have hired someone to do it. You see that big ape nurse of his?" Chris asked.

"Blankenship says the Januses were a devoted couple. Been married a long time."

"Did he say how she was adaptin' to his medical problem?"

"Just that she's been worried about the decline in his health recently. I mean, she knew he was gonna croak and all, but that don't mean she was looking forward to it. Apparently Blankenship was only the hubby's personal physician. He didn't treat the wife."

"Who's her doctor?"

"Dr. Clifford Purnell. I got his address."

"How old you figure Janus is?"

"Looks older than dirt. Could be the disease though."

"I asked Teddie before I left," Chris said. "Janus is sixty."

"So? That ain't that old."

"There's somethin' about a guy his age married to someone Elaine Barrie's age that creeps me out. He's old enough to be her father."

"Why would that bother you? I thought it was common practice 'down home' for good old boys to marry twelve-year-olds."

"Janus says there weren't any problems between him and his

wife, but I think he wasn't telling me everything," Chris said.

"Why would he lie?"

"I don't know. His problems had to have put some strain on their marriage. We got this young woman, good looking, married to this sick older guy who probably hasn't been able to get it up for over a year. You think she turned into a nun overnight?"

"Maybe she stocked up on batteries." Carmen shrugged. "You think she was prowling around?"

"What would you do?"

"I'd wait for him to bite the dust, collect the insurance, and *then* find a horny young stud."

"You wouldn't try to find another man before your hubby kicked off? She took that suite about the same time Janus's health started its nose dive and the maid did say she wasn't always alone."

"You shouldn't be surprised if he lied about that. Not likely he's gonna want the world to know if she was cheating on him. Besides, Blankenship said Janus rented the penthouse and the lease is in his name."

"He gave me the names of her best friend and her manager. Guess we could start with them in the mornin'." Chris glanced at her watch. "Make that in an hour or so."

"What about the people in her show?"

"Must be forty people in that. You might have to break out a new notebook."

"You seen her show?"

"Yeah. You?"

"Shit. It's hard enough keeping up with real life without cluttering it up with fantasyland," Sandoval said as she looked out the side window.

Chapter Three

CHRIS WALKED INTO the squad room carrying two Styrofoam food containers while balancing two large cups of coffee on top. She managed to make her way to her desk and set the stack down.

"One coffee with everything," she said handing a cup to Carmen. "And one scrambled with sausage and hash browns. Sans grits."

It had been after six by the time Shaw and Sandoval returned to their precinct and started filling out their preliminary reports on the demise of Elaine Barrie, the toast of Broadway. Looking for any excuse to avoid paperwork, Chris volunteered to run out for fast food breakfasts.

"Where's the hot sauce?" Carmen asked as she popped open her food container.

"Jesus, Carmen. Can't you eat one damn meal without that crap? Give your stomach a break this early in the mornin'," Chris said, sitting down across from her.

"Just hand it over," Carmen said, snapping her fingers at Chris.

Chris reached into her jacket pocket and tossed four small packets onto her partner's desk.

"You should eat more of this, Chris. It spices up your sex life. Make you real hot stuff," Carmen said, making a little clicking sound.

"Really? Maybe that's where I went wrong with Jill."

Carmen laughed and threw a packet of hot sauce at Chris.

"I'll have a patrol car stop by the theater and pick up a copy of the program for Barrie's show. Thought it would give us a bunch of names plus maybe some pictures to associate with the names," Carmen said as she washed down a bite of her breakfast with a swig of steaming coffee.

"Good idea," Chris said as she shoveled scrambled eggs into her mouth.

"The captain hasn't released the story to the press yet, but a couple of reporters were snooping around while you were gone. They know something big's up."

"Can't keep a story like this quiet for long," Chris shrugged. "Someone probably already offered the maid a fifty and now she's negotiatin' a better deal with the *Enquirer*. You wanna wake up the manager or agent or whatever he is or shall I do the honors?"

"Don't matter. You do him and I'll wake up the best friend."

THE PHONE AT Malcolm Gallagher's home on Long Island rang three times before he picked up the receiver.

"This had better be the most important phone call I have ever received," Malcolm Gallagher growled into the phone.

"Malcolm Gallagher?"

"Yeah."

"Mr. Gallagher, this is Detective Christine Shaw, NYPD, Midtown Precinct. I'm calling to notify you that your client, Elaine Barrie, was killed last night," Chris said bluntly. She had always found a direct approach to bad news to be the best method in cases like this.

"If this is a joke, I'm not amused," Gallagher snapped.

"Mr. Gallagher, I wish this was a joke, but it isn't," Chris said. "I need to ask you a few questions."

"I don't...shit...do you know wha—"

"I'd prefer not to discuss this over the phone, sir. Could you meet me at, say, nine?"

"Where?"

"I can meet you here at the precinct or your office. Doesn't really matter."

"Does Carl know?"

"He's been informed and has given a preliminary statement."

"How—"

"Your office or the precinct, Mr. Gallagher?" Chris repeated.

"Uh...my office, I suppose. I can meet you sooner if you want. I won't be able to get back to sleep now anyway. Jesus, I can't believe this."

"I'm sorry to be the one to tell you, Mr. —"

"What about the show? Are they going to cancel tonight's performance?"

"I wouldn't know anything about that. Things are pretty sketchy right now."

"I can be at my office by seven-thirty. 4934 West 57th Street," he said, abruptly disconnecting the call without a goodbye.

Chris stared at the receiver for a moment. "Warm guy," she mumbled as she stuffed another spork full of food into her mouth and pushed the phone closer to Sandoval.

"HELLO," A WOMAN'S voice barely managed to croak. She cleared her throat and tried again. "Hello."

"Della Summers?" Carmen asked.

"This is Marissa Parilli. Who the hell is this?"

"I was given this number for Ms. Summers."

"Just a minute," Marissa said.

Carmen heard rustling. Whoever Marissa Parilli was, she hadn't bothered to cover the phone's receiver.

"Who the hell is it this early?" a woman's muffled voice asked.

"A woman. Nice voice. Should I be jealous?"

"You know damn well there's no one else," she answered.

"Maybe it's Elaine," Marissa said with a sneer.

"She wouldn't be up this early," the second voice said, followed by more rustling. "This is Della Summers," the second voice finally responded.

"Ms. Summers, this is Detective Carmen Sandoval, NYPD, Midtown Precinct."

"What can I do for you this early in the morning, officer? Am I blocking the dumpster again?"

"No, ma'am. I was given your name by Carl Janus. He suggested we might want to talk to you."

"I wouldn't believe anything that prick said if I were you," Della said.

"He said you were Elaine Barrie's best friend. Is that true?"

"Yeah, I guess so. I've known her a long time. Why?"

"Miss Barrie was killed last night and we'd..."

"What do you mean she was killed?" Della cut Carmen off. "How?"

"I can't go into specifics about her death right now, but we'd like to talk to you. Maybe you'll be able to shed a little light on her movements yesterday."

"I don't believe this," Della said almost to herself. "I talked to her after the show last night."

"Would you be willing to come down to the precinct sometime this morning?" Carmen asked.

"Of...of course. I'll do whatever I can."

"Say about nine? Ask the desk officer for Detective Sandoval."

"At nine," Della muttered as she hung up the phone.

JUST BEFORE SUNRISE was the coldest part of the day, and the dark early morning clouds didn't help. Chris pulled the collar of her overcoat up on her neck again as she waited for Sandoval to join her for the drive to Malcolm Gallagher's office. The rain had stopped, at least for the moment, but she knew it wouldn't be long before she would be up to her ass in snow. The first year or two she had been in New York, she thought the snow was picturesque. Now it was an annual nuisance. Even the sight of pristine fields of snow and the white skeletons of the trees in Central Park failed to inspire the awe it once had. The only good thing was that the freakin' muggers who used the park as their personal hunting ground were slightly less active.

Chris wanted to stop at the medical examiner's office on her way to interview Malcolm Gallagher, but the lab assistant she spoke to on the phone told her that Featherstone was still working on the autopsy and probably wouldn't be finished before eight-thirty, if then. Probably taking pictures for his scrapbook, Chris thought. Of course, Elaine Barrie was going to be a high profile case. Maybe Featherstone just wanted to be extra careful and not screw things up like those morons in California had in the O.J. case.

"He say seven-thirty?" Sandoval asked as she got into Chris' car.

"Yep."

"Then you better step on it, cowgirl, or we'll be late."

"So what? Even if we mess up his appointment calendar, he probably doesn't have another client who brings in the cash flow Elaine Barrie did."

Midtown Precinct was less than a ten minute drive from Gallagher's West 57th Street offices. As the two detectives exited the elevator the hallway was quiet. The offices occupied the entire third floor of the building, and pictures of his clients lined the walls on both sides of the hallway. Chris recognized a few of the posed faces, but was clueless about others.

"Looks like the pictures hanging in the beauty salon where I get my hair cut," Carmen said, glancing at the pictures.

Halfway down the hall, Chris paused in front of a striking photograph of Elaine Barrie. It was hard to tell how old the picture was, but Chris thought it had been taken recently. Elaine was simply dressed in the portrait, with her chin resting on her folded hands. The hazel-green eyes had been accentuated by lighting, not dull and lifeless the way Chris had seen them a few hours earlier. A slight curve upwards at the corners of Elaine Barrie's mouth hinted at a smile.

"You stuck in that spot or what?" Carmen chided.

"Just thinkin' what a shame it is," Chris said almost apologetically.

Carmen tapped at a partially open door at the end of the hallway and pushed it open. Malcolm Gallagher was seated behind a large carved oak desk and looked up when the door opened. Another younger man, dressed in wrinkled khaki pants and a faded blue polo shirt was staring out the window overlooking Central Park. He looked like he hadn't quite reached his thirties yet.

"I'm Detective Shaw. I spoke to you earlier. This is Detective Sandoval," Chris said as she approached the desk.

"Ordinarily, I'd say it's a pleasure to meet you, but considering the circumstances I'm sure you can understand my feelings. This is my son and business associate, Todd," Gallagher said, indicating the younger man standing near the window. "I'm expecting my attorney to join us soon. Please have a seat."

Great, Chris thought. I haven't even asked him a question yet and he's already thinkin' he needs a fuckin' attorney. "I hope you don't mind answerin' a few questions, Mr. Gallagher," Chris said. "Most of them are preliminary and an attorney shouldn't have any objections."

"I made coffee if you'd like some," Gallagher offered as he glanced at his wristwatch. "It may not be as good as my secretary makes, but it's hot."

"Maybe later," Chris said. "But thanks anyway." It was obvious Gallagher was stalling.

"I'm not sure how I can help you, Detectives," Gallagher said as he sat behind his desk and adjusted his body.

"When was the last time you saw Miss Barrie?" Chris asked. She heard the ding of the elevator in the distance followed by the sound of rapidly approaching footsteps. The tapping of the footsteps sounded like those of high heels.

Gallagher rose again and smiled as someone entered his office. "Detectives, my attorney, Grace Gallagher," he said.

"Good morning, father," a tall, attractive strawberry-blonde in a gray pin-striped power suit said as she kissed Gallagher's cheek lightly. "My apologies for being late." Without a moment's hesitation she turned to face the two detectives. "May I see your identification, please?" she asked in a husky voice.

Chris thought her heart would stop as she took in the willowy blonde. Everything about the woman screamed soft, seductive femininity except her eyes which seemed to carry a warning of danger. Chris pulled her badge and identification from her belt and held it out. Grace took the wallet and glanced at it for a moment before she smiled crookedly and handed it back. Chris smiled as her eyes met Grace Gallagher's. She liked blondes, especially tall, willowy ones, and even though this one was clearly above her pay grade, admiring the terrain rarely got her in trouble. The marbled blue-gray eyes didn't hurt either. She watched as Grace examined Carmen's identification and handed it back. Whatever the earthy scent was that Chris inhaled, she was sure it was as expensive as it was arousing.

Chris cleared her throat and repeated her last question. "When was the last time you saw Miss Barrie?"

"We both saw her last night after her show," Todd offered quietly and resumed staring out the window.

"We'll need to interview you separately," Chris said. "In the meantime, you'll need to leave until I complete my interview with your father. Detective Sandoval can accompany you and take your statement."

Todd glanced at his sister as Carmen stood.

"It's all right, Todd," Grace said quietly. She turned back to the detectives. "I'm the attorney for both my father and brother. No questioning may take place outside my presence." She looked at Chris and smiled. "I'm sure you understand."

Without looking at Todd Gallagher, Chris said, "Sure enough. Don't leave until we have a chance to speak to you." Chris took a deep breath. She hated fucking lawyers, no matter how good-looking they were. They always made things more complicated than they needed to be.

"We'll meet you in your office in a little while, Todd," Grace said with a smile.

After Todd left the room, Carmen sat back down and crossed her legs as she leaned back in her chair. She glanced at Chris. "I'll take notes," she said. "Can't read your handwriting anyway."

Once she was satisfied that Todd Gallagher had left the office, Chris continued her interview with Malcolm. "About what time did you see Miss Barrie last night?" she asked.

Malcolm opened his mouth to speak, but Grace's hand on his shoulder stopped him and he looked up at her. "You don't mind if we record this conversation, do you?" she asked.

Chris looked at her, a question in her eyes. "Because of the nature of my father's business, negotiating contracts and representing the best interests of his clients, we've found recording their conversations to be enormously useful in case of a dispute about what was said during their discussions," Grace said, maintaining a smile that was beginning to annoy Chris.

"*We* would find it enormously useful if we were provided a copy of the recording," Chris said with a touch of irritation in her voice. "Is there anything else before we get on with this preliminary interview?"

"Does that mean other interviews might occur in the future?" Grace asked.

"That depends on what we might find as we get further into our investigation. That is, of course, provided we ever get through the first interview," Chris said tightly, her eyes narrowing.

"Take a breath," Carmen muttered under her breath.

Chris riveted her eyes on Malcolm. "What time did you see Miss Barrie last night?" she reiterated.

"The final performance yesterday was at eight. She performed a matinee yesterday as well. Wednesdays can be a terrible drain. Her husband is quite ill, you know," Malcolm said.

"So what time did you see her after the last performance?" Chris persisted.

"Must have been around ten-thirty or eleven," Gallagher answered with a shrug. "Maybe a little later."

"Do you go to every show?" Carmen interjected.

"Lord, no! I mean, it's a great show, but I couldn't possibly sit through every performance. I'd never get anything else done. No, I had a business matter to discuss with Elaine yesterday so I dropped by the theater near the end of the last show."

"What business matter was that?" Chris asked.

"I doubt that's relevant to your investigation, Detective Shaw," Grace interrupted.

"We'll have to be the ones who decide what's relevant and what isn't, Ms. Gallagher," Chris responded. Suddenly she didn't like Grace Gallagher, but couldn't put her finger on exactly what she disliked about her. Perhaps it was by doing her job Grace was interfering with Chris' ability to do hers. "These are only preliminary questions," Chris said. She looked back at Malcolm. "Go on, sir."

Gallagher glanced up at his daughter. "It was only a business discussion. None of it matters now." He returned his attention to the two detectives. "Elaine was planning a new album and we were renegotiating her contract with the recording company. She's been with the same label since she began, but they were pressing her to record a different style. Frankly, she didn't like it."

"Was she thinkin' about changin' recordin' companies?"

"We discussed it, but I think her old company realized they could potentially lose a proven money maker. They were going to cave in eventually rather than lose her."

"Did you meet with her last night at the theater?"

"In her dressing room, yes."

"Was there anyone else there when you spoke to her?"

Gallagher thought for a moment before answering. "Well, Del came in for a moment while I was there, but she left before Elaine and I got around to discussing the contract. Todd was probably there as well."

"Della Summers?" Carmen asked.

"Yes. She's always around. If you see Elaine, Del's usually nearby. They were very close. I took her on as a client to make Elaine happy a few years ago."

"Apparently after the show, Miss Barrie went to her suite at the Montclair," Chris said. "Did you accompany her?"

Malcolm hesitated to take a drink from his coffee cup. "No. I left the theater with her, but I got in my car and she went across the street toward the hotel."

"Have you ever been to her suite at the Montclair, Mr. Gallagher?" Chris asked.

"Of course. I am her manager."

"Of course," Chris repeated. "Was anyone with her when she went to the Montclair or did you see anyone waiting for her outside the hotel?"

"Quite honestly, Detective, I didn't stick around to see. I promised my wife I'd be home earlier than usual last night and was already running late by the time Elaine and I concluded our chat."

"What time did you arrive home?"

Malcolm shrugged. "One, one-thirty."

"We've been told by another witness that Miss Barrie was at the suite frequently and not always alone," Chris said.

"I'm sure she had visitors from time to time," Gallagher said with a shrug.

"The witness intimated the visitors were always male and spent the night," Chris pressed.

"Detective Shaw, I am — or was — Elaine's business manager. I was not her keeper nor was I her conscience. What she did, or didn't do, in her private life certainly wasn't any of my business."

"But if her reputation was called into question, that could have damaged her career, couldn't it?" Chris asked.

"It might have. But Elaine didn't get where she was by being stupid. She would never have done anything to harm her career."

"Still," Chris continued, "if her career took a nosedive due to whatever she did privately, I imagine your revenues might have taken a little dip as well."

"What are you suggesting, Detective?" Grace interrupted.

"Not a thing, Counselor," Chris said with a smile. She noticed that Malcolm's face had begun to flush and his neck looked like his shirt had suddenly shrunk and was choking him. "Just that Miss Barrie must have been a pretty lucrative client."

"As a matter of fact, Elaine is, or was, the most productive client I have, Detective Shaw," Gallagher said with a slight bite in his voice. "So if you're suggesting I had anything to do with her death, then you would have to assume I was the dumbest person on the plant to deprive myself of the benefits from that productivity for any reason."

"If Miss Barrie was havin' a little fling on the side, who might it have been with?" Chris asked.

"I'm sure I wouldn't know. I've already told you that I never meddled in her personal life."

"It would be easy to understand if she did play around a little. I mean, after all, her husband seems to be a little...indisposed."

"If you have questions about Elaine's private life perhaps you should speak to Carl. He probably won't tell you much. He protected Elaine like a bulldog from everyone and I don't mind telling you that he and I aren't exactly fond of one another."

"Why's that?"

"I tried to sell Elaine on the idea of making a screen test a few years ago. Thought Carl was going to have a stroke. Come to think of it," Gallagher said with a smile, "that would have almost been divine providence."

"He doesn't like movies?"

Gallagher looked up at the ceiling and said, "'Elaine was created to perform in the legitimate theater only. She is not a whore willing to sell her talents to the highest bidder.' And that is a direct quote from the ever pompous Mr. Janus."

"As her husband, how much influence did he have over her decisions?" Chris asked.

"She listened to him, but even she didn't always agree with him. They had some monumental disagreements before Carl became ill. Almost legendary battles in front of lots of witnesses. Ask anyone about Carl. He was always extremely demanding of Elaine."

"Why didn't she leave him if he was that bad?" Chris asked.

"That wasn't an area where Elaine confided in me." Gallagher shrugged. Chris watched as he quickly glanced at his expensive wrist watch.

"She must have been pretty young when they married," Chris said.

"Too damn young, but she wouldn't listen to me. Wouldn't listen to anyone where Carl was concerned. Granted, he is a legend in the theater himself and being married to him didn't exactly hurt her career, but she could have gone so much farther if that ass would have let her."

"Was there anyone you can think of who might have wanted Ms. Barrie to disappear?" Chris asked.

"As far as I know no one wished her ill. That doesn't mean someone, like her understudy, for example, wouldn't have liked for Elaine to come down with a case of laryngitis. Is there anything else I can help you with, Detective Shaw? I have an appointment in about thirty minutes," Gallagher said, standing up and buttoning the jacket of his suit.

"If we think of anything else, we'll drop by," Chris said as she slipped her notebook into her pocket. "Would anyone be at the theater today?"

"The theater is dark on Mondays. Elaine insisted on one day off during the week. If you need to speak to the other cast members, however, I'm sure they can be rounded up."

"So the show will go on despite Miss Barrie's absence?" Chris asked.

"Possibly. I can call the producer and ask what he plans to do if you'd like," Gallagher offered.

Gallagher hung up his phone ten minutes later and cleared his throat. "Everyone, cast and crew, will be at the theater this afternoon at two. I spoke to Oliver Levinson, and he promised to contact everyone. Surprisingly, he suggested the performances for the next couple of days might be cancelled."

"Is Levinson the producer?" Chris asked.

"Yes, it's his production. You would want to talk to him anyway," Gallagher said. "He discovered Elaine at a little bistro in the Village when she was eighteen or nineteen. I should warn you though it might be difficult to talk to him about Elaine right now."

Chris waited for Gallagher to continue.

"It's just that Oliver regarded Elaine as practically his daughter. He was quite upset when I told him about her death."

"We still need to speak to your son," Chris said when Gallagher stood.

Malcolm nodded and said, "Grace, please escort the detectives to Todd's office."

Chris stood and walked toward the door of Gallagher's office. She opened it and waited for Grace to exit. Before they left, she said, "I'll need you to come to the precinct today or tomorrow. We need your fingerprints, just in case. We're only beginning our investigation and will possibly have more questions for you." Chris shifted her gaze to Grace Gallagher and grinned. "You're invited to the party as well, Counselor. We wouldn't want to violate anyone's rights."

Grace bowed her head slightly in acceptance. "I wouldn't miss it, Detective. Now if you'll follow me I'll show you to my brother's office."

Despite her earlier annoyance at Grace's occasional interruptions during the interview with Malcolm, Chris forgot her irritation as she watched the sway of Grace's hips and the movement of firm, invitingly rounded buttocks beneath her sleek skirt. Long, curvaceous legs carried her gracefully down the tiled corridor. Chris thought there could be worse ways to begin a day. Grace stopped and tapped on a door, opening it without waiting for an invitation to enter.

Todd Gallagher sat at his desk reading a small stack of papers and examining a spreadsheet unfolded next to the stack. He picked them up quickly when the door opened and shoved them into a desk drawer. His smile held no warmth or welcome as he invited Chris and Carmen to be seated. His hair was more disheveled than it had been and he made a half-hearted attempt to make his clothing more presentable before he sat.

"Is there a hidden recording device in this office as well?" Chris asked as she settled into a chair.

"No," Grace answered with a smile. "No negotiations take place in Todd's office." Before Chris could ask, Grace added, "I'll bring your copy of my father's interview when we come to the precinct to have their fingerprints taken."

"What fingerprints?" Todd asked.

"The police want your fingerprints to eliminate you as a suspect, Todd," Grace explained.

"Do I have to do that?" he protested. "I haven't done anything."

"It's just a normal procedure, Mr. Gallagher," Chris said.

"Well, it's not normal for me!"

"It's all right, Todd. I'll be there with you to protect your rights," Grace said softly as she patted his shoulder.

"We've already established that you were with your father for at least a portion of Miss Barrie's final performance last night. What time did you arrive at the theater?" Chris asked.

"About nine-forty-five or ten, I think," Todd answered. "I met my father there."

"You didn't go together?"

"No. I stopped to eat dinner before I went to the theater."

"Where was that?"

Todd shrugged. "I don't know the name. Some little place a block or two from the theater."

"What did you have for dinner?"

"What possible difference does that make?" Grace asked.

Chris smiled. "I might want to eat there some time if the food is good."

"I can recommend the hot roast beef sandwich with mashed potatoes," Todd said, looking bored.

"What's your job title here, Mr. Gallagher?" Chris asked, looking around the office.

"I'm a financial analyst. My father insists that his clients have a portfolio as soon as their careers reach a certain level."

"What's the purpose for that?"

"In their professions there's no guarantee they will have steady work. He likes to make sure they have some financial security between jobs."

"Did Elaine Barrie have a portfolio?"

Todd nodded. "A rather large one. My job is to advise the clients when they should consider selling a stock and perhaps purchase a new one."

"Your father mentioned that Della Summers is a client. Does she have a portfolio?"

"Not through the agency, but I think she had someone else set one up for her."

"Were you with your father when he spoke to Miss Barrie backstage?"

"For a few minutes. I wasn't paying much attention."

"Too busy checking out the ladies backstage, huh?" Chris asked with a grin.

Todd laughed and nodded. "You bet," he said.

"When did you leave?"

"I don't know exactly. I was supposed to meet a friend for a drink and it was getting late."

"Where did you meet your friend?"

"O'Malley's on Lex. It's on my way home anyway."

"We'll need your friend's name as well."

"Is any of this relevant to anything?" Grace asked.

Chris looked at her and smiled. "Probably not, but you never know, Counselor." She returned her attention to Todd. "Did you see either your father or Miss Barrie leave the theater after the show?"

"No. I left before they did. They were still talking in her dressing room the last time I saw either of them."

Chris glanced at Carmen. "Can you think of anything else we need to ask about right now."

Carmen flipped through the pages of her notebook and shook her head. "I think that covers everything for now."

Chris stood and extended her hand to Todd. "Let us know if you think of anything later, Mr. Gallagher, and keep yourself available in case we have more questions."

Grace opened the office door. "It's been a pleasure, Detectives," she said as they walked into the hallway.

Chris looked at her and cocked an eyebrow. "Not yet," she said.

"WE GOT TIME to stop by the ME's office?" Chris asked as she stopped for a red light at eight-thirty. The sidewalks were beginning to fill with men and women making their way toward the high-rise office buildings and the high-price stores that lined Fifth Avenue.

"Sure. Della Summers isn't supposed to be at the precinct until nine. I'll call and tell the desk sergeant to have her wait."

"What did you think of Gallagher?" Chris asked as the traffic in front of her began to move.

"The father didn't act as upset as I might have expected, but some people handle these things better than others," Carmen said. "It's a little unusual that he had his attorney there for the preliminary questioning."

"If I just lost a cash cow like Elaine Barrie I'd be worryin' about when my creditors were gonna start callin'. Let's pull his financials."

"He's right, you know. Why would he harm her when his livelihood depended on her?"

"Maybe she'd decided to throw her business elsewhere. If Gallagher and Janus didn't get along, maybe Janus was tryin' to convince her to find other representation. Janus admitted last night...or this mornin'...whenever... that he didn't like Gallagher. Remember to ask the friend about that."

"What'd you make of the son, Todd?" Carmen asked. "He seemed a little...I don't know...out of place or something."

"I'll check his background. See what his purpose in life is other than drawin' a paycheck from dear ole dad."

"While you're at it, you might want to run financials and phone records for both of them," Carmen suggested.

"I already got somebody on that for each party we interview."

"That include the lady lawyer?" Carmen asked.

"Maybe I'll handle that one by myself."

"I bet you'd love that," Carmen said with a laugh.

"I don't mind getting my hands a little dirty," Chris smirked.

CHRIS PULLED HER vehicle into an official parking space in the rear of the building that housed the medical examiner's office. She hated visits to the ME. People who handled the bodies either never talked or spent their time making speculative remarks about the victims. She was used to seeing mangled victims at the scene of a crime, but there was something unsettling about seeing them again at the morgue, naked and exposed, gray chalkiness replacing the living pink cells of their bodies, the inner person open and exposed under harsh examining lights.

Chris and Carmen took a service elevator to the floor where Featherstone's office was located. His long time secretary, Thelma Trent, was transcribing taped notes when the two detectives entered the office. Thelma had been the secretary for the medical examiner's office as long as Chris had been in New York, but she had never been able to guess the woman's age. Probably somewhere between thirty and infinity. Thelma smiled when she saw them come through the door and stopped the tape player.

"Well, well, well, if it isn't CS Squared," Thelma quipped. Since the day Chris and Carmen had been partnered, there had been no shortage of jokes about their matching initials. In fact, Carmen had even begun signing her paperwork "CS2" to avoid confusion. Apparently the levity had also found its way to the ME's office.

"Mornin', gorgeous," Chris greeted her with a smile.

"You're here early and as full of shit as usual," Thelma said.

"Has Arthur sent his tape on the Barrie case up yet?" Chris asked, avoiding further social amenities.

"Having a bad morning, Chris?" Thelma asked with a wink.

"No, but we have someone comin' in to answer a few questions in half an hour," Chris answered.

"I think Arthur's still in the lab. Let me call down and see."

When Thelma hung up her phone, she swiveled her chair back toward Chris and Carmen.

"Arthur said it will be a while before he dictates his findings. If you want a quick overview, he suggests you join him downstairs."

"Thanks, Thelma," Chris said.

The lab and autopsy rooms were located in the basement of the building and were at least twenty degrees cooler than the upper floors. They found Arthur Featherstone peering into a microscope in one of the labs.

"So what can you tell us, Artie?" Chris asked as he continued looking at a slide.

"Penetrating blunt force trauma to the right temporal region," Arthur answered without looking up, his glasses pushed up on his forehead. "Probably dead before she hit the floor."

"Did you identify a weapon?" Carmen asked.

"Yeah, but it sounds like something out of one of those really bad detective movies," he said as he stood and moved to a nearby table. He picked up a long, thin object. "Brass poker from the bedroom fireplace. Isn't that original? No prints, just smudges. Neat killer. Replaced it with the rest of the fireplace tools after it was wiped down." He pointed at the curved end. "See this part? It's used to turn or move logs. She was struck with enough force that this part penetrated the skull. It made for a very nasty and very lethal weapon."

"The body tell you anything?" Chris asked.

Arthur returned to his microscope and pulled his glasses down on his nose before jotting a few notes on a clipboard lying next to the microscope.

"There are bruises on her back, neck, and upper arms, which

suggest that she put up a pretty good fight. Bruises on the back conformed to a picture frame in the hallway, so she either ran into it or, more likely, was pushed against it. With some force, I might add. Deep bruise. There was an as yet unidentified substance on her left upper arm. Something sticky almost like axle grease. I've sent it to the lab."

"Any signs of sexual assault?" Carmen asked.

"I found a few carpet fibers mixed in with her pubic hair, but there was no semen present."

"Could there have been more than one assailant?" Chris asked.

"Maybe. Her hair was damp when I examined her at the scene. She could have been attacked as she left the bathroom after showering. Just speculating, of course."

"Was she raped?" Chris asked.

"I'm thinking not. Forensics found some longer hairs under the body that didn't belong to the victim, but they could have already been on the carpet and missed by housekeeping or were shed by the killer. We'll run a few tests to see if we can get any DNA," Arthur explained as he pushed his glasses up and returned to his microscope. "She was pregnant at the time of her demise, by the way."

"How far along was the pregnancy?" Chris asked, trying to cover the surprise in her voice.

"Not very, maybe four or five weeks. It's possible she didn't even know herself yet. My wife never knew until she was around six weeks. Might want to check with her personal physician."

"Guess that makes her private life a little less private," Chris said.

Arthur looked up at Chris, "There was something else a little strange. From the looks of the body she must have put up a helluva fight, but none of her fingernails were broken. She should've scratched the shit out of whoever was attacking her, right?"

"Yeah," Chris nodded.

"When I did the autopsy all of her fingernails were intact, not even a dent. She was wearing artificial nails," Arthur explained. "The French kind with the white tips."

"The killer could have cleaned under them," Shaw said.

"Practically gave her a fucking manicure," Arthur nodded.

"Great. Just great," Chris said, exhaling. "Got any other useful information for us?"

"Didn't have much in her stomach. Probably didn't eat after the last show. What was in her stomach showed she'd eaten a good meal several hours before she died, probably before her last show. Prime rib, potato, salad with balsamic vinegar dressing, and tea. When was the last time anyone saw her?"

"Her agent says he left her between eleven-thirty and midnight," Chris said.

"The maid found the body a little after two," Carmen said.

"That gives you a pretty narrow window of opportunity. The good news is no drugs, no booze in her system. Very health-conscious lady," Arthur said as he picked up his clipboard once again. "Certainly not anticipating dying."

"Can you run a paternity test?" Chris asked. "Might help narrow the field down a little."

"I'll see what I can do," Arthur said. "I'll need DNA samples from any male suspects though."

Chapter Four

AT NINE-FIFTEEN Carmen Sandoval stopped at the precinct front desk to pick up her messages. Patrol officers were already bringing in a variety of individuals for booking. According to the desk officer, Della Summers was waiting in the break room.

"Ms. Summers?" Carmen asked, sticking her head into the officers' break room.

A woman Carmen estimated at late thirties or early forties stood up, nearly knocking over a cup of coffee as she rose. Carmen crossed the room and managed a sympathetic smile.

"I'm sorry to keep you waiting, Ms. Summers," Carmen said as she extended a hand toward Della. "I'm Detective Sandoval."

"No problem," Della said, coughing slightly.

"Why don't we find someplace a little more private?" Carmen said as she glanced at the police officers sitting nearby.

Della ran a hand through short brunette hair and nodded. Carmen glanced over her shoulder at Della and made a quick mental inventory of her attire. Tan jeans over desert boots and a blue work shirt with thin red and white stripes. Della looked uncomfortable as Carmen led her to an empty interrogation room.

"Can I get you another cup of coffee?" Carmen asked as she closed the door.

"No, thanks," Della answered, looking around the uninviting room.

Carmen pulled out a chair and sat down, motioning to a chair opposite her as she took her notepad from the pocket of her blazer.

"I apologize, but this is about the best place we have around here," Carmen said with a smile. "And I'd like to tell you how sorry I am about the loss of your friend."

"Thanks," Della said quietly.

It appeared that Della Summers wasn't going to be volunteering information even if she was willing to answer questions. She sat and waited for Carmen to ask something.

"How long have you known Miss Barrie?" Sandoval began.

"Since...uh...," Della closed her eyes for a moment and then reopened them. "Nineteen ninety-one. Sorry, but I had to do a little subtraction."

"Her husband told us you were her best friend."

"I suppose so," Della shrugged.

Carmen leaned back in her chair and looked at Della as the

woman fiddled nervously with the buttons on her shirt sleeve and waited.

"Since you were close to her, can I assume she might have shared information about her private life with you?"

"Depends," Della said with a shrug. "She didn't tell me everything she did."

"Have you been to her apartment at the Montclair?"

Della looked at Carmen. "Yeah, a few times."

"When was the last time you were there?"

"I don't know. Maybe a week or so ago."

"You weren't there last night?"

"No."

"Where were you?"

"Why?"

"We're just trying to account for everyone and establish a timeline."

"I was at home. And before you ask, I wasn't alone. My roommate was home as well."

"Is that the woman I spoke to this morning when I called?"

"Yes."

"What can you tell me about Miss Barrie's relationship with her husband?"

"What do you want to know about it?"

"Well, how did they get along? Any problems?"

"No more than usual, I guess. They fought sometimes."

"About what?"

"Business."

"They had a business relationship?"

"That's how they met. Carl was Elaine's director in the first show she did."

"And they hit it off?"

Della frowned and rubbed her forehead as if trying to decide what to tell Carmen about the complex relationship between Elaine Barrie and Carl Janus. After taking a deep breath she said, "They hated each other."

"Stop! Everyone freeze!" Carl Janus yelled loudly as he half ran, half walked down the aisle of the empty, darkened theater. "House lights!"

He took the steps onto the stage two at a time, looking around at the cast, posed like statues. He turned and looked at the seats in the theater.

"Oliver!"

"What Carl?" a man seated halfway back answered.

Carl turned and walked to where Elaine Barrie was standing

and took her by the arm. He returned to the front of the stage, pulling her behind him.

"Congratulations, Oliver. This is possibly the first single-dimensional leading lady I've ever encountered in the theater," Carl said.

"What's the problem, Carl?" Oliver said as he rose from his seat and moved toward the stage.

"Do your glasses need an adjustment?" Carl asked. "What did you see happening on the stage?"

"Well, I was really listening to..." Oliver began.

"Then we won't have a problem as long as you fill this theater every damn night with blind people. But if one sighted person gets through the door this production is going to go down faster than the Titanic."

"What are you talking about?"

"Her!" Carl said pointing to Elaine.

"She sounds great!" Oliver said.

"But that's it. I can't remember ever seeing a show where the leading lady rooted herself in the middle of the stage and never moved. This girl moves like a brick with legs."

Carl turned to Elaine and said, "Do your legs bend, honey?"

"Of course," Elaine snapped.

"Coulda fooled me since I haven't seen you do anything but walk around up here like the tin man from *Wizard of Oz*. But at least he had a personality."

"What would you like me to do, Mr. Janus?" Elaine asked.

He brought his face close to hers. "I'd like you to remember that people will be paying thirty-five fucking hard-earned dollars and up to come in here, sit down and be entertained for two goddamn hours. If they wanted to see you stand still and sing a song, they could pay a helluva lot less at a cabaret in the Village," he seethed.

"Maybe I don't understand how I should move. Maybe you should show me," Elaine said. "Isn't that your job?"

Carl grabbed her arm again and took her to one side of the stage away from the others. When he stopped, she jerked her arm away from him. Getting close to her once again, he said, "Look at those people over there. Don't look at me, goddammit! Look at them. Their jobs and their paychecks depend on what *you* do. Now look at Oliver. His reputation, not to mention a sizable chunk of his change, depends on what *you* do. Look at the backstage crew and the musicians in the pit. Their jobs and paychecks depend on what *you* do. Is this beginning to penetrate that thick skull and sink into that minuscule brain of yours? Everything depends on what *you* do! Why Oliver Levinson would choose a complete novice escapes me, but he did and we're all waiting for *you* to do something."

Tears began to well up in Elaine's eyes, but she blinked them back.

"Look, I know you can sing, honey, but there's more to theater than that. You have to sell this show. Everyone else is here to showcase you. Your voice alone isn't enough to carry this production. We open in three weeks so if you can't cut it, say so and we can find someone else who can sing *and* walk at the same time."

Elaine looked defiantly at him, lifting her chin slightly. "I can do it."

"Then do it, for Christ's sake, and do it damn quick."

She returned to her place on the stage as Janus and Oliver Levinson returned to their seats.

"Whatever possessed you to hire someone with no experience, Oliver?" Carl asked as he sat down.

"I hired her for her voice, Carl. I hired you to teach her everything else," Oliver answered.

"I ain't God, Oliver. I don't do miracles."

"Sounds like Janus was pretty rough on her," Sandoval said.

"Climbed on her back and stayed there the whole run. If he'd talked to me like that, I'd have spit in his face and walked," Della said.

"But she didn't."

"No. And Carl was on her every waking hour. Nothing she did was good enough for that bastard. It was a wonder she was able to go on when the show opened. By then she was working on nothing but adrenaline."

"Was the show successful?"

"Yeah. We had a good run. About a year, I think. Janus took home a Tony for Best Director that year."

"You were in the show, too?"

"Elaine made sure I was in every show she did. I became her sounding board, I guess. Listened when she was pissed off and celebrated when she was successful. Elaine took care of the people around her."

"Was she difficult to work with?"

"No. Never."

"I'll tell you, Della, Elaine Barrie and Carl Janus seem like an odd match."

Della laughed. "Yeah, everybody said that." Della leaned forward on her elbows. "No one could believe it when Elaine married Janus. Shit! He was old enough to be her father. I thought Gallagher was going to flip out."

"Her manager?"

"Yeah. Now there's a real prick. Makes Carl look like Mother Teresa."

"What do you mean?"

"I mean all Gallagher wanted out of Elaine was money. At least Carl wanted a good performance. If Malcolm Gallagher could have gotten away with it, he'd have booked Elaine anywhere for a buck. But he lost most of his influence over her after she married Carl. Gallagher thought she was stupid, I suppose, but Elaine was one smart lady. Knew a whole lot more than she let on."

"Do you know why Miss Barrie took the apartment at the Montclair?"

"So she could rest between shows. But actually Carl leased it for her," Della said.

"A housekeeper at the Montclair told us that Elaine wasn't always alone in the apartment."

"She had a lot of friends."

"Well, the housekeeper intimated that most of her visitors were men and some of them stayed there all night."

"Really?" Della said, looking down at her lap.

"You know who any of them might have been?"

"I was Elaine's friend, but I didn't keep track of her social life."

"It's possible one of those visitors might have killed her, Della."

"That's not pos..." Della began.

"Why isn't it possible?"

"What Elaine did isn't anyone's business."

"If you know any of the men, we need to question them. If they didn't hurt Elaine, they might still be able to help."

"Have you asked Carl about this?"

"He said they weren't having any marital problems."

"Then they weren't. Elaine loved Carl. She wouldn't have cheated on him. Look, are we about finished here?" Della asked.

"Will you be around if I need to speak to you again?"

"Does that mean I shouldn't skip town?" Della laughed.

"Yes."

"Don't worry, I'm not going anywhere," Della said, standing up.

Carmen closed her notebook and opened the door for Della. Della brushed past Carmen, hitting her arm on the door jamb.

"Damn!" Della said as she grabbed her right forearm.

"You all right?" Carmen said when they were in the hallway.

"Yeah. My roommate's cat scratched me a couple of days ago. Still hurts like hell. Wish she'd get rid of the damn thing."

Chapter Five

A FEW MINUTES after two that afternoon, Chris and Carmen ducked into the lobby of the Lerner Theater. The rain had returned with a vengeance and a howling wind was blowing the cold wetness down the canyons formed by the buildings on either side of the street. The wind driven rain felt like tiny knives as they drove themselves against Chris' head and neck.

Chris shook the water from her overcoat and looked around the blue and gold interior of the theater lobby. It looked different empty. The last time she had been in the Lerner Theater a hundred people had been milling around waiting for the evening performance to begin. Now she noticed there were a few worn places in the carpet and the brass railings seemed less shiny. The theater itself seemed to have lost some of its magic.

"You believe the cat scratch story?" Chris asked as she draped her coat over her arm.

"Well, she wasn't trying to hide it. I'll see if I can talk to the roommate tomorrow and check for kitty litter."

"Did you bring the program?"

"Yeah, but everyone's supposed to be here."

They walked up a flight of six steps leading into the main auditorium. The only lights on were those on the stage where about twenty men and women were standing in small clusters. As Chris made her way down the aisle, she saw three men seated in the row in front of the orchestra pit. One of the men turned, saw Chris and Carmen, and stood up.

"Are you from the police department?" a bald man with horn rimmed glasses asked as the detectives reached him.

"Yes, sir. I'm Detective Shaw and this is Detective Sandoval."

"Oliver Levinson," he said. "Everyone in the cast and crew is here except Del Summers."

"We won't delay you long, Mr. Levinson."

"It doesn't matter," Levinson said, shaking his head. "I've decided to shut the show down for the remainder of the week. We'll have to make a few adjustments..." he began until his voice caught and he looked down at the carpeting. "Without Elaine it won't be the same show," he said softly.

"Do you think people won't come to see the show without her?" Chris asked.

"Elaine *was* the show, Detective Shaw. People paid to see her, not an understudy." Levinson paused to gather his emotions and cleared his throat. "I'm sorry. These gentlemen are Gordon Amalfi, the director, and David Galway, my co-producer."

"I assume you'll want to speak to the cast members," Amalfi said. He was wearing an off-white Irish cable knit sweater that accented his blue eyes.

Chris looked at the people on the stage who were staring back at her.

"Were there any cast members who were particularly close to Miss Barrie?" Chris asked.

"Probably just Kent. Kent Devine. He's known Elaine since she arrived in New York. I believe they once lived together for a time," Levinson said.

Chris laid her overcoat over a seat and unbuttoned her blazer. "Anyone else?"

"Del."

"We've already interviewed Ms. Summers. Miss Barrie's husband gave us her name," Carmen said.

"How is Carl taking this?" Levinson asked with obvious concern.

"About as well as you would expect," Chris said.

"Things were bad enough for Carl already, but now, without Elaine..." Levinson's voice trailed away again.

"Do you know Mr. Janus well?" Chris asked.

"Since before his accident."

"What accident?"

"Well, Carl used to be an actor himself. Actually on the verge of getting his big break when he was hit by some damn fool drunk driver after a performance. He recovered for the most part, but I'm sure you must have noticed the scars on his face. Anyway, he refocused himself and dove into a behind-the-scenes role as a director," Levinson explained.

"And a damn good one," Amalfi contributed. "Everyone thought his life was set, especially after he and Elaine married."

"Why's that?" Chris asked.

"Well, Carl was sort of a boat without a rudder. He knew everything there was to know about the theater, but immersed himself so deeply in it that he forgot to learn anything about people. Oh, he could direct the hell out of them. He just couldn't relate to them."

"Until he met Miss Barrie," Chris said.

"Right," Levinson said with a smile. "You remember how much he changed don't you, Gordon?"

Amalfi laughed. "It was like watching a metamorphosis, Detective Shaw. I can't ever remember seeing Carl smile until he and Elaine became a couple."

"They seem like an unlikely pair," Chris said.

"Yeah, but it was their differences that made them so great together. Not that Carl didn't fight it with every ounce of strength he had."

"He didn't pursue her?" Carmen asked.

"Hell, no!" Amalfi said with a smile. "Elaine chased him until the poor bastard couldn't run any more. Then she just ran him down. I was Carl's assistant on another show then."

At forty-five Carl Janus was at the peak of his career. Every show he directed did well and he was in demand. His handling of performers was harsh even though there was never any doubt he knew how to get the best out of even secondary players.

"Goddamn actors," Carl fumed as he returned to his seat in the theater and the rehearsal resumed.

"You're lucky they don't walk out, Carl," Gordon Amalfi said, taking a deep breath. "Why do you treat them like that?"

"Because now they can redirect their energy. They hate me bad enough to show me they can do it because they think I think they can't. Make sense?" Janus said as he slid down in his seat and rested his knees on the seat in front of him.

"Reverse psychology?" Amalfi asked.

"Yeah. If it stops working and they all walk out, I'll be forced to find a new motivational technique. But right now this one is still working," Carl said. "Kill the house lights! Let's see how bad they can fuck it up this time."

"I see you've still got that soft touch, CJ," a voice behind Janus and Amalfi said.

Janus looked over his shoulder. Elaine Barrie had slipped into the theater and was sitting two or three rows behind them.

"Who the fuck let you in?" Janus asked with a frown. "This is supposed to be a closed rehearsal."

Elaine shrugged. "The door was open."

"Well, what the hell do you want? We have a lot of work to do here," Janus snapped.

"I can wait until you're through," she said, leaning back in her seat.

A few minutes later, Janus got up.

"House lights! Everyone take five," he hollered. He turned around and leaned his hands on the back of his seat. "I'm not going to sit here all goddamn day with you staring at the back of my head. What do you want?"

"I need some advice," she said,

"Do I look like Dear Abby?" Janus asked.

"I'm rehearsing a new show and having a little trouble."

"Still haven't figured out how to walk and sing simultaneously?" Janus sneered.

She laughed lightly. "No, I finally got that one. It's something else."

Janus looked at Amalfi. "Gordon, go up there and talk to Janine. Remind her she has to face the audience when she speaks her lines. And tell that idiot Bennett that he doesn't need to understand his character's motivation. He's a fucking actor, not a psychoanalyst."

Amalfi smiled and trotted to the stage.

"Okay, so what's the problem?" Janus asked Elaine.

"It's a little embarrassing, CJ," she said.

"Spit it out, for Christ's sake! The producers are paying me by the hour," Janus demanded.

Elaine took a deep breath. "I'm having a problem with my leading man."

"You're kidding me, right?"

"No. I can do the scenes, but I can't stand Gavin Lewis. He's a pompous ass."

"He's a prick, but a damn good leading man. You're lucky he agreed to work with you."

"He's propositioning me, on stage, during every performance."

"It's the theater, Elaine. Who's your director? He should be able to straighten Lewis out."

"Marc Jacobson."

"He's a good director. Just tell him your problem."

"He and Gavin are like brothers."

"Then grab his balls and squeeze them until his voice changes."

"It's a good show and will probably have a long run. But I need Gavin to dial it down."

"Then quit the damn show and find another one you can handle with your limited talents," Janus replied with a shrug.

"I can handle this one," Elaine said standing up. "Until yesterday he had only been suggestive. Then suddenly he became gropey and had the nerve to suggest we 'get together'."

"Then pretend he's someone you'd want to touch you. Make it a concentration exercise."

"Can't you help me?"

"I just did."

"No, CJ. I mean you're the most annoying man I know. Just read through the lines with me and help me find a way to ignore him."

"You want me to molest you while you say your lines?" Janus said with a wry grin.

"Yes. Well, sort of. At least annoy me so I can practice ignoring him."

"That's the stupidest thing I've ever heard, sweetheart."

"Will you do it?"

"Don't you know someone else who can annoy you?"

"No one has ever annoyed me as much as you, CJ."

Carl barked out a laugh. "Is that your idea of a compliment?"

"Yes, I think so."

Janus shook his head. "We'll be breaking in a couple of hours. Come back then."

"Great!" Elaine smiled.

"And don't tell anyone about this."

As Elaine was walking away, Amalfi returned and sat down.

"What did she want?" Amalfi asked.

"She wants me to annoy her," Janus said as he sat down.

"Sounds like typecasting to me," Amalfi said with a laugh.

A little over two hours later Elaine walked down the aisle to the stage. Janus was already on the stage sitting at a table with a script in front of him.

"This show any good?" she asked.

"It will be, but right now it sucks. Let's see a scene," he said.

"I marked one," she said, handing him a script.

Janus pushed his chair away from the table. "How gropey does Gavin get?"

"It's never anything the audience would see. The kiss is the worst part."

"Well, it's a fucking love scene, Elaine. Maybe he's just trying for a little authenticity."

"That doesn't mean we need to drop to the stage and get it on."

"Okay, okay. You start."

Janus turned his back to her and she reached out to touch his arm.

"I wish you wouldn't leave, Tony."

Janus spun around to face her. "What would be the point of staying? I'd only want you more. We know it can never work."

Elaine stepped closer to him and touched his face. "There has to be a way we can be together without hurting anyone else."

Janus placed a hand on Elaine's waist. "I don't know, Colleen."

Elaine laughed. "Do you remember our trip to the country?"

"Of course. How could I forget?" Janus said. As he spoke his line, his hand slid down to her hip and squeezed it.

Elaine threw her arms around Janus's shoulders. "I sometimes wish we could keep reliving that day over and over."

Janus pressed his head next to hers and whispered, "After this rehearsal let's go to my place where I can show you how much of a man I really am." At the same time his hand wandered onto her buttock and squeezed again. He heard her breath hitch before she spoke her next line.

"Why is life so difficult, Tony? Why couldn't I have met you before I married James?"

"By the time I finish fucking you you'll be begging for more, you hick," Janus whispered with his cheek against hers.

"That was low," Elaine whispered back before she continued with her lines. "What can we do?"

"There's nothing we can do. I can't hurt Leslie any more than you can hurt James."

"I love you, Tony."

"I love you, too."

"End of scene," Janus announced.

"Except for the kiss."

"How'd I do?"

"That was pretty close to Gavin."

"You seemed to handle it fine, Elaine."

"By the time we get to the kiss, I already know he's going to force his tongue down my throat and I tense up," Elaine said.

"Which way do you turn you head?" Janus asked.

"What's the difference?" She shrugged.

"Because if you turn your head to the left the audience won't be able to tell what you're doing. One, they won't see your mouth and, two, your hair will obstruct their view of his mouth. You could be staring at his chin for all they know."

"Really?"

"Tell Jacobson and Gavin you're coming down with a cold or something. Gavin is vain enough not to want to catch anything that might put him out of business."

"And the audience can't see it?"

"No. Tilt your head to the left," Janus ordered.

Elaine tilted her head and Janus put his arms around her and lowered his head toward her. He stopped just short of her face.

"If we had an audience right now, they'd swear to God we were playing tonsil hockey."

"Fascinating," Elaine said softly.

Janus looked at her and his arms loosened their hold.

"Kiss me," Elaine breathed.

"What?"

"You heard me," she smiled

He released her and stepped back. "It'll work. Trust me."

"I'm sure it will. But I want you to kiss me."

"That's enough, Elaine. You're just a kid."

"I'm a grown woman, not a child." She stepped closer to him. "Don't you want to kiss me, CJ?"

"As a matter of fact, I don't."

"I've wanted to kiss you since the first time you yelled at me."

Before Janus could back away any farther, Elaine put her arms around him. "Finish the scene," she demanded as her finger traced the scar down his cheek.

"This is why you really came here, isn't it?" he asked.

"I don't know what you're talking about," Elaine said with a coy smile.

"Everyone knows, except apparently you, that Gavin is gayer than a goose and Marc is his lover. They've been together for years. Gavin would never consider kissing you, let alone fucking you."

"I—"

Janus stopped her by covering her mouth with his, drawing her into a long, lingering kiss. When he brought the kiss to an end, he said, "But I would."

"I was hoping you'd say that," she said as she brought their lips together again.

"They were married less than six months later," Amalfi said with a chuckle. "She set Carl up. I think it surprised her when he kind of turned the tables on her."

"Sounds like pre-meditated seduction." Chris smiled.

"That's the way Elaine was. She saw something she wanted, she went after it. Had a lot of drive for a twenty-year-old," Amalfi said.

"The funny thing though," Levinson added, "she really loved Carl."

"We've heard they had a few fights," Chris said.

"Huge fights," Levinson said. "But never about anything except work. You know, how to approach a part, which show to do. Never anything personal."

"I've seen them practically come to blows on the stage and an hour later look like newlyweds over dinner," Amalfi added.

"Doesn't sound like your average marriage," Chris observed.

"It's what made it work for them though," Levinson said. "Fire and ice."

"Who was fire and who was ice?" Sandoval asked.

Amalfi and Levinson looked at each other.

"I don't really know," Levinson said sheepishly. "I guess they were both a little of each."

Chapter Six

CHRIS AND CARMEN divided the cast members and crew in half and began a series of interviews that consumed the remainder of the afternoon. Levinson let them use two dressing rooms for the interviews. Halfway through, Chris took a break and entered the room where Carmen had just completed questioning a very attractive, buxom blonde who managed to wiggle between Chris and the door frame on her way out. The woman looked at Chris and smiled as she passed her. Chris leaned partially out the door and watched her walk away.

"You're drooling," Carmen said from behind her.

"How come you get all the good lookin' ones and I get my father?" Chris asked, giving a little wave as the blonde disappeared around a turn in the hallway.

"I can interview the men for a while if you want, but then I'd never get you out of here. I, for one, do have a social life. Why don't you come with us tomorrow night?" Carmen shrugged. "Loosen up a little."

"Us?"

"Yeah, me and Ruben are doing some dancing," Carmen said while performing a small wiggle in her chair.

"Sounds like fun. You, me, and good old Ruben. No thanks."

"Mama's going, too."

"Goodie. At least I'd have a date."

"There's a contest at the club, so we thought we'd give it a shot."

"What's the grand prize? A one way ticket to San Juan?"

"You're a fucking bigot, Shaw," Carmen said with a straight face.

"Who me? A good old barefoot redneck gal from Texas? Nah!"

Carmen laughed, which made Chris smile. She liked to hear Carmen's throaty, full laugh.

"Find out anything interestin' yet?" Chris asked.

Carmen flipped through the pages of her notebook.

"Elaine Barrie was a bitch. No, wait, she was a saint. Oops! Here she was the devil incarnate. Not to mention the frequent, and ever popular, perfectionist, hard worker, super talent."

"Let me know if you get a consensus. So far I got zip that I'd repeat in mixed company. The men seem to have lusted after her ass unsuccessfully. That doesn't include the ones who thought they'd still have a chance to bed her if she had remained alive long enough."

"Wishful thinkers?"

"Yeah. I got about four more. How about you?"

"Just a couple."

CHRIS PICKED UP a cup of coffee and returned to her temporary office. When she entered a middle-aged man with an excellent haircut was already seated at the table. Chris sat down and flipped to a new page in her notebook.

"I'm Detective Christine Shaw," she said to start the conversation.

"Kent Devine," the man said, flashing a smile that must have cost a fortune.

Chris looked up and smiled. "Mr. Levinson told me earlier that you were close to Miss Barrie."

"I've known her since she first arrived in the city."

"Then you've known her longer than Della Summers."

"Yeah, I think Del met her about six months after I did."

"Mr. Levinson also said that you and Miss Barrie once lived together. Is that right?"

"For about a year and a half. But it wasn't what you're thinking, Detective. I gave her a place to stay until she got on her feet. She was extremely young and this city has a tendency to eat its young."

"She must have been pretty wobbly to live with you that long."

"Elaine was very insecure about her talents."

"When did she move out?"

"After she got her first real gig."

"Did that make you mad?"

"No. Why would it?"

"Nothing romantic between you?"

A slow smile moved across Devine's lips. "We had a few moments. But it wasn't anything serious."

"Just a quickie to relieve your tension every now and then?"

The smile disappeared from Devine's face. "Don't make it sound like Elaine was cheap or easy, Detective Shaw. She wasn't."

"Then why don't you tell me how she was," Chris said, laying her pen down and picking up her coffee cup.

Devine leaned back. "Elaine was...it's hard to find the right word. Innocent, untested, eager. Back then, I mean she was only eighteen, I thought she was too sweet to make it here. But she was a fast learner. And she *never* used sex to get what she wanted."

"How did you feel when she married Carl Janus?"

"It didn't matter to her what I thought. She asked me to give her away."

"Do you like Carl?"

"No one liked Carl, except Elaine," Devine said with a shrug. "This is the theater, Detective. Once you hit the theater door, the gloves come off and the claws come out. The nicest person you'd meet on the street becomes an instant bitch once she steps on the stage."

"Did Elaine turn into a bitch?"

Devine smiled and shook his head slowly. "That's why I didn't think she'd make it. She never changed. Always was that sweet kid from West by God Virginia trying to break into the big time. If Carl didn't do anything else for Elaine he taught her about the theater and how to block out some of its pettiness. That's why you shouldn't believe half of what those idiots out there tell you. Most of them were jealous of Elaine's success when they should have been grateful they had a job."

"When was the last time you saw Miss Barrie?"

"I talked to her for a few minutes after the last performance yesterday. Just idle chit-chat about the show, and I asked how Carl was doing."

"You ever been to her suite at the Montclair?"

Suddenly Devine appeared to be nervous. He pulled a cigarette from a pack in his pocket and lit it before answering. "We've all been there. Elaine threw a Christmas party for the cast and crew there this year. About a week before Christmas."

"Since you were such an old friend, were you ever there alone with her?"

Devine took a deep drag on his cigarette. "Yes," he answered as he expelled smoke.

"Rekindlin' an old flame?"

"Don't be ridiculous!" Devine bristled. "I already told you there was never anything serious between Elaine and me."

"It's been my experience that you don't always have to be serious about a woman to get in bed with her."

"Elaine never would've cheated on Carl. She wasn't like that," Devine said quietly.

"Yeah, that's what everybody tells me. Too bad we have a witness who says Miss Barrie entertained men in her suite and a few of them spent the night."

"That's a damn lie!" Devine spit out as he stood up, knocking his chair over.

"Sit down, Mr. Devine," Shaw said calmly. "Is it possible someone else used the suite besides Miss Barrie?"

Devine sat his chair upright. "Anything's possible, I suppose."

Chris looked at Devine. "Look, I'm not tryin' to dig up dirt on

Miss Barrie. But, and this is only a but, if she did entertain men in that suite, it's possible one of them might have been responsible for her death."

Devine continued to puff on his cigarette without speaking. Finally he crushed the cigarette out and looked at Chris. "You ever see her perform, Detective?"

"Several times. Never disappointed."

"You should have seen her last performance," Kent said, casting his eyes up and closing them. "It was magical, inspired."

"How so?"

"It's hard to explain. She'd done the role dozens of time. She always gave a bravura performance, but that one was different, like she was doing it for the first time and was still excited. I don't know, it was just special somehow. When she sang the final song in the show, the love song, I wanted to cry. It was so filled with emotion."

"The one she sings to the lover she never got to say goodbye to?" Chris asked. "I've seen the show."

Kent patted his chest over his heart. "She was singing to Carl," he said softly. "Even though she knew she was going to lose him, she wasn't ready to let him go. It was sad, but joyous at the same time."

"Would the audience have noticed?"

"Probably no one except the cast members would have noticed the change in her demeanor." He shrugged. "Or maybe it was only my imagination."

"And you didn't go to her suite after the show," Chris restated.

Devine shook his head and half smiled. "You might want to talk to Damon Hunter and Alex Webb."

"Are they cast members?"

"Not in this show. They were in her last one, about a year and a half, two years ago."

"And what do you think they can tell me?"

Devine shrugged. "I have no idea, but I know they've been to the suite."

Chris decided not to pursue the reason Hunter and Webb might have been to Elaine Barrie's suite at the Montclair, especially since it had been leased after the last time she worked with them.

"Do you know where I can reach them?"

"Alex is in an off-Broadway show at the Cherry Lane in the Village. And you'll probably find Damon crawling around with a pack of cockroaches somewhere. The Actors' Guild will know if he's lurking someplace."

When Devine left the room, Chris took a small evidence bag from her coat pocket and used her pen to scoop the cigarette butt into it before sealing and labeling it.

Chapter Seven

AS CHRIS LOOKED at her reflection in the bathroom mirror and ran a comb through her hair, she made a mental note to not embarrass herself that night. She should never have let Carmen talk her into going to the Club Cabana. The thought of spending the evening tolerating Ruben Montanez and watching gyrating Hispanics sling their bodies around at breakneck speed to Latin rhythms made her shudder. But Carmen had pushed all the right buttons and she admitted she was tired of looking at the cracking paint on her apartment walls. Although she always hated it when Jill was gone, the homecomings had been something to look forward to. Chris wondered what she was doing at that moment, but doubted Jill was as alone and lonely as she was. Chris never knew what she'd done to deserve being dumped and left bleeding. Her ashtrays were just full, she guessed, and it was time for a trade-in.

An hour later, Chris took a deep breath and swung open the front door to the Club Cabana. Throbbing Latin music assaulted her eardrums as soon as the door cracked open as if the music had been waiting, ready to pounce on the next unsuspecting person brave enough to enter. The club was dark with gaudy flashing lights. Chris' pupils didn't know whether to contract or dilate and within a minute they gave up and allowed an endless procession of pulsating white and yellow dots to dance across her vision. Blind and deaf, she thought. Who could ask for more than that from a night on the town? She stepped away from the door and leaned against the wall and, to her amazement, her senses made adjustments to the sound and lighting. Through a blue-gray haze of cigarette smoke, Chris could see dancers already pulsating to the music. It took her a little longer to find Carmen and her insufferable boyfriend, Ruben Montanez. She saw Ruben first and had to smile. He must have visited Carmen's uncle because he looked like a Puerto Rican pimp. He was wearing tight black pants and a jacket over a shiny white shirt that Chris assumed was satin. As Ruben danced and turned, Chris saw that the top two or three buttons of the shirt had been left open, revealing a muscular chest covered by enough gold chains and crosses to supply every priest in the diocese. With every move the jewelry around Ruben's neck jumped and Chris hoped Carmen didn't get close enough to lose an eye.

Chris made her way toward the dance floor, excusing herself a dozen times before she reached the table where Carmen's mother was sitting, sucking on a thin red straw which was embedded in a slushy pink concoction. Little white and green umbrellas kept the straw company. Mercedes Sandoval was a slightly chuffy woman in her late fifties. She had been wearing the same hairstyle as long as Chris had known her, a neat French twist that was always held in place by what looked to Chris like a long alligator clip. When she reached the table, Chris bent down and kissed the woman on the cheek.

"How're ya doin', gorgeous?" she asked with a broad smile.

Mercedes got up and threw her arms around Chris' shoulders, squeezing her tightly. The plumpness of the older woman's breasts forced Chris to arch her back slightly as she returned the hug.

"You here just in time, Christina," Mercedes said with a thick accent. It always amused Chris that when she had been to Carmen's home, Mercedes only spoke English when she was speaking to her. Otherwise, the remainder of her conversation was in rapid, staccato Spanish.

"Contest ready to start," she said, patting Chris' arm.

Before Chris could sit, a harried waiter swooped down to take her order. Chris asked for a shot of bourbon with a beer chaser and sat down.

An emcee took a microphone and announced the beginning of the dance contest. Two dozen couples took the floor for the first round and the music began again.

"Meringue," Mercedes announced. "Carmen's best dance."

Chris looked onto the dance floor and had no trouble locating Ruben again, but it was the first time she had seen Carmen since she arrived. She let out a low whistle and glanced at Mercedes.

"Carmen look good, no?" the woman smiled proudly.

"Too good for Ruben." Chris smiled back.

Carmen was wearing a tight, form-fitting red dress, but Chris had no idea what the fabric might have been. Something in the material caught the light and reflected it as she moved. Thin straps held the dress up and Chris noticed there wasn't a whole lot to be held up. Basically it covered her body from just above her breasts to mid-thigh. It took her a few minutes, but Chris finally realized the reason she hadn't spotted Carmen earlier was because of her hair. At work she kept it up in a manner similar to her mother's. Tonight it hung loosely well below her shoulders. The lights from a glitzy spinning globe over the dance floor periodically swept over her, illuminating her reddish brown hair. It was the first time since they had become partners four years before that Chris had seen Carmen out of her traditional work clothes. Carmen was attractive, but shit, tonight she was flat out sexy.

Ruben and Carmen made it through four rounds before being weeded out. When they reached the table where Chris and Mercedes were seated, there was a brief exchange in Spanish among Ruben, Carmen and Mercedes.

"What happened?" Chris asked. "I thought you were doin' great."

"Ruben thinks the judges were paid off and Mama thinks they just don't know good dancing when they see it," Carmen said after she took a long drink from a glass in front of her and ran a napkin across her chest to soak up the sweat.

Ruben plopped dejectedly into a chair and wrapped an arm around Carmen's shoulder. He kissed her on the cheek and picked up another glass.

"Next time," Ruben said.

"Don't get worked up over it, Ruben," Carmen said. "It's just for fun."

Ruben watched the remaining four couples as they continued their competition.

"Just wait," he said, pointing onto the floor. "You see that couple there? I seen her talkin' to one of the judges before we started. How much you wanna bet they'll be the winners? She probably promised the guy a blow job."

"Ruben!" Carmen hissed.

Ruben finally realized he and Carmen weren't alone at the table and looked embarrassed.

"I'm sorry, Senora Sandoval. I apologize," he said as he patted Mercedes' hand.

"You better learn to watch your mouth," Mercedes said, sipping at her pink drink again.

Ruben looked across the table at Chris. "And how are you this evening, Shaw?"

"Happier than a hog in slop," Chris said smiling at Carmen, who rolled her eyes and laughed. Ruben and Mercedes just looked confused.

"It's okay, Mama," Carmen said. "Apparently that's how they talk in Texas."

"Tell me, Shaw," Ruben started, running his index finger around the rim of his glass. "Do people in Texas dance?"

Chris tossed back her shot and took a drink from her beer.

"We've been known to stumble around the dance floor from time to time."

"But not like this, eh?" Ruben asked.

"No. Not like this. We like to save our heavy breathin' for the bedroom," Chris said.

Carmen tried to kick Chris under the table but missed. Chris looked at her and held up a finger, wagging it at her. "Nice try," she said.

"So, Shaw, when you dance, what you do? Folk dances?" Ruben continued to goad her.

"I'll tell you, Ruben. My daddy told me there was only one kind of dancin' that was worth a damn," Chris explained.

"Yeah, and what is that? A polka?"

Chris leaned her forearms on the small table. "A nice slow dance. You see the whole idea is to hold your woman real close and let your body press against hers so she knows you want her. Hell, after what you were doin' out there, a person wouldn't have the energy to do anything...romantic."

Every time she was in the same room with Ruben Montanez the same thing happened. He seemed obsessed with the idea of irritating her for some reason she had never exactly figured out. It was no secret he disliked the idea of his girlfriend being partnered with a lesbian. While it was obvious Carmen was completely into men, Chris suspected Ruben didn't trust her entirely. Chris reminded herself that, although it would be easy to make Ruben uncomfortable, Carmen would be the one who'd pay the price later. She was too good a friend to put in an awkward situation and Chris bit her tongue.

"You look great tonight, by the way." Chris smiled at Carmen.

"Thank you."

"You should wear your hair down more often," she said.

"It gets in my way at work," Carmen said.

"Your mother is getting tired, Carmen," Ruben announced.

"We've got a big day tomorrow anyway," Chris said.

"Did you get addresses on Webb and Hunter?" Carmen asked as she slipped a jacket over her dress.

"Yeah. I left a message on an answering machine for Hunter and told him to call me at the precinct in the morning. I figure we can catch Webb at the theater sometime after lunch," Chris said as she finished her beer.

"See you in the morning then," Carmen said as she turned to walk away.

Chapter Eight

CHRIS WAS HALFWAY back to her desk with a cup of coffee when Carmen arrived for work the next morning. Her hair was back in its usual style and the tight red dress had been replaced by loose-fitting light gray wool slacks and a navy blue blazer over a white turtleneck.

"Morning," she said as she dropped her purse into her desk drawer.

Chris nodded at her. "Coffee's fresh."

"Great!" Carmen said.

Chris was thumbing through the reports from the night shift when Carmen returned and sat down. She sipped at her coffee quietly for a few minutes before setting her cup down and leaning forward.

"Listen Chris, about last night. Ruben..." she started.

"Forget it, Carmen. I shouldn't have been tryin' to mess with his mind," Chris said without looking up from the reports.

"Well, it's just that..." she tried again.

"He didn't give you any shit later about invitin' me, did he?"

"He'll get over it. But I was think—"

"Detective Sandoval," a uniformed officer said as he walked up to Carmen's desk.

Carmen slapped her hand down on her desk and glared up at the officer. "What! Goddammit, can't a person carry on a conversation around here without being interrupted?" she said with exasperation in her voice.

"I'm sorry, Detective, but there's a man at the front desk who says he has to talk to whoever is in charge of the Barrie case," the officer said.

Chris sat up at her desk. "Who is it?"

"An Alex Webb. Said he just found out about it. Looks pretty shook up."

Carmen looked at Chris. "Send him back," she said.

Chris and Carmen stood as they watched Alex Webb come toward them. His hair was blond and looked mussed up, as did his clothing. From the look on his face it didn't look like he'd had much sleep.

"Mr. Webb," Chris said. "I'm Detective Shaw and this is Detective Sandoval."

Webb nodded at them and glanced around the squad room.

"I've never been in a police station before," he said lamely, unsure of what he was doing.

"Would you like a cup of coffee?" Carmen asked.

Webb ran a hand through his hair and nodded. "Uh, yeah, I guess so. Black, please."

"Why don't I meet you in Room Two, Carmen," Chris said.

Alex Webb fell into a chair in the interrogation room and covered his face with his hands. A minute later, Chris set a steaming cup in front of him before she and Sandoval sat down across from him.

"When did you find out about Miss Barrie's death, Mr. Webb?" Chris asked.

"Kent. Kent called me yesterday afternoon. I couldn't believe it," Alex said almost to himself.

"Kent Devine?" Chris continued.

"Yeah. He said he had already talked to you and thought you'd want to speak to me as well."

"We were planning to drop by the Cherry Lane this afternoon," Carmen said.

"I called the theater this morning and told them I needed a couple of days off. After I found out...I couldn't have gone on anyway."

"When did you last see Miss Barrie?" Chris began.

"I haven't seen her in a while, but she came to see my show about a month ago," Webb said.

"Did you talk to her?" Chris asked.

"Not that night. She called me the next day. Said she loved it. She was a wonderful woman."

"Had you ever worked with her professionally?" Carmen asked.

"A couple of years ago. A fabulous experience. She was extremely generous and willing to help a newcomer."

"Have you ever been to her suite at the Montclair?" Chris asked as she leaned forward in her chair.

"She didn't have a suite at the Montclair when I worked with her," Webb hedged.

"I know, but have you ever been there?" Chris pressed.

Webb hesitated for a moment and looked at Chris and then Carmen. "I was there once or twice."

"Did you spend the night?" Chris went on.

"Why would I, Detective? Elaine was my friend. That's all." Chris noticed that Webb's hand was shaking slightly as he picked up his coffee.

"Can we get a picture of you for our files, Mr. Webb?" Carmen asked.

"Well...I guess my agent has one, but why do you need my picture?" Alex asked.

"We have a witness who saw men enter Miss Barrie's suite. She said some of them stayed all night, but didn't know their names," Carmen explained. "Would she recognize your face, Mr. Webb?"

Chris thought Webb was going to break down. Webb looked up at the light hanging overhead, squeezed his eyes shut, and took a deep breath.

"Yes, she might," he finally answered quietly.

"So you did spend the night in Miss Barrie's suite?" Chris asked.

Webb smiled slightly. "That's a very delicate way of putting it, Detective Shaw."

"Would you like to explain your relationship with Miss Barrie to us, Alex?" Carmen asked.

"I'm not sure I can. It seems so bizarre now. But at the time..." he paused. Chris and Carmen waited for Webb to continue.

"Look, I don't want you to think badly about Elaine."

"Whatever it is can't hurt her now," Carmen said. "We just want to find whoever killed her."

"I know." Webb nodded. "It was actually a business arrangement. Elaine's husband is sick. Been sick for quite a while. Anyway, about a year ago, I think, I got a message that Mr. Janus wanted to see me at his place."

"Was that a big deal?" Chris asked.

Webb's eyes widened slightly. "Would it be a big deal if the police commissioner or the mayor wanted to see you?" he asked.

"Go on." Carmen smiled.

"Carl Janus might be sick, but he still slings a lot of weight around the theater district. He has a reputation as a star maker. So, naturally, I went to see him. I thought it might be about a part or something, but it wasn't."

"What did he want?" Chris asked.

"Well, he knew that Elaine and I had worked together and that I liked her...as a friend, you know? He explained a little about his illness and then offered me a job."

"In a play?" Carmen asked.

"He wanted to hire me to be Elaine's...Elaine's companion," Webb said with his eyes closed.

"Excuse me," Chris said in disbelief.

Webb opened his eyes and they were clear.

"He asked me to be with Elaine socially. I thought he was crazy, but he persisted. Said he needed someone he could trust, said Elaine had always spoken well about me."

"He offered you money be with his wife?" Chris asked, not

fully believing what she was hearing.

"Not money. In exchange Carl said he would make sure I always had work in the theater."

"Jesus Christ!" Chris said, looking at Carmen. "Her husband was her pimp."

"No! No! It wasn't like that," Webb protested. "Carl loved Elaine. He only wanted her to be happy."

"By arrangin' for her to sleep with other men?"

"It wasn't like that, Detective Shaw. I would be more of a companion."

"Just exchangin' one favor for another."

"I couldn't understand it myself and initially I turned him down flat."

"But eventually you forced yourself into her bed. That right?" Chris asked sarcastically.

"I talked myself into spending time with her, but I wasn't forced to do anything."

"Did he threaten to ruin your career if you said no?"

"No. And I swear that before I finished talking to him that day I almost felt sorry for Carl. It was obvious how much he loved Elaine. And that sounds even more ridiculous," Webb said. He leaned his arms on the table and lowered his head as if thinking. "You see, his illness made it nearly impossible for him to...to...well, you know. He said he couldn't stand the thought of a woman as young and vital as Elaine spending God knew how long...unsatisfied."

"Wasn't the 'in sickness or health' bit part of her wedding vows?" Carmen asked.

"I'm sure it was, Detective," Alex snapped, "but remember that it wasn't Elaine making the suggestion."

"Can we assume then that you accepted Janus's offer?" Chris asked.

"Yes, I'm ashamed to say that I did. I feel funny talking about it though. Part of the deal was that I could never reveal anything about our arrangement to anyone, but I guess it can't hurt her now."

"What was Miss Barrie's reaction to the arrangement?"

"Initially she was furious with Carl."

"But she got over it."

"She was very comfortable to be around. I always thought she was kind of vulnerable."

"How long did your liaison with Miss Barrie last?" Chris continued.

"Look, Detective, you don't have to believe me and I wouldn't really blame you if you didn't, but I swear to God that I never...*never* went to bed with Elaine. We pretended for Carl's sake, but I slept on the couch every time I was there."

"Didn't you find Miss Barrie attractive?" Chris asked.

"Of course I did. She was beautiful, but she was my friend. And, to be honest, it all seemed a little sordid to me, no matter how well-intentioned Carl was."

"So how long did this arrangement last?" Carmen asked.

"Maybe three or four months. Carl never let anyone hang around long enough to get too comfortable."

"There were others?" Chris asked incredulously.

"I was the second," Webb said.

"Do you know any of the others?" Chris went on.

"I only know that Damon Hunter was the first one approached by Carl, but he didn't last long. Elaine told me she didn't like him."

"You know him?"

"Yeah, unfortunately. He's a world class pig. Thinks he's God's gift to women. I was shocked when I found out Carl had hired him. Somehow Damon found out about me and Elaine and needled me about it constantly, asking questions about what we were doing and making perverse remarks about what he said they did. I knew he was lying, but he strutted around like a damn peacock, shooting his mouth off."

"Was there anyone else that you know of?" Chris asked.

"Just Kent."

"She slept with Kent Devine?"

"As far as I know he was the last one. Didn't he tell you?"

"Not directly."

"I don't think there was much going on between Elaine and Kent. They've been friends forever."

"He said they once lived together."

"Yeah, but that was only so Elaine wouldn't have to sleep on the streets. Platonic, you know."

"Did you see Miss Barrie the night before last?"

"No. After my performance that night I was too exhausted to do anything except go home and crash."

Chris stood up. "Keep yourself available, Mr. Webb, in case we have other questions for you."

"I hope you catch the bastard who did this, Detective. You know, it's funny, but in the three or four months Elaine and I were together, we spent most of our time talking. She helped me get ready for the part I'm doing now. I know that sounds strange because she was a very desirable woman. Quite seductive. Somehow it would have felt like sleeping with my sister or something," Webb said, shaking his head sadly. "I'm really going to miss her."

Alex Webb left the room, depositing his coffee cup in a trashcan as he left.

"Do you believe that shit?!" Chris exclaimed as she stuck her pen inside the cup, lifted it out of the trash, and handed it to Carmen.

"Looks like we'll have to start over and question a few people again," Carmen said.

"Jesus Christ! I can't believe a man would attempt to fix his wife up with other men. Or that she would go along with it. I need some fresh air."

Chris splashed water on her face in the squad's locker room and watched in the mirror as it dripped from her chin. She hadn't expected the twists she knew so far in the Barrie case. She didn't want to believe any of it.

Chris Shaw had been an admirer of Elaine Barrie's since before she arrived in New York six years earlier. She had seen her sing a few times in clubs and followed her career as it took off and soared. If Chris had been a different kind of person, she could easily have become a stalker, following Elaine Barrie around trying to get closer. The first time she had seen Elaine, she thought she was the most beautiful woman she had ever seen. Of course, her seat had been some distance from the stage, but in her memory Elaine had glowed in the spotlight that fell over her body, shining brighter than the lights of the city itself.

Chris remembered flying into LaGuardia in the middle of the night and looking down into the heart of the city as her plane descended. She thought then, and still did, that from the air, from a distance, New York was the most fascinatingly beautiful city on Earth, with its seamier side hidden in the darkness behind the lights. Was it possible that Elaine Barrie, like the city, had only been beautiful from a distance, her seamy side hidden behind the spotlight?

Chris was still drying her face when she returned to her desk. As she sat down, she saw a note in Carmen's handwriting. Damon Hunter, *numero uno*, had called and agreed to come to the precinct after lunch.

Chapter Nine

CHRIS DIDN'T NEED a formal introduction to recognize Damon Hunter. Alex Webb had called him a pig and Kent Devine had called him a cockroach. She knew both were true before Hunter opened his mouth. He was well-dressed as he strolled toward Chris' desk, his black hair shiny and combed back. With his swarthy, Mediterranean looks, he reminded her of a bad Valentino impersonator.

"You Shaw?" Hunter asked as he sauntered up to Chris, eyeing every woman in the squad room as if they were selections on a menu while he sucked on a straw in a Starbuck's cup.

"Yeah," Chris replied. "Follow me."

As she led Damon Hunter to an interrogation room, she was glad Carmen had taken longer than usual for lunch. She was certain Hunter would have come on to her. As soon as they were seated, Chris got to the heart of the matter. Hell, she already knew about the arrangements with Carl Janus. Why beat around the bush?

"So, you wanna tell me about your arrangement with Carl Janus?" Chris asked bluntly.

"Who told you about that?" Hunter asked, apparently not surprised that the police knew about it.

"Doesn't matter. I understand you were Miss Barrie's first extracurricular partner," Chris said.

Hunter smiled broadly at Chris and unzipped his jacket. "That's correct."

"You know, Mr. Hunter, I don't understand why you would agree to such a relationship," she said.

"Really?" Damon said.

"I mean, you appear to be an attractive enough man. Seems like you could find women for yourself without all this contract business."

"I don't have trouble finding women, Detective. But it isn't every day a man is handed the chance to sleep with a woman as well-known as Elaine Barrie on a silver platter."

"Were you surprised when Carl Janus contacted you about spendin' time with his wife?"

"A little, but I didn't argue with him. I knew who he was and Elaine and I had worked together. Very attractive lady and I didn't have to do the dinner bit. She was just there, waiting for me to join her, you know? Who would walk away from a deal like that?"

"Did Janus pay you to spend time with Ms. Barrie?" Chris asked, ignoring Hunter's question.

"Not with money. Just a promise that my future would be...secure."

"What do you assume he meant by that?"

"That I wasn't going to have any trouble finding work in the theater. But the old fucker lied."

"You think he broke the agreement?"

"Look, Detective, I wanted a secure future in the theater. Janus wanted someone to satisfy his wife when he couldn't get it up anymore. He thought being with another man would make her happy."

"And did you make her happy, Mr. Hunter?"

A slow smile crossed his lips as he looked down at his hands. "Yes," he finally answered. "Every time."

"Did she seem happy with the arrangement?"

"She resisted the whole thing at first, you know. Said she felt guilty because I wasn't her old man. But she got into it later on. In the end, we were both...satisfied, if you get my drift."

"How did you deal with her resistance?"

"I didn't force her to do anything she wasn't willing to do. So if you're thinking rape, you can flush that idea right out of your suspicious little mind," he answered defensively. "I gave her exactly what she wanted and what I was hired to give her."

"Maybe it was simply a social arrangement so Miss Barrie could be seen in public."

"That wasn't my understanding," Hunter said with a shrug.

"Ever get into anything kinky?" Chris asked.

"My, but you're curious about Elaine's bedroom activities," Hunter said with a smirk.

"Miss Barrie told someone that you hurt her. If Janus found out about it, maybe he decided you were the one who violated the agreement."

"I bet that dyke, Della Summers, told you that, right? Shit, Elaine probably told her that to make her jealous."

"Why would Della be jealous?"

"Because she wanted Elaine herself, but Elaine was strictly into men. Where's the thrill in two women pretending to fuck one another?"

Chris smiled to herself. If Hunter only had a clue what two women together could do to one another sexually he might be jealous. She had noticed that he always said he had sex with Elaine Barrie, but never that he made love to her. Self-centered prick that he was.

"You think Carl Janus was jealous of your physical

relationship with his wife?"

"Maybe he didn't think he would be, but hell, he was a man with a beautiful wife and he knew she was sleeping with other men. Knew what they used to do with each other and pictured her doing that with another man. If it was me, just thinking about it would start to get to me. No one's that open-minded."

"Do you think he might have killed her because he became jealous?"

"I don't see how." Hunter laughed. "As far as I know, he can't even hold his own dick when he takes a piss."

"He could have hired someone to do it for him."

"I suppose so. Ain't like he's hurting for cash."

"How many times were you and Ms. Barrie together?"

"I didn't mark the dates on my calendar."

"Was she resistant after the first time?"

"Never had another problem," Hunter said shaking his head. "Became a real eager beaver. Like I said, she really got into it after a while. She was usually already in bed, ready and waiting when I got there. Like she couldn't wait."

"How long did these...meetings usually last?"

"You're asking a lot of beat-around-the-bush questions, Shaw. Why don't you just ask me for the gory details and get it over with?"

"I'm not interested in the details of your sexual forays with Miss Barrie, Hunter."

He leaned forward and rested his elbows on the table, never taking his eyes off Chris.

"But you're curious as hell about how she was in bed, aren't you? Anyone would be. Only natural. But, for a dyke, such as yourself, I'm sure your curiosity is driving you crazy. Everyone wants to know what the rich and famous are really like once they go home and turn out the lights. Do they screw each other the same as regular people or is there something special and exotic about it? I can see the curiosity in your eyes, Detective. What you'd really like to know is what it felt like to touch her, to feel her body respond, to drown in her kisses."

"That's not the purpose of this interrogation," Chris said even though Hunter was right. She did want to know about those things, but wasn't sure Damon Hunter was the guy she wanted to tell her. As Chris watched, Hunter closed his eyes and leaned back in the chair again.

"It was everything you probably think it would be. Maybe more," Hunter began. "Elaine was a sensuous woman who wanted a man's body near hers, touching her. She wasn't afraid of her own sexuality and could drive you to a point where all you wanted was to consume her any way you could. She loved that. Not that she was a tease. It heightened the experience. You begged for it, but she withheld it just long enough," Hunter smiled. "Never let me take her before she was ready and thought I was too. Touching her was like running my hands over fine silk, not that imitation shit, and her body almost melted into mine. Sweaty and hot, sweet and yielding, glistening in the candlelight."

"That's enough," Chris said.

"No, no, it's only the beginning," Hunter smiled. "It was what she did next that was really exceptional. Her mouth..." he went on.

"I said that's enough. None of this has anything to do with her death."

Hunter opened his eyes and smiled at Shaw. "You're right. But I don't know anything about how she died, only how she fucked."

"Did you see her the night she died?"

"Yeah, but it was the first time since we ended our little rendezvous about a year ago. I took a friend to see Elaine's show and went backstage to give her my regards."

"Did she usually go to her apartment after a show?"

"No. Unless she had a meeting with someone or it was a matinee day. She rested up between shows and, as far as I know, never had visitors then."

"If she usually went home after a show, when did she meet with you?"

"On dark days."

Chris looked at Hunter and knew he was lying.

"You know, days when she didn't have a show," Hunter explained. "Off days. They're called dark days."

"So on the day she died, it wasn't an off day?"

"No. She should have been with Janus after the show."

"Any idea who she might have been meetin'?"

He shook his head. "Was she dressed when they found her?"

"I'm afraid I can't tell you that."

"Well, if she was dressed, she might have met someone on a business matter, but that seems pretty unlikely. She never discussed business without Janus present. If she wasn't dressed, then maybe she decided to find a man for herself for a change."

"Was there anyone she seemed to be interested in?"

"If there was, I didn't notice," Hunter said. "She liked men who were tough and outspoken, sort of dominating. She and Janus argued all the time and, I tell you what, I think it turned her on."

"Arguin' turned her on?"

"Seemed like it. I was supposed to meet her one day and she was late. Told me she and Janus had a disagreement. She was still a little hyped up about it, on edge, but it was the best sex we ever had. I mean, she was always good, but there was something different about her that day. I can't think of a word to describe it. She couldn't get enough. I thought if a disagreement led to what she was doing then I ought to pray for them to have a really big blow-up, you know."

"Like she was takin' out her anger at her husband on you."

"Yeah, but not by being mad at me. More like she wanted to give me more of herself to make up. Didn't bother me in the least."

"How long were you Ms. Barrie's lover, Mr. Hunter?"

"Couple of months. Then Janus found someone else for her. No one ever stayed more than a couple of months. Guess he was afraid she'd get attached to them or something."

"Do you know any of the other men she slept with?"

"I heard a rumor she was sleeping with Kent Devine now, but can't say for sure."

"So the relationship between Elaine and Kent Devine is only a rumor?"

"Yes. But I did see him going across the street toward the hotel with her a couple of times."

"On dark days?"

"No, on matinee days mostly."

"So she could have been sleepin' with him on matinee days?"

"It wasn't her usual thing, but I guess it's possible. You'd have to ask Kent about that."

"Sounds like Mr. Janus only sought out men who knew his wife. Why not a total stranger?"

"Theater is the only world he knows and feels comfortable in. But, once again, you'd have to ask him about that. I've done a lot of different things in the theater, but mind-reading wasn't one of them. Sorry."

"Was there anyone you noticed who seemed out of place after her last performance? A stranger who got backstage? Anything like that?"

"No one gets backstage without a pass. I didn't see anyone unusual hanging around the theater when I left, but I wasn't really looking."

"Did Ms. Barrie have any visitors with passes after the show?"

"Just Gallagher, but he's there after a lot of performances. Keeping an eye on his fifteen percent."

"Her manager?"

"Yeah. Malcolm Gallagher. Lech extraordinaire. When I went backstage I thought I saw his kid leaving."

"Todd?"

"I guess that's his name. He hung around sometimes making sure Daddy's money was safe."

"What time was that?"

Hunter shrugged. "The performance ended about ten-thirty. Maybe about twenty minutes after the show ended."

"Did Gallagher know about the arrangements made by Mr. Janus?"

Hunter looked puzzled for a moment. "You know what? I really don't know. He could have. I never thought about it."

"They've been together a long time."

"Since before she married Janus, I think. I heard he wasn't happy about that union one little bit."

"I guess that's all the questions I have for now, Mr. Hunter. Keep yourself available in case I think of something else later," Chris said standing up.

Hunter pushed himself away from the table and stretched as he stood.

"With Elaine dead, I guess the show will go on with her faithful understudy. Personally, I give it about a month before it's curtains for good."

"Understudy no good?"

"She's not Elaine Barrie."

Chris watched Hunter strut down the hall toward the front doors, wondering how much of his statement could be believed and how much had been wishful thinking on his part. According to Alex Webb, Hunter's time with Elaine Barrie had been exceedingly brief. There wasn't any doubt that Hunter had a monumental ego. If Elaine had rejected him, he might have conjured up what might have been. She certainly wasn't in a position to dispute his story. Still, his story bothered Chris. She didn't want any of it to be true and the Elaine Barrie in her mind wouldn't have acted in the salacious manner Hunter had suggested. It was possible that her behavior had led to her death. It was just as possible that it hadn't.

It took Chris the better part of an hour to write up the report on her questioning of Damon Hunter and to bag the Starbuck's cup he'd left on the table of the interrogation room. When she finished, she didn't feel she knew Elaine Barrie any better than when she started. Why she felt the need to understand her wasn't clear to Chris. She had never needed to get into a victim's head before. She knew why, but didn't want to think about it. She would have liked to have known Elaine Barrie as a person and not merely a personality. But which Elaine would she have met: the loving wife of Carl Janus, the best friend of Della Summers, the sweet woman Alex Webb knew, or the sexual predator of Damon Hunter's memory. Chris began to believe that Elaine Barrie might have been all of those things, and if that was true she must have been the greatest performer who ever drew breath.

Chapter Ten

CARMEN KNOCKED ON the door of loft apartment 4C and waited. It had taken her a while to locate the building in the TriBeCa area south and east of Greenwich and SoHo. It was a long way from her apartment in Spanish Harlem, economically as well as physically. A few seconds later, a slender, statuesque woman in her thirties partially opened the door. The woman's eyes had a sultry look as they scanned slowly up and down Carmen's body.

"I'm looking for Della Summers," Carmen said.

"For what?" the woman asked in a throaty voice.

"I need to ask her a few questions," Carmen answered, holding her detective's shield up for the woman to see.

The door closed, and Carmen heard the chain guard slide before the door re-opened.

"She's in the shower. Who should I say is here?" the woman asked as she rested her weight on one foot and brushed long dark hair away from her face.

"Detective Sandoval, Midtown Homicide."

"This about Elaine?"

"Yeah."

"Del doesn't know anything that can help you, Detective," the woman said off-handedly.

"I just need to clear up a few things from our earlier conversation. Are you Ms. Summers' roommate?"

"Among other things," the woman said, running her tongue across her upper lip.

"Well, if you could tell her I'm here," Carmen said, feeling slightly uncomfortable.

"Will I need to leave you two alone?"

"No. That won't be necessary. I'm afraid I didn't get your name."

"Ma-rees-sa," the woman pronounced slowly.

Marissa wandered slowly toward the back of the apartment, glancing over her shoulder at Carmen and smiling. As soon as she was out of sight, Carmen took a deep breath and exhaled. She looked around briefly to see if there were any signs of the cat Della said had scratched her and wondered if the animal in question might be named Ma-rees-sa.

The apartment seemed to be well-furnished with furniture that obviously hadn't been purchased at a flea market or discount store.

On closer inspection, Carmen saw that the paintings mounted on the walls were not prints, but appeared to be originals. A glass wall offered a good view of the surrounding area and opened onto a narrow balcony.

Carmen was still standing in the middle of the living room when Della Summers came down the hall. She was wearing jeans and a t-shirt. From the way she moved, it appeared to Carmen that she hadn't taken time to put on anything underneath her clothing. Her hair was wet and a towel hung around her neck.

"Sorry, Detective," Della said with a smile. "Did Marissa offer you something to drink?"

"I'm fine," Carmen said. "I had lunch a little while ago and decided to swing by here on my way back to work."

"What did you want to know?" Della asked as she settled on the couch and drew her bare feet under her.

"Just need to clear up a couple of points. By the way, how's your arm?"

Della glanced at her bandaged forearm. "Better, thanks."

"Where's the cat?"

"Wha...oh, it took off yesterday. Probably found a new boyfriend somewhere."

"Too bad."

Della was beginning to look a little edgy and readjusted herself on the couch.

"That why you came here, Detective Sandoval, to check on our cat?"

"Would you mind showing me the scratches on your arm, Miss Summers?"

"For what?" Marissa interrupted.

"Well, it's possible Miss Barrie scratched her attacker..." Carmen began.

Della leaped up from the couch. "You think I killed Elaine?" she asked, shaking her head.

"That's ridiculous," Marissa added, going to Della's side.

"Why is it ridiculous?" Carmen asked.

Della had stopped communicating and stood shaking her head.

"Because there is no way in hell Del would have killed Elaine," Marissa said, taking a step toward Carmen. "She...she..." Marissa sputtered.

"She what?" Carmen asked as she stood to face Marissa.

Marissa glanced over her shoulder at Della and turned back toward Carmen.

"She loved Elaine."

"They were old friends, so what?" Carmen challenged.

Marissa threw her hands up in exasperation. "Not that way,

you idiot! How'd you ever get to be a detective anyway? Del has been in love with Elaine for years. She might kill *for* her, but wouldn't touch a hair on Elaine's head."

Carmen stepped to where she could see Della.

"And did Elaine feel the same way, Della?" Carmen asked.

Della looked up quickly, and Carmen saw tears pooling in her eyes as she shook her head.

"Did you argue about it?"

"This is total bullshit!" Marissa said loudly.

"If you don't butt out of this conversation, Ma-rees-sa," Carmen said, rolling the r, "I'll place you under arrest for obstructing my investigation. *Comprende?*"

Marissa put her hands up in surrender and walked away.

"Sit down, Della," Carmen said. "Let's talk about it."

Della sat down on the edge of the couch and took a deep breath and held it for a moment.

"We didn't argue about it," Della finally said softly.

"But Elaine knew you were gay?"

"Yes." Della smiled slightly. "Almost from the very beginning."

Della Summers was washing glasses behind the bar when she looked up and spotted Kent Devine across the semi-dark room. He flashed her a smile and waved before walking to the bar. At first Della hadn't noticed his companion, but when the young woman's face was finally illuminated by the lights over the bar, it took Del's breath away momentarily.

"What can I get you today, Kent?" Del asked as she continued to look at the woman. She estimated she was still in her teens, perhaps eighteen or nineteen.

"The boss in?" Kent asked.

"In the counting house, counting out his change," she answered, motioning to the rear of the bar with her head. "Who's your friend?"

"This is Elaine, from West by God Virginia," Kent said with a grin.

Del dried her hand and extended it across the bar. Elaine's grip was stronger than she expected.

"We're trying to find her a job. You know, just until she gets her big break," Kent said, with a wink.

"Ah, an actress," Del said. "She looks too young to be working in a place like this, Kent, but tell Gus I can use some help around the bar."

Kent told Elaine he would be right back and walked to a door in the back of the club.

"You want a drink?" Del asked. "Like water or tea."

"Thanks," Elaine said as she looked around.

Del poured a glass of tea and shoved it across the bar toward Elaine.

"Been here long?" Del asked as she continued washing and drying glasses.

"A few months."

"You got a place to stay, until your big break, that is?"

"I'm staying with Kent for now. Until I get enough money for a place of my own. I don't know about the big break thing," Elaine laughed lightly and drank her tea.

Del watched the young woman who seemed mesmerized by what she was seeing.

"Have you been working here long?" Elaine asked.

"Too damn long. I'm still waiting for my big break."

"Are you in the theater?"

"Ain't we all, honey?"

"I don't think I'm really good enough for the theater, but it's exciting anyway."

Kent returned a few minutes later and rested a hand on Elaine's shoulder when he reached the bar.

"Thanks for the tip, Del. You start tonight," Kent told Elaine.

"Elaine," Del said, "why don't you look around the club? You know, get the lay of the land."

When Elaine had wandered off, Del reached across the bar and touched Kent's arm.

"How old is that girl, Kent?"

"Nineteen, why?"

"She looks too young to be legal. What are you up to with her anyway?"

"Nothing."

"Don't give me that shit. You're sleeping with her, aren't you?"

Kent simply smiled at Della. "Why don't you get me a beer, Del?"

"How long before you figure she'll be back on the bus for West Virginia," Del asked as she handed Kent his beer.

Kent leaned his elbows on the bar and sipped his beer.

"Maybe never. I admit we've fooled around some, but I tell you what, Del, that girl can sing."

"We can all sing," Del snorted.

"Not like her. You wait. You'll see."

"And you think she's going to get her big break working in this joint?"

"How long did Elaine work at the club?" Carmen asked.

"Maybe six months. Sure enough, Kent was right. The girl could sell a song like nobody you ever heard. I never heard a voice as pure. Like silk drifting over your soul. Anyway, one night Oliver Levinson strolled into the club, just slummin' I suppose. As soon as Kent saw Levinson, he got Elaine on the stage to sing a duet with him. And the rest, as they say, is show biz history. A regular fucking fairy tale."

"How did you and Elaine become such close friends?" Carmen asked.

Della thought about it for a moment. "I really don't know. Levinson wanted her for a new show he was putting together and she quit the club. Then one night about a month later she appeared around closing time."

Della folded her bartender's apron and stashed it under the bar. When she stood up, Elaine was sitting at the bar.

"Got any tea?" Elaine asked with a smile.

"Jesus, Elaine. I didn't hear you come in."

"Didn't mean to scare you."

"We're closing."

"I know. Do you have a few minutes?"

"Sure. What's up?"

"I don't know anyone in town except you and Kent and need to talk to someone."

"Where's Kent?"

"He's a nice guy, but I can't always talk to him."

"You got a problem?"

"No," Elaine said, pausing. "Listen, Del, if I can get you a part in Levinson's show, would you take it?"

Del laughed. "No, I'd rather stay here shleppin' drinks."

"I'm serious."

"Of course I'd take it."

"He needs another dancer. It's not a big part or anything, but I'd like for you to be in the show with me. I'd feel better if I knew at least one other person on the stage."

"Why are you doing this, Elaine? You don't know me from shit."

Elaine leaned back on the bar chair. "I just need a friend, Del. Someone I can talk to when I need to."

"How good a friend ya lookin' for?" Del smiled as she leaned forward against the bar.

"I know you're gay, Del, but I'm not. I like you and you're easy to talk to. I don't care about your private life. I just need a friend I can trust. Who knows, maybe this is your big break. Be my friend and I promise that when I work, you'll work."

"And she's gotten me on with every production she's been in since," Della said. "A very good friend."

Marissa reappeared, carrying a glass of water. She sat down next to Della, slipped an arm around her, and handed her the glass. Della smiled at Marissa and sipped the water.

"I hope you understand," Carmen said, clearing her throat, "but I have to ask. Was there ever anything between you and Elaine besides friendship?"

Marissa opened her mouth to speak, but Della stopped her.

"I don't want you to get the wrong idea, Detective," Della said quietly. "I won't deny that I was attracted to Elaine. She became a very seductive woman and could turn on the charm with anyone, man or woman. But, to answer your question, no, there was never anything except friendship between Elaine and me."

"I'm assuming she told you more personal things than you told me yesterday," Carmen said.

"It wasn't a blow-by-blow description, but I got a fair idea about what her private life became."

"How was her relationship with her husband?"

"I thought she was crazy when she started going out with Carl and that she should be locked up in a rubber room when she told me she was going to marry him."

"You didn't like him?"

"I thought it was a fling at first, you know. But she was serious as a heart attack. Then I thought maybe she was using him to help her career, but that wasn't her style. She never stepped on anyone to get as far as she did and she absolutely didn't make it by sleeping around."

Della stopped and sipped more water. "Carl's all right," she finally said. "One thing I know is that he was crazy in love with her and she deserved someone like that."

"Did she still confide in you after her marriage?"

Marissa laughed. "You bet. Even spent the night here a couple of times, yakking all damn night."

"How did you feel about that?" Carmen asked, looking at Marissa.

"Just caused me to lose some sleep." Marissa shrugged.

"Were you jealous of the relationship between Della and Elaine?"

"Shit, no!"

"Miss Barrie was a wealthy woman," Carmen said.

"Hell, Detective, I earn more than Elaine did in her best year. How else do you think we can afford a place like this?"

"Marissa's a stockbroker," Della explained.

"You're not in the theater then," Carmen said.

"Too risky a venture for me. Give me good, solid stocks and bonds any day."

"How long have you been together?" Carmen asked.

"Five years, almost," Della said.

"Did Elaine tell you about Damon Hunter and Alex Webb?"

"Oops!" Marissa said. "Secret's out, Del."

"She told me," Della said, frowning. "She hated it."

"What did she tell you about Hunter and Webb?"

"Not much about Alex. He worked with her in her last show. Nice guy, but a little unsophisticated. Elaine thought he hadn't been with many women before. No Lothario. But she liked him. I'd be surprised if there was ever anything intimate between them. He was like a little brother to her."

"And Hunter?"

"That's a different story. He was an animal. Only time I ever heard her say she hated someone."

"What did Hunter do that she found so distasteful?"

"Rape is pretty distasteful, don't you think?" Marissa asked bluntly.

"Hunter raped her? Did she report it?" Carmen asked.

"And tell you guys what? The man my husband hired to spend time with me, raped me? Who's gonna believe a bullshit story like that?" Marissa laughed.

"Even a prostitute can be raped," Carmen said.

"And I'm sure you spend all your free time looking for guys reported by prostitutes, Detective," Marissa snorted.

"Did Elaine tell her husband about the rape?"

"As far as I know, she only told him Hunter hurt her. One thing I know is that Damon Hunter had better apply to plumber's school or something because Carl Janus will make sure he never works in the theater again. Elaine only saw him that one time."

"So anything else between them, beyond that one time, is a lie?"

"Absolutely."

"Is Hunter the kind of man who might strike back if he thought his career had been destroyed because of Elaine?"

"Probably. Now that I think about it, I saw him at the theater the night Elaine was killed. But I don't know if she talked to him or not."

"Malcolm Gallagher said he was the last person to see her that night," Carmen said.

"Might have been. I know he was with her when I left. I checked on her before I came home."

"Did you always do that?"

"No, but she and Gallagher were having a pretty loud argument about something and I thought she might be looking for an excuse to get rid of him. And I wanted to congratulate her on a great show. She really outdid herself in the last performance."

"You don't know what they were arguing about?"

"No. When I stuck my head in her dressing room I could see that Elaine was pretty upset with Malcolm. They had lots of disagreements about the direction of her career, especially recently. So I figured it must have been the same this time. When I looked in Todd was telling Malcolm to calm down and back off. They could discuss it later. Whatever *it* was."

"He wanted her to go to California, right?" Carmen asked.

"The guy had visions of palm trees dancing in his head. Elaine might have given it a shot later, but with Carl sick, there was no way she was going to launch into something new. It was hard enough for her to keep going with the show and recording."

"Why did she?"

"Carl wanted her to. For Carl, the performance is everything. He loves the theater. It was his whole life, even after he married Elaine. Carl always said the same thing. The people in the audience have spent hard-earned bucks to get a good show and they had better get one every damn performance."

"Mr. Janus didn't seem to be the kind of person who would have been happy about his wife being with other men," Carmen observed.

"Carl's a pragmatist," Della said. "His illness made most physical intimacy on his part out of the question. Elaine was less than forty. He thought, however warped that thinking was, that she needed someone she could be intimate with."

"Surely after her trouble with Hunter, he saw his plan wouldn't work," Carmen said.

"That's why Elaine sort of directed him to Alex Webb. He was harmless and liked Elaine enough to never hurt her. I suppose that's how she finally ended up with Kent as well. You know about him?"

"Yes. He's given us a statement."

"He probably didn't tell you much about their relationship. Elaine liked him from the beginning, but they hadn't had a romantic relationship since she was nineteen, and even that wasn't too serious. Elaine created a fantasy to keep Carl happy."

"And Carl wasn't jealous?"

"Elaine said they never talked about it. Once she was home, life was your average husband and wife thing. Even when she stayed at the Montclair she called him every night."

"Do you think I could see those scratches on your arm now?" Carmen asked.

Della took a deep breath and began peeling the bandage away from her forearm. Four dark red claw marks appeared on the soft underside of her forearm. She looked at them and held her arm out for Carmen to see.

"Looks a little red," Carmen observed. "Has a doctor looked at your arm?"

"I took her to my personal physician the next day," Marissa said. "Dr. Julius Maynard. His office is in Manhattan."

Chapter Eleven

"IF HUNTER RAPED her once, he might have tried it again," Chris said when Carmen recounted her visit with Della Summers.

"It's only second-hand information, Chris. For all we know, Elaine made it up," Carmen said. "Happens all the time."

"Jesus, it sounds like they're talking about four or five different women," Chris said, her frustration showing. "Everyone who knew her describes her behavior differently."

"She was a woman, what do you expect?" Carmen shrugged.

"Maybe predictability."

"You think people act the same all the time? Must've been nice growing up at Disneyland."

"I know people act differently sometimes, Carmen, but not all the damn time. Look at these interviews. Here she's a slutty nympho. Here she's practically a saint. In this one she's elegant and refined. Pick one, they're all different."

"I know you don't date men, okay, but it's the same thing with women. So here's the way it goes, just so you don't think you're special next time or something. Girl goes out with guy. Girl sizes guy up. You know, what kind of guy he is, what she thinks he expects, how he looks at her, and so on. You with me so far?"

"Yeah."

"Then once she thinks she's got it figured out, that's how she acts right up until they're standing in front of the priest."

"That's the stupidest thing I ever heard. Why wouldn't she just act like herself? You think that's what guys, or a woman for that matter, wants? A fake."

"Hey, you damn skippy," Carmen said. "You go out on a date expecting some good-looking chick with manners and wind up with Petunia Pig, you gonna ask her out again? Pure survival tactic. You want that second date you better put on one good show the first time. After they marry you, then you can be yourself."

"Then the only story we can believe is Carl Janus's."

"Unless she changed for him when he got sick."

"So, what? You think Elaine Barrie was like some kind of chameleon, changing her personality to suit every person she was with."

"Why not? She made a living pretending to be someone she wasn't."

"Then if she was this ideal woman to everyone who knew her,

why would anyone kill her?"

"Hell, I don't know. Maybe she ran into someone who didn't like lizards."

Chris smiled at the remark.

"So now what?" Carmen asked.

"I guess we'd better talk to Janus again since obviously everything wasn't peaches and cream the way he said it was."

Carmen looked over the top of a file folder she had been reviewing. "Well, at least you didn't say hunky-damn-dorry. You got any plans for tonight?" she asked.

"I sure as hell don't plan to watch another dance contest," Chris grumped.

"Mama told me to invite you for dinner. She's cooking up your favorite. If you don't have other plans, she thought you might want to join us."

"Depends on who 'us' is."

"Just me, Mama, and Frankie."

"Works for me. Can I bring anything?"

The phone on Chris' desk rang before Carmen could answer.

"Shaw," she said, leaning back in her chair.

"Arthur Featherstone here," the deputy medical examiner said.

"What's up, Artie?"

"Wanted to let you know the final report on the Barrie case is being typed up and should be on your desk by morning. I've already authorized the release of the body."

"Thanks. Anything else?"

"Nothing that raised a red flag for me. By the way, better break out your good clothes. The press has already been here. I'm sure you and Carmen are next. Once the papers get started, the commissioner's liable to be all over you."

"Like a pack of dogs on a three-legged cat," Chris mumbled to herself.

As she hung up, she looked at the clock hanging on the wall next to her desk. Four-thirty.

"How about we pack it in for today?" she said.

"Sure," Carmen shrugged. "You gonna follow me?"

"I hope Mercedes has something to drink at home. I could really use something right now," Chris said as she picked up her overcoat.

CHRIS OPENED THE first of what she hoped would be several beers a little more than half an hour later. The early news was on and she leaned back on the afghan-covered sofa to watch. Being the polite country girl she was, she offered to help with dinner, but

Mercedes ran her out of the kitchen with a combination of English and Spanish threats.

"The top story from Manhattan today is the murder of Broadway superstar, Elaine Barrie," the solemn-faced announcer reported as a picture of the victim appeared magically behind his head. "For more on the story, Elizabeth Herrera, reporting live from the Lerner Theater."

"Hey, Carmen!" Chris yelled. "It's on the tube!"

Carmen rushed into the living room, still buttoning her blouse. For a split second Chris caught a glimpse of white lace against Carmen's olive skin.

"Thank you, Bob. Elaine Barrie, a star of the highest magnitude on the Broadway stage, was found murdered the night before last in her suite at the Montclair Hotel. The death was made public only today when the New York City Medical Examiner's Office released its final report. Miss Barrie, the wife of famed director, Carl Janus, was found in the early morning hours of December twenty-seventh. According to Deputy Medical Examiner Arthur Featherstone, Miss Barrie was killed after her last performance the evening of December twenty-sixth. Cast members in her latest production have all expressed shock and the show, which is at the Lerner Theater, across the street from the Montclair, has been cancelled for the remainder of the week."

"Do the police have any suspects, Elizabeth?" the announcer interrupted.

"Uh, apparently, the police are questioning the people who knew Miss Barrie, Bob, but so far we haven't had a chance to speak to the detectives in charge of the case."

"Thank you, Elizabeth," the announcer continued, breaking his remote connection. "We will keep you updated on this case as we receive more on the story. In other news..."

"Well, that didn't say much," Carmen said as she slipped her shoes on.

"Guess we'll be ducking reporters now. Maybe you should handle them, Carmen. You're better looking than I am."

"Surely you don't expect me to disagree with that." Carmen laughed.

Mercedes stuck her head into the living room. "Dinner ready."

Chris and Carmen took seats at the table.

"Frankie be a little late," Mercedes announced. "Got some business."

Chris wondered if Frankie Sandoval was preparing to screw up again. The last time, he had boosted the car of a family friend who hadn't pressed charges against the eighteen-year-old. Frankie had been one of those late-life babies and Chris often wondered if he hadn't been accidental. Carmen was fourteen years older and the fact that she was a police officer hadn't deterred Frankie from committing petty crimes. Since Carmen's father died, Mercedes had a tough time keeping the boy in check.

"How is Frankie?" Chris asked innocently.

"He's a pain in our collective asses," Carmen said.

"Don' talk about you brother like that, Carmenita," Mercedes said.

"How long are you gonna put up with his crap, Mama? He's headed for hard time if he doesn't straighten up."

"Don' you give him trouble when he gets home. Maybe you talk to him, Christina."

"Leave Chris out of this, Mama. Frankie isn't her problem. Did you talk to his counselor?" Carmen asked.

"Jes."

"And? Is he going to school or not?"

"Sometime."

"I'll talk to him," Chris said. "This is great, Mercedes."

The compliment about her cooking made Mercedes smile and Chris hoped the conversation wouldn't circle back to Frankie.

CHRIS CARRIED THE last of the dishes into the kitchen and stacked them next to the sink while Mercedes busied herself around the kitchen.

"You a good woman, Christina," she said.

"Thanks. Now how about you get off your feet for a while and watch TV and let me pay for dinner by cleanin' up in here?" Chris said.

"No, no. You our guest," Mercedes protested.

"Hell, Mercedes, I eat here often enough to be out of the guest category. Get outta here."

"I worried about Carmenita."

"Why? She's doin' great at work."

"She still see that *bendejo*, Ruben. He no good for her."

"They seem to get along okay and he's got a good job with the city."

"He not a good man."

"There's not many good guys left," Chris said, "but Carmen can handle herself. I wouldn't worry about her if I were you."

"Is time Carmenita settle down. Find good man like my Francisco and make the babies."

Chris wasn't sure what to say about that. The picture of Carmen bouncing babies on each hip made her smile. Other than the fact that she thought Ruben Montanez was an asshole, Chris had never dared to delve into her partner's personal life.

By the time Mercedes gave up and left the kitchen, Chris had finished washing most of the dishes. She was working on the last pan when Carmen came in.

"Mama stick you with the dishes?" she asked.

"Nah, I volunteered. I'm almost done and then I better get home."

"What should I do about Frankie, Chris? I feel so damn helpless and I should know what to do."

"Maybe you should drag his ass to family counselin' or something. Or maybe it's just a stage. You know how teenagers are."

"Yeah, I suppose," Carmen said.

"You think he's runnin' with a gang?"

"I haven't seen any evidence of it, but when your sister's a cop you might not broadcast it at home."

"Maybe you should scare the shit out of him. If he thinks he's tough, I know a few guys who could take care of that pretty quick," Chris said, rolling her shirtsleeves down and buttoning the cuffs.

"I know the Barrie case is important, Chris, but if things sort of get out of hand with Frankie, I might have to take a day or two off."

"So do it. Take care of your family, Carmen," Chris said as they walked back into the living room.

Chris took her overcoat from a coat rack next to the front door.

"I'll go down with you," Carmen said.

"That's okay. It's cold out there."

Carmen grabbed a down jacket anyway and followed Chris to her car.

"Your mother's worried about you," Chris said.

"Yeah, I know. She thinks my reproductive organs are gonna shrivel up and go away if I don't start pumping out babies soon."

Chris laughed. "Something like that."

"Jesus, that woman will talk to anybody about anything."

"She loves you," Chris said softly. "You're lucky you still have a mother."

"Yeah, I know. I just wish she'd realize times have changed. If I got married tomorrow, she'd expect me to quit working and stand over a stove all day cooking frijoles and waiting for my man to come home like she did."

"Most men wouldn't mind that," Chris said with a smile.

"Is that what you expect from a woman, Chris?"

"I'm probably not the best person to ask, Carmen. My mama used to say I'd know the right one when they came along. Thought I had it, but I was obviously wrong." Chris rubbed her hands together. "What do you want from a man?"

Carmen shrugged. "Someone who cares about me, I guess. I mean there has to be something beside their talents in bed, right?"

Chris looked away and swallowed, almost ashamed to admit that was exactly what she looked for. Since Jill's sudden departure with Captain Wonderful, the only things Chris had looked for was a woman who was moderately attractive after three or four drinks and willing to catch a cab home. "A sense of humor helps, too, especially with our jobs," Chris finally answered as she started to shuffle around in an attempt to keep warm. "Look, I need to get home before I turn into a Popsicle," she said.

Chapter Twelve

ROBERT BLANKENSHIP PULLED his stethoscope from around his neck and opened a black medical bag.

"I think we're going to have to increase your medication, Carl," he said, dropping the stethoscope into his bag.

Ted Warner propped Carl up on a stack of pillows and helped him re-button his shirt.

"How much longer do you think I have, Rob?" Janus asked.

"I'd like to think positively," Blankenship said.

"Somehow your voice doesn't sound very positive," Carl chuckled. "It doesn't matter anyway. No matter what you do, we all know what the outcome will be. You've done the best you could."

"I think you should consider checking into the hospital where I can keep a closer eye on you."

"No. I think I'll stay here. You and Ted know what my wishes are about that."

"But we have a better chance for more time in the hospital."

Carl smiled warmly at his doctor. "Without Elaine, I don't have a reason for hanging around. Funny, but I was sure I would be the one waiting for her."

"She wouldn't want you to quit, Mr. Janus," Ted said.

"There's a memorial for her tomorrow, Rob. I have to be there," Janus said flatly.

"I'll go with you. No funeral?"

"I made arrangements to have her body shipped back to West Virginia. She should be buried with the rest of her family."

"But what about..." Blankenship began.

"Ted has already taken care of that. When I die, he'll ship me to West Virginia. I bought a place next to Elaine."

"I thought you hated West Virginia."

"I do, but Elaine loved it. I'll be able to tolerate it as long as we're together."

"What time is the memorial?" Blankenship asked.

"At three. Showtime. Bring a camera so you can record all those false tears. Should see some fine acting."

"Give them a break, Carl. Everyone is going to miss Elaine."

Their conversation was interrupted by the buzzing of the doorbell. Warner left the room quickly to answer it. When he returned a few minutes later, he was accompanied by Christine

Shaw. Janus frowned slightly when he saw her.

"More questions, Detective Shaw?" Janus asked.

"A few," Chris said. "I'm glad you're here, Doctor, I was going to give you a call."

"What can I do for you?" Blankenship asked as he snapped his bag shut.

"Is there someplace we can talk privately?" Chris asked.

"Ted," Janus said. "Why don't you show Detective Shaw and the good doctor into the living room? I promise not to sneak in and eavesdrop on your conversation."

CHRIS LOOKED OVER her shoulder at a smiling Carl Janus who seemed at ease and surprisingly cheerful. As Chris and Blankenship followed Ted, she couldn't help but glance around the Janus's apartment. She had been too pre-occupied to notice much during her previous middle-of-the-night visit. As they entered the large living room, Chris paused when she saw an almost life-size portrait of Elaine hanging over the fireplace mantle. What struck Chris were her eyes. They were a vibrant hazel that leaned toward green. She had a Mona Lisa smile and appeared to be very relaxed. She was seated on a straight back chair with one arm resting on the chair back. She was wearing a low-cut, white, cossack-style blouse over a long emerald green skirt that draped onto the floor. Whoever painted it had mainly concentrated on her face and hands. As Chris stared at the portrait, Blankenship stepped beside her.

"It's a lovely portrait, isn't it?" Blankenship asked with sadness in his voice.

"Yes. When was it done?" Chris asked.

"Two or three years ago, I think. It was an anniversary gift for Carl."

"How well did you know Mrs. Janus, Doctor?"

"Not very well, I'm afraid. I spent a lot of time with Carl, but I only spoke to her a few times. Mostly about his health," Blankenship answered.

"Was she concerned about it?"

"Of course," the doctor said. "Any wife would be. It's heartbreaking to see a man as strong and alive as Carl decline. ALS can be a rapidly progressing disease."

"How long do you think he has?"

"Well, since he's refused to check into a hospital, I would think probably nine months tops."

Ted asked if there was anything they needed before he turned to leave them alone, but Chris stopped him.

"I'll need to speak to you as well, Mr. Warner," she said.

Warner looked confused. "About what?" he asked.

"Just a few questions about Mr. and Mrs. Janus. I assume you were here when she was."

"Yes. I have the room next to the master bedroom."

"Good. Have a seat," Chris directed.

Warner and Blankenship both sat down and waited, unsure what help they could be in the investigation into the death of Elaine Barrie.

"Did Mr. Janus confide in either of you?" Chris began.

"About what?" Blankenship asked warily.

"Personal information," she said.

"Anything Carl Janus might have told me is protected by the doctor-patient privilege, Detective," Blankenship said.

"How about you, Ted? You're not a doctor. Janus ever talk to you about his wife or their relationship?"

Ted looked at Blankenship and then back at Chris.

"No," he finally said.

"You said your room is next to the Januses. Did you ever hear them argue? Ever hear loud voices coming from their room?"

"Their private life was none of my business. I didn't interfere," Ted said.

"I asked if you ever heard them argue, not what you might have done about it," Chris reiterated.

"I might have heard them argue once or twice," Ted said so softly that Chris could barely hear him.

"All married couples argue, Detective Shaw," Blankenship said.

Ignoring the doctor, Chris continued with Ted, "How long have you been Mr. Janus's nurse?"

"Since not long after he was diagnosed with ALS," Ted answered. "She didn't want him to be alone."

"So you've been here, what, about two years?"

"About."

"Did you ever hear what Mr. and Mrs. Janus argued about?"

"None of my business."

"Did Mrs. Janus sleep in the room with her husband?" Chris asked.

"Yeah, when she was home."

"How many nights a week was she home?"

"I don't know," Ted shrugged. "Four. Three or four. Sometimes more. Some nights she stayed at her place at the Montclair."

"It's not that far from the Lerner Theater to here. Why wouldn't she come home every night?"

"Mr. Janus wanted her to stay at the Montclair. I have to wake him up every couple of hours for his medication or to reposition him in bed. He said Miss Barrie needed to be rested before a performance."

"Thank you, Ted. I appreciate the information," Chris said.

Ted and Blankenship both rose to leave.

"If you could stay for a moment, Doctor," she said.

Blankenship stood and leaned against an overstuffed chair as Ted left them alone.

"I know a lot of information about Mr. Janus is confidential, but there are a couple of questions about the ALS itself I'd like to ask," Chris said.

"I'll tell you what I can, Detective Shaw, but I won't violate patient confidentiality," Blankenship warned.

"I understand that. A patient with this disease, what kinds of limitations would they have?"

"It starts fairly benignly with some weakness in the extremities, but can spread quite rapidly. I've never known a patient Carl's age to survive more than three or four years."

"Would it strike one part of the body faster than others?"

"It generally might be an overall sensation or feeling of weakness, almost not noticeable. Then gradually the patient will begin to lose control and use of the muscles in the extremities. Carl began to lose the use of his legs within a few months. Now he has very limited use of his left arm and the right is virtually useless. I've already told Detective Sandoval most of this," Blankenship said.

"The heart is a muscle, right?"

"Yes, and as soon as the disease invades that muscle, it's all but over. Carl's heart has been compromised, but that's been a recent complication."

"I assume for a patient with the disease a sex life would be out of the question then?"

Blankenship eyed Chris carefully. "What are you getting at, Detective?"

"Nothing in particular. Just curious."

Blankenship drew a deep breath.

"Initially the patient can enjoy a relatively normal sex life, but it would diminish as the disease progressed."

"Would the patient's partner still be able to arouse the patient?"

"Sometimes, but not always. That involves an involuntary reflex."

"Well, I guess that's about it, Doctor Blankenship. I appreciate your help," Chris said.

Before she left the study to return to Janus's bedroom, Chris glanced at Elaine's portrait again and wondered who she really was. When she entered the bedroom, Janus was sitting up in bed, reading. He smiled as Chris came toward him and used his left hand to remove reading glasses from his face.

"You like the theater, Detective Shaw?" Janus asked.

"Very much."

Janus pointed to what he was reading. "A script for a stage play," he said. "Can you believe anyone would still send one to me?" Janus smiled.

"I hear you're the best."

"Maybe, but this play is a pile of shit. Never make it. Too complex. The audience needs something straightforward that they can either identify with personally or that helps them escape from an otherwise mundane existence for two or three hours."

Janus closed the script and tossed it next to him on the bed. "What can I do for you, Detective? I'm sure you didn't come here for a lecture on the theater."

Chris looked around and pulled a chair next to the bed. She unbuttoned her jacket and looked at Janus. She felt profoundly sorry for the man, but didn't know any way to escape questioning him about his wife's possible extramarital activities.

"Durin' our investigation into Mrs. Janus's death, a few things have come to light that I need to ask you about."

"Will it help you find who killed her?"

"I think so. We've interviewed a number of people, including Alex Webb and Damon Hunter," Chris said, looking for a reaction from Janus. "Do you know them?"

"I believe they had both worked with Elaine in one of her shows," Janus answered calmly.

"According to a witness who saw them, they also spent time in the Montclair suite with her." Chris wasn't sure why she was beating around the bush, but she had hoped for more reaction from Janus.

"I suppose that's possible. Elaine tried to keep up with some of the people who worked with her."

Chris cleared her throat and looked at the floor. "Well, Mr. Janus, both of these men have said that you hired them to have social liaisons with your wife," Chris blurted out.

Janus blinked a few times and sucked in a deep breath. "That's true," he finally said.

"You'll have to excuse me if I'm havin' a tough time understandin' that, sir," Chris said.

"I don't expect or need for you to understand it, Detective Shaw," Janus said in a voice that was suddenly strong and hard. "I'm sure you can understand why I'd prefer to keep that a private matter."

"I'm sure. Were these arrangements your idea or your wife's?"

"Elaine would never have suggested such a thing. She would never have been unfaithful to me." Janus's voice had softened somewhat.

"But she was," Chris said.

"No! She never was. You think I don't know what she did? Hell, Alex Webb wouldn't have slept with Elaine if she'd been the one suggesting it. Kent has been with her most recently and I'm sure they never did anything either. When Elaine suggested Alex and Kent, I knew what she was up to and didn't want to ruin her scheme."

"What scheme?" Chris asked.

"If you've spoken to Damon Hunter, then I'm sure you already know what kind of man he is." Chris watched his fingers slowly curl into a loose fist. "He raped Elaine, you know."

"She told you that?"

"She didn't have to. I knew there was something very wrong after she met with him."

"Then why would you persist in having her with other men?"

"I don't know whether I can explain my relationship with Elaine to you or not. Or whether you would understand it if I did," Janus said and then paused. "Elaine was my only wife. Don't know why I waited so long to marry. Waiting for Elaine, I suppose. There used to be rumors that I was gay. Quite amusing actually. But I can assure you that I wasn't inexperienced where women were concerned. Christ, Detective, I didn't make it to forty-five without losing my virginity or discovering what a wonderfully divine creature a woman can be. I simply didn't find one I'd want to wake up next to every damn morning. Until I met Elaine. She was so shy and so loving that there aren't enough words for me to describe her. But, to get to the heart of it, however crass it might sound, Elaine was an extremely sexual woman. I can't remember being with a woman who rejoiced in making love as much as she did. I used to ask her where she learned what she knew about sex. All she would ever tell me was that she read a lot when she was younger." Janus laughed. He closed his eyes and continued laughing lightly, almost to himself for several moments. When he finally reopened his eyes and looked at Chris, she saw sadness for a time past in his eyes.

"Ah, well, anyway," Janus resumed, "after my illness reached a certain point, I couldn't stand the thought of a sexual creature such as Elaine being alone. She told me once that a good sex life like ours kept her performances alive. I didn't want her to lose that either."

"So you came up with this...solution?"

"I took the suite at the Montclair, and like a fool, contacted Hunter. He was a nice looking man and I made him an offer he really couldn't refuse."

"But it didn't work out the way you planned?"

A pained expression came on Janus's face and he chewed his lower lip. "I caused Elaine to be hurt. I'll never be able to forget that or forgive myself for subjecting her to an assault like that. The only thing I could do was ruin Hunter as far as the theater was concerned."

"Did you and your wife argue about the arrangements you proposed?"

"Yes, many times before I contacted Hunter."

"Why do you think she agreed to go along with it?"

"To make me happy, I suppose. Sounds a little O'Henry-ish doesn't it?"

"*Gift of the Magi*," Chris said.

"You know O'Henry?" Janus asked with a smile.

"I was a lit major in college," Chris admitted.

"Must be why you're a policewoman. No money in literature these days," Janus sighed.

"Have you considered, Mr. Janus, that your arrangement might have led to your wife's death?" Chris asked.

"I've thought about it, but I hope not," Janus answered as tears began forming in his eyes. "If I wasn't already at death's doorstep, I think I would take my own life if what I did cost Elaine hers."

"We've interviewed both Hunter and Webb."

"Did Alex tell you he had slept with Elaine?" Janus asked.

"He said he slept on the couch."

"Well, if I know Elaine, I think it's fair to say that was all he did. Sleeping together and making love are not the same thing, despite the way people interchange those phrases today."

"You think the same was true for Kent Devine?"

"I wouldn't doubt it. Elaine told me that before I met her she had been with Kent, but that it hadn't been a serious thing for either of them."

"Sort of casual sex?"

"I dislike that term, Detective. Sounds cheap, certainly non-committal. She was very young then, probably more curious than anything else."

"Or maybe Kent was taking advantage of her youthful inexperience."

"Whatever it was, I believe it evolved into a very good friendship. Kent would never have harmed her."

Chapter Thirteen

"WHERE THE HELL have you been?" Carmen demanded as Chris came into the squad room.

"Stopped by to chat with Carl Janus. Why?" Chris asked.

"Because you left me stuck here with those fucking piranha reporters."

"I thought we agreed last night that you'd handle them because you were better lookin'," Chris said with a grin. "So what did you tell them?"

"The usual bullshit."

"Oh, you mean, we're lookin' into it, we've questioned a number of witnesses, we're goin' over the forensic evidence. That bullshit?"

Carmen smiled. "I don't know why they even bother talking to us. We always tell them the same thing."

"Well, I reckon it's so they can point out how uncooperative we are and tell everyone how incompetent we are when we don't have it solved within two or three days," Chris said as she glanced through the messages on her desk.

"Yeah, I *reckon*," Carmen said in a mocking voice. "Did you get a DNA sample for Janus?"

"Yeah. He consented to a swab."

"What did hubby have to say?"

Chris gave Carmen a brief synopsis of her conversation with Carl Janus.

"Well, at least he didn't deny it," Carmen shrugged.

"And I don't think he had anything directly to do with her death. Now if we'd found Damon Hunter dead, Janus would have been my first suspect."

"You almost sound sorry for Janus, Chris."

"I don't know what to think about him. He only wanted his wife to be happy, even if he was a little misguided in the way he went about it."

"How do you think the rape happened?"

"I think Hunter went to the Montclair like he was supposed to, she tried to explain she wasn't interested, but would keep up a pretense for Carl, and Hunter wasn't interested in pretendin'. I'd love to nail his ass for it, but it ain't gonna happen. The best Janus could do was blackball the guy."

"So what are our options now?" Carmen asked. "Hunter could

have killed her because of what Janus did to him. Della Summers knew about the men and could have killed her because she got jealous. For that matter, Ma-rees-sa, could have been jealous of Elaine and bopped her. Maybe Alex Webb isn't the innocent Opie he seems to be. He might have decided to go the whole nine yards and knocked her off so he wouldn't be ruined like Damon. Kent Devine might have tried to rekindle an old flame and been rejected. And now you think we can eliminate the husband. Wow! We got it down to twenty suspects instead of twenty-one."

"I think we can cross Blankenship and the nurse off our list, too," Chris said.

"Shit." Carmen shook her head. "They weren't even on my list."

Chris poured a cup of coffee and took it back to her desk. She opened a file and picked up her phone, looking at the file as she punched in a number. She listened for a minute and then rolled her eyes as her call was forwarded to an answering service telling her that Dr. Clifford Purnell was out of town for the week and referring his patients to the physician covering for him. Chris jotted down a note and hung up.

"Did Frankie get home last night?" she asked.

"Yeah, the dumb shit finally rolled up after midnight. Drunk as a skunk and demanding dinner."

"And what did you do?"

"I made Mama stay in her room so she couldn't cook for him and told him where the fucking kitchen was. I shoulda thrown him out and then arrested him for public intoxication, but I didn't want to fight with Mama again."

"Have you checked on a family counselor?"

"Yeah, I called earlier. We're supposed to go Monday if I can keep Frankie around that long."

"I've been thinkin' about it and maybe you should let him have enough rope to hang himself. Some people have to learn the hard way."

"That's what Ruben says," Carmen said.

"Well, who'd have thought Ruben Montanez and I would ever agree on anything?"

"I wish I knew why you hate Ruben so much," Carmen said.

"I don't hate him, Carmen. Hate's a strong word. I don't like him. If I hated him I could be really nasty."

"So why don't you like him?"

"Doesn't matter," Chris mumbled.

"It matters to me."

"I guess because he's such a pompous ass, struttin' around like he knows more than anyone else. Mr. Macho pretendin' to be a

Puerto Rican John Travolta or somethin'. He's a fuckin' paramedic, for Christ's sake, not Albert fuckin' Schweitzer. Plus he treats you like a possession."

"'Scuse me for asking," Carmen said, holding her hand up.

"I think you can do better, that's all. What're you doin' this weekend?" Chris asked.

Carmen smiled, "Why? You gonna take me away from all this to look for Mr. Right?"

"Yeah, maybe you'll run into some rich guy."

Carmen snorted, "Yeah, some rich *white* guy."

"Got somethin' against white folks?"

"No. I just don't socialize with many white people. They clash with the color scheme in my neighborhood."

"Well, what am I? Chinese?"

"Speaking of Chinese, you hungry?" Carmen asked, changing topics.

Chapter Fourteen

AS CHRIS PILOTED her car through the city streets, she wasn't in a hurry. It was going to be a long afternoon and she might as well be as relaxed as possible. She had been to Carmen's apartment many times before, but usually after dark. Today, she decided to take a more scenic route, if such a thing was possible in New York's Spanish Harlem. She had to smile thinking about her first few months in the city when she couldn't find anything.

As she rounded the corner onto Lexington Avenue at 118th Street, three or four blocks from Carmen's apartment building, she spotted a familiar figure leaning against a chain link fence. Even though she knew Carmen wouldn't want her to, Chris pulled to the curb and got out of the Trans-Am. Frankie Sandoval recognized her immediately. Two other young men about Frankie's age glanced over their shoulders at Chris as she strolled toward them, pausing in the middle of the street for a moment as a truck passed by. The three men managed to get through an elaborate and well-choreographed handshake and began sauntering away from Frankie by the time the truck was gone.

"Hey, Frankie, what's up?" Chris asked as she reached the curb.

"Nothin'. Just hangin'," Frankie shrugged.

"You get a job yet?"

"Why?"

"Well," Chris said, leaning against the fence, "I heard you weren't going to school anymore, so I figured maybe you got a job."

"Carmen been talkin' to you 'bout me?"

"When you spend all day workin' with someone you gotta talk about somethin'. Your name came up."

Frankie pushed himself away from the fence. Chris noticed a sullen look about him she hadn't seen before. And his dress matched what most of the street punks she had encountered lately were wearing. Droopy, baggy pants, perfect for concealing any number of weapons, and a long black trench coat.

"She ain't got no right talkin' 'bout me wit' you. I don't need you all up in my business."

"Carmen's worried about you, Frankie. Looks like she has reason to be," Chris said, casting a glance at his friends who had stopped a block away.

"She should be worried about her own self. I can take care of myself. Don't need help from no woman."

"Then maybe you should find a place of your own and quit moochin' off Mercedes and Carmen. Of course, you won't be able to get much of a place with what you'd earn moppin' floors at Mickey Dee's."

"There's other ways to make money. Easy ways."

"And probably illegal, too." She nodded toward the other two youths. "Who're your friends there?"

"Just some guys."

"From a gang?"

Frankie shrugged and Chris was beginning to become irritated at the boy's diffident attitude.

"What you doin' here anyway?" Frankie asked. "Ain't no work day."

"Carmen and I are doin' a little overtime on a case."

"Yeah, right," the teen snorted. "Maybe you plannin' to do a little undercover work wit' her, too, huh."

"Be careful where you're goin' with that, bud," Chris said looking hard at her partner's brother.

"Hey, bitch. I ain't your bud, okay," Frankie said, waving his arms around in a macho display Chris always found ridiculous. "You wanna fuck my sister that's your business, but Ruben he done beat ya to it. All you be gettin' is sloppy seconds. Besides, Carmen ain't got the hots for no white dyke like you no how."

Chris grabbed Frankie by the collar of his coat and slammed him against the fence. The fence bounced Frankie back toward Chris, who slammed him into it again, still hanging onto the boy's coat. As Frankie bounced toward her the second time, she jerked him close to her face.

"You need to learn to have more respect for people, Frank. I'll do you a favor and not tell Carmen what you just said. If I was you–"

"You don't got no –" Frankie began.

"Shut up, you stupid little shit!" Chris seethed. "If I was you, I wouldn't be bad-mouthin' the *woman* who's keepin' clothes on your back and beans in your belly."

Chris released him as she shoved him backward into the fence, forcing him to grab the chain link to remain upright. As Chris turned to leave, Frankie cursed at her, and even she knew enough street Spanish to understand what the boy was saying. From the corner of her eyes she saw the other two moving back toward Frankie. She pointed at them and called out, "Back off!"

They paused as she whirled around and pointed at Frankie.

"Next time I hear you been givin' your mother or sister shit, Frankie, I'll come back and kick your ass from here to Hoboken.

You might get away with walkin' all over them, but this is one dyke you better not fuck with. Got it!"

Chris got in her car and slammed the door shut. She hadn't intended to get into a confrontation with Frankie and thought she had probably done more damage than good. Secretly, Chris believed Frankie was right about Ruben and decided to drive around to cool off before she picked Carmen up for the memorial service.

Nearly an hour later, Chris was knocking at the door of Carmen's apartment. When she opened the door, Carmen looked ticked, and Chris wondered if Frankie had come home and told her about their encounter.

"You're late," Carmen snapped. "I been sitting around here over an hour."

EVEN THOUGH CHRIS made the best time she could through the mid-afternoon traffic, the service at the Lerner Theater had already been underway for ten minutes when they rushed into the theater lobby. They moved quietly as they entered the back of the auditorium and stood in the shadows against the back wall. The auditorium was filled with those who had both admired and hated Elaine Barrie. An enormous picture of her was suspended against a black backdrop and there were hundreds of flowers on the stage and lining the steps on either side of the proscenium. A spotlight illuminated the picture of an apparently happy Elaine Barrie. Various pictures of Elaine in scenes from her shows were continuously projected onto stationary sets on either side of the black backdrop.

Chris spotted Carl Janus immediately. He was strapped into a wheelchair and sitting in the aisle near the front. Seated to his right was Robert Blankenship. Ted Warner sat in the left aisle seat.

"Where's the body?" Carmen whispered as she leaned over to Chris.

"Janus had her taken to West Virginia so she could be buried with other members of her family," Chris whispered back.

"Talk about slumming," Carmen said.

"I don't think she'll mind much."

An infinite number of people, some known to Chris and Carmen and more than a few strangers, took turns eulogizing Elaine Barrie. After a while they all began to sound repetitious to Chris and she wandered into the lobby. Posters advertising Elaine's final show were still in their metal and glass frames, draped in black bunting. Wreaths with black ribbons hung on the glass doors to the theater. The whole building seemed to be in mourning.

Three-quarters of an hour later, the auditorium doors opened and Chris watched as Ted Warner lowered Carl Janus's wheelchair down the six steps into the lobby. Janus glanced momentarily at Chris and nodded slightly as he was wheeled toward a black Lincoln that was waiting at the curb. As Robert Blankenship passed, Chris stopped him.

"How's he doin', Doctor?"

Blankenship shook his head slightly. "He quit taking his medication. Apparently, Ted wasn't making sure Carl was really swallowing them. I found where he'd been squirreling them away this morning. When I told you he had about nine months left, that was if he took the medication."

"And now?"

"Maybe half that."

"When did he quit takin' the meds?"

"The day he learned about Elaine's death," Blankenship said as he walked away.

Chris was saddened to hear what Janus was doing, even though she understood it. The man had less than six months left on the planet and had lost the only person who made his life worth hanging onto. With her gone, and unable to leave his apartment, death had become a welcome alternative.

A large group of men and women walked slowly past Chris on their way out of the theater. She recognized a few of them from play posters and the newspapers. The police photographer she'd requested was taking pictures of everyone leaving the memorial service, although not particularly discreetly. She nodded at Malcolm Gallagher as he escorted an attractive well-dressed and well-groomed older woman to a waiting limousine. He held the door open for the woman and waited for his son and daughter to enter the vehicle. Grace Gallagher glanced at Chris and her lips curled into a slight smile. Chris nodded as their eyes met before returning her attention to the dispersing crowd. She spotted Levinson and Galway as they retrieved their coats from the theater cloakroom. Not far behind them, Kent Devine stopped to speak to Della Summers and another woman. From what Carmen had told her, Chris assumed the second woman was Marissa Parilli. She was a very attractive woman dressed for Wall Street success. Della didn't seem to be handling Elaine's death well and Chris was sure the tear-jerker memorial service hadn't helped. Marissa put an arm around Della and escorted her out of the building.

Chris moved to where Kent was standing. "Nice service," she said.

"Total bullshit," Kent said without smiling. "Elaine would have hated it. Half the women in there were secretly jumping for joy because the competition has been decreased by one. Now they might get a chance at parts they would never have been considered for if Elaine was still alive."

"Well, it's not against the law to wish someone dead," Chris said.

"Good thing, Detective, or you'd need more officers in the theater district," Kent said with more than a touch of bitterness in his voice.

"Do you have a minute?" Chris asked.

"Well, I was really planning..."

"It'll just take a minute," Chris insisted.

Kent picked up his coat and followed Chris into an alcove near the cloakroom.

"You know, I wish you'd been a little more forthcomin' with me, Mr. Devine," she began.

"About what?"

"The nature of your relationship with Miss Barrie."

"You mean Carl's little 'arrangement'?" Kent said with a smile.

"For starters."

"I presume you've spoken to Alex and Damon," Kent said, slipping his coat on.

"Why didn't you tell me you were number three?"

"I didn't see any reason to."

"Were you and Miss Barrie lovers?"

"Once up a time," Kent said, looking at the floor. "A million years ago."

"How about durin' your current relationship?"

"I already told you. There was nothing physical between Elaine and me. I was doing her a favor to keep Janus off her back."

"Come on, Kent! You must have known that she was puttin' out for Alex and Damon."

Kent laughed. "Alex Webb was terrified of Elaine. For him it would have been tantamount to screwing the Virgin Mary. Strictly platonic."

"Did Elaine tell you that?"

"Alex did. How many guys are going to admit to another guy that they were handed a woman like Elaine and couldn't do it?"

"Damon Hunter doesn't seem to have had the same problem," Chris suggested.

"Hell, Elaine wasn't interested in that prick either. But he bragged around that he was sleeping with her."

"Did you know he raped her?" she asked. From the stricken look on Devine's face, Chris was sure he hadn't known.

"Fuck!" Kent ranted as he walked in a small circle. His face had turned the color of ash. "This is Carl's fault. He's the reason Elaine's dead. Him and his warped ideas about what would make her happy."

"I think he already realizes that, even if it is a little late," Chris sympathized.

"Jesus, no wonder she..."

"She what, Kent?"

Devine leaned against the wall of the alcove, resting his head back and staring at the ceiling.

"Poor Elaine," Kent said, almost to himself.

"You want to tell me about it?" Chris asked.

Devine took a deep breath. "Why not? Nothing I say can hurt her now."

Kent slid down the wall until he was sitting on the floor, with his arms resting on his knees.

"You already know that Elaine and I had a little thing when she was much younger."

"Yeah," Chris said, sitting down next to him.

Devine glanced over at her and a small smile crossed his face. "She was really beautiful, you know," he said.

"Very," Chris agreed, waiting for Devine to continue.

"Ah, hell," Kent said, running a hand through his graying brown hair. "It was Elaine who approached me about replacing Alex. I thought she was out of her mind, but she begged me. Said it was for Janus's sake. She was worried about keeping *him* happy, if you can believe that."

"You think she loved Janus as much as everyone says?"

"Everything she did revolved around him. Especially after his health took a turn for the worse. She worried so much about him that I don't think she ever really thought about her own happiness."

"So you agreed to this pretend relationship?"

"Yeah. One of the best performances of my life. Elaine and I would meet in her suite and play cards or rehearse lines or try out recipes on each other. Very exciting stuff, but not exactly what other people thought it was. She was fun to be with, very relaxed and charming."

"Did you spend the night there?"

"Lots of times. That couch in the living room is more comfortable than it looks."

"And that's how you spent your time together?"

Kent closed his eyes and inhaled deeply. "Until a couple of weeks ago. Then everything changed."

"You made love to her?" Chris asked softly.

Kent nodded. "Neither of us planned for it happen."

Kent Devine opened the door to Elaine's suite and waited for her to enter.

"Why don't you check to see what's in the refrigerator?" she said. "I'll be back in a minute. I have to call Carl before he falls asleep."

Kent threw his coat over a chair and fished around in the refrigerator until he found a slab of cheese and some fruit. A bottle of wine was lying on the bottom shelf. By the time Elaine reappeared dressed in casual slacks and an oversized peasant blouse, Kent had arranged cheese, fruit and crackers on a plate and was pouring wine into two glasses.

"Looks good," she said, picking up a grape and popping it into her mouth.

"You talk to Carl?" Kent asked.

"Uh huh."

"How's he doing?"

"I don't know really. Some days he seems okay and others..." she said letting her voice trail away.

"I'm sorry, Elaine. You don't deserve this and neither does Carl."

"And here I thought you didn't like my husband," she said.

"I don't, but he seems to make you happy. Or did."

"The first fourteen years were the happiest of my life, Kent. But this last year has been...difficult. It breaks my heart to watch Carl wasting away and there's not a damn thing I can do except pretend it isn't happening. Guess that proves money can't buy everything."

"I hate to ask this, honey, but what are you going to do, you know, after?"

"You mean after Carl dies? You know what he'd say, of course," she smiled.

"The show must go on, no matter what." Kent laughed as he sipped from his wine glass.

Elaine laughed, too. "I was thinking I might take a few months off anyway. We were planning a trip to Europe before he got sick. Maybe I'll go for the both of us."

Kent reached across the counter and squeezed Elaine's hand.

"You're a good woman, Elaine. I hope Carl knows how much you love him."

Elaine smiled at Kent. "I know what everyone said when we got married. That I only married him to advance my career. That I was using him. That he was an old fool who got carried away by his glands. But that was all bullshit, Kent. I would have left the theater in a second if he had wanted it."

Kent looked at her and saw tears running down her cheeks. She wiped them away with the sleeve of her blouse.

"I miss having him hold me in his arms. I miss having him close to me. I didn't realize how much I needed him to feel whole."

Kent moved around the counter and took Elaine in his arms.

"I know you miss the old Carl," Kent whispered, stroking her hair while he let her cry.

When she had composed herself, she raised her head and let Kent wipe new tears from her face.

"You've always been such a good friend, Kent. You don't know how much it's meant to me."

"We've had a few good times, haven't we?"

"Lots of wonderful memories," she smiled.

Kent still had his arms around her to comfort her.

"Would you do a favor for an old friend, Kent?"

"You know I'd do anything for you I can," Kent answered.

She looked into his eyes. "Be Carl for me, just for tonight."

Even though he knew she was seeing Carl Janus and not him, Kent kissed her cheek and didn't speak as Elaine wrapped her arms around his neck and sought his lips with hers.

"So you see, Detective Shaw, even though we made love, Elaine wasn't making love with me. She was making love with Carl. She was so fucking lonely," Kent sighed. He looked at Chris and said, "Even when we were younger, she never made love to me like that. So much tenderness...such passion..."

"Must've been tough for you," Chris said quietly.

"The toughest part is I'll probably never be lucky enough to find a woman who'll love me as much as Elaine loved Carl."

"There you are," Carmen said. "I thought you'd left without me."

Kent and Chris got up and joined Carmen at the cloakroom.

"I appreciate your candor, Mr. Devine," Chris said, shaking Kent's hand.

Kent nodded, jammed his hands in the pockets of his coat, and walked away.

Chapter Fifteen

"THAT'S INCREDIBLE!" CARMEN said as Chris drove through the darkening streets away from the theater district. The sun was hidden by the canyon-like walls and the last rays of sunlight struck the upper windows of the buildings and reflected off one another.

"She used Devine and essentially cheated on her husband without really cheating," Chris said.

"That the only time?" Carmen asked.

"Apparently. He said it only happened a week or two before she died."

"I gather Janus doesn't know about it."

"I don't think so, and I sure as hell ain't gonna tell him."

"But if he knew, it would give him a motive, Chris," Carmen said.

"You're not gonna tell him either, Carmen. Understand?" Chris said forcefully as she looked across the car at her partner.

"Yeah, but..."

"But nothing. Carl Janus didn't kill his wife, and he didn't hire someone to do it. Even if he knew what happened between Elaine and Devine, he wouldn't have killed her over it. It was what he wanted anyway, for Christ's sake. Okay?"

"Don't get all bent about it, Chris."

"I'm not bent. I just wish I knew more about her, that's all."

"Sounds like you have a thing for her."

"That's absurd."

"Never seen you need to get into a vic's head before."

"Since most of our vics are junkies, gang bangers, and whores, I guess I never thought there was anything in their heads worth knowin'. Elaine Barrie was more complex than that."

It was just after dark when Chris pulled to the curb in front of Carmen's apartment building and left the car running.

"You wanna come up?" Carmen asked.

"Think I'll go home, throw a TV dinner in the oven, and take a shower. Now that we've interviewed most of the people of interest, Monday, we need to check out the hotel surveillance tapes. Maybe someone interestin' will turn up."

"Okay. And then what?"

"As much as I hate it I think we should speak to Hunter again. See if he's luggin' around the mother of all grudges about being blackballed by Janus."

"Need to put the manager, what's his name, on our list, too."

"Gallagher."

"Yeah. Della said she heard him arguing with Elaine after the show that night. He said he talked to her. In my family there's a pretty big gap between talking and arguing," Carmen said.

They were talking when the door on the passenger side of Chris' car opened suddenly, causing them both to reach for their weapons. In the glow cast by the dome light, Chris saw Ruben Montanez's mustachioed face.

"Shit!" Chris said, re-holstering her revolver. "That's a damn good way to get your stupid fuckin' head blown all over the street, Montanez."

"If I was a bad guy, Shaw, you'd already be dead," Montanez said without smiling.

Ruben was still glaring at Chris when he spoke to Carmen. "What you doing out here anyway? I been waiting for you," he said. "I tol' Mercedes I'd drive you both to church. If you can drag yourself away from Shaw here maybe we won't be late."

"You said you were working tonight," Carmen said crossly.

"This what you do when I'm busting my ass at work?"

"And just what is it you think we were doin'?" Chris asked.

"Stay out of this, Shaw. This is between me and Carmen," Ruben ordered.

"Not when your head is stickin' inside my car, it isn't," Chris said leaning toward Carmen's side of the car.

"Why don't you two knock this estrogen versus testosterone shit off?" Carmen said.

"Why don't you and your big mouth get on up out of the car, Shaw?" Ruben said loudly.

"Gladly," Chris said, opening her door and slamming it shut behind her.

Chris and Ruben met on the sidewalk next to the car as Carmen got out and slammed her door. Ruben pointed a finger in Chris' face.

"Stay away from Carmen, understand?" Ruben shouted.

"And how do you recommend we work together if I do that, Ruben," Chris shouted back.

"Stay away from her after work. She ain't working today."

"Unfortunately, our job isn't like yours. We don't sit around on our asses playin' cards and tryin' out new recipes waitin' for a goddamn bell to go off before we react like Pavlov's fuckin' dogs."

Carmen stepped between them. "Stop it!" she yelled.

The window of an apartment on the second floor of Carmen's building flew open and a man stuck his head out. "Knock it off down there before I call the cops," he yelled.

"We *are* the cops, asshole," Chris yelled back at the man. "Close that goddamn window before I arrest you for interferin' with police business."

The window banged shut and Chris turned her attention back to Montanez.

"I'm warning you, Shaw," Ruben said.

"You ain't doin' shit!" Chris said in sheer frustration. "Except standin' out here in the street flappin' your fuckin' lips and pissin' me off."

Montanez took a step toward Chris, but Carmen pushed him back. Ruben reached up and knocked her arms out of his way.

"That's it, bud," Chris said venomously. "You touch my partner again and I'll take your fuckin' head off and use it for a soccer ball."

"You some big tough dyke cop, Shaw. I ain't the one carryin' a gun," Ruben said.

Chris pulled her service weapon out of its holster and laid it on the hood of her car. Then she took her wallet with her badge out of her jacket pocket and placed it next to her gun.

"That's in case you have a problem about strikin' a police officer," Chris said. "What's your excuse now, macho man? You want a piece of me, come on and get it. I don't have all night!"

Ruben glared at Chris, but didn't move toward her.

"Well, what's it gonna be, Montanez?" Chris said, stepping closer to him. "Need a little incentive?" She reached out quickly and slapped his face. He looked shocked and his body trembled with anger.

"That's enough, Chris!" Carmen said.

"No, it's not!" Chris snapped. "Don't you want to see what your boyfriend here's got?"

Carmen stepped between them again and pushed Chris back.

"He's not worth it, Chris. They'll haul your ass up on charges."

"He treats you like shit, Carmen."

"I can handle this. Just get back in the damn car and get out of here."

Chris looked at Carmen's face and took a deep breath. As she turned away to get into the car, Montanez said, "I know how you people are. You just tryin' to get Carmen in bed, Shaw. If you ain't already done it."

Carmen spun around and glared at Ruben. "That's a fucking lie and you damn well know it, Ruben."

"If I was sleepin' with her, she wouldn't still be goin' out with your sorry ass," Chris shouted.

"You lookin' for some hot Puerto Rican pussy to see what you been missin'," Ruben spat.

There was nothing Carmen could do as Chris stepped around her and grabbed Montanez. One swing put Ruben on the ground, and it took every ounce of strength she could summon to leave it at one. Chris massaged her fist, grabbed her gun and wallet off the hood of her car, and walked back to the driver's side of her vehicle, leaving Ruben on the ground with blood running from his nose. As she turned on the ignition, Carmen tapped on the window.

"I'm sorry, Chris," she said as the window lowered.

"Let me know if the asshole wants to press charges," Chris said as she shifted her car into gear.

AS CHRIS PULLED away, Carmen shoved her hands into the pockets of her coat and walked toward the entrance to her building.

"Carmen!" Ruben said loudly.

She stopped and took a deep breath, exhaling a white cloud into the cold night air. "What?"

Ruben held a handkerchief to his bleeding nose as he walked unsteadily to where she was standing. "I want you to request a new partner."

"Why would I do that, Ruben?"

"I don't want you working with that bitch. Understand?"

"No, I don't. This isn't my problem and it isn't Chris'. You're the only one with a problem, Ruben. *You* understand?"

Ruben checked the handkerchief. His nose had stopped bleeding, but blood had dripped onto his jacket and shirt. He reached out and took Carmen by the arm.

"You expect to stay my woman, you get a new partner."

Carmen jerked her arm away from Ruben. "Maybe I'm not your woman!"

"You're fuckin' her, aren't you?"

"Whatever you think is going on is only happening inside your tiny little head. Chris is my friend and my partner."

He grabbed her arm again. "You think I don't see the way she looks at you?" he hissed.

Carmen put her hand on top of his and smiled at him. The smile disappeared quickly as she grabbed Ruben's pinkie finger and pushed it back nearly to his wrist. He howled in pain and released her arm.

"I'm filing charges for assault in the morning," he said, rubbing his hand.

"Won't do you no good," Carmen said as she went up the steps to her building. "I'm the only witness, and I didn't see a damn thing except you tripping over a nasty crack in the sidewalk." She shrugged. "Maybe you can sue the city."

CHRIS DROVE DOWN Park Avenue toward Manhattan. She needed a drink and didn't feel like drinking alone. Two fights in the same day. First Frankie and now Ruben. Obviously she wasn't making any friends among the male Hispanic population of the city. Physical reactions like that weren't like her, and she wondered if she was losing her grip. She had been working with Carmen Sandoval for four years and had never considered her anything more than another police officer.

The murder of Elaine Barrie was the first big-time homicide in Midtown Precinct in over a year. If it had been some junkie who'd been killed it wouldn't have bothered Chris nearly as much. Junkies had families too, but somehow they never seemed surprised when they were informed of a death. Prostitutes were pretty much the same way. Jump in the sack with a total stranger, knowing they were in danger of running into some whacko or religious wingnut trying to purge the sin from their bodies to save their souls the hard way.

But the Barrie case was different. A beautiful woman who had everything to live for except the one thing she couldn't have. There was no real evidence she'd been promiscuous, a drunk, or a drug addict. She'd simply been lonely. The same kind of lonely Chris was feeling at that very moment.

She hadn't been to the bar that had once been her favorite hangout in over a year. Not since Jill had flown home, then flown the coop with a woman who could have been the poster girl for recruiting airline pilots. Chris parked her car and strolled into Crossroads, giving her eyes time to adjust to the dim lighting and the rainbow of colors splashing on the walls from a disco ball hanging over the small dance floor. She walked up to the bar and tapped the wooden top. A girl, who didn't look old enough to drink, appeared from out of nowhere.

"Beer," Chris said. "Whatever's on tap is fine." She dropped a five on the bar and picked up the frosted mug the girl set in front of her, telling her to keep the change.

Chris leaned against the bar and gulped down two or three large swallows of the cold beer. She smiled as she thought how great it would have tasted with a plate full of spicy Texas barbecue or a mouthful of deep dish pizza made only the way Orlando's in Dallas could make them. She would need to get something to eat on the way home. By the time her mug was empty, she was feeling a little less sorry for herself and ordered a refill. She watched the couples on the dance floor and fought the feeling of unhappiness that began to worm its way back into her mind. The memory of Jill's body pressing closely against hers as they moved across the floor still created a familiar tingle in her crotch. Jill had been a great dancer. A tall, leggy red-head, Chris had loved the way Jill's hand on her neck felt as she nuzzled into Chris.

Chris shook her head to throw the memories away and pushed away from the bar. The women she saw now were strangers, not the same crowd that had filled Crossroads the last time she had been there. Oh well, women were like that. The patrons ebbed and flowed with the whole scene changing once any of them found even a temporary partner. Chris leaned against a wall near the dance floor and brought a foot up to rest against it as she watched and sipped her beer. She had her own theory about dancing as a form of foreplay before something more primal and intimate. The dancers ranged from expert to incompetent, but all had one thing in common, the desire to feel another woman in their arms. Her foot slipped off the wall and she stood up straighter when she saw a gorgeous strawberry blonde walking toward her. The woman's gently swaying hips whispered a familiar invitation.

"I'm surprised to see you here, Detective," Grace Gallagher said.

"Trust me, Counselor, the surprise is all mine," Chris replied.

"You come here often."

"Used to."

"Are you alone?"

"Not at the moment," Chris said, hoping she was projecting her most charming smile.

"How's the investigation going?"

"Pretty much sucks, but I can't really discuss it."

Grace did her best to look offended. "I'm hurt," she said through pouty lips that made Chris' stomach flutter.

"You'll recover. Do you dance?" Chris asked when a song she liked began. "Or are you one of those women who come here to sit on her ass and stare at other people havin' fun?"

"That was either a challenge or an insult."

"It's been suggested from time to time that I work on my people skills," Chris said as she set her mug on a ledge along the wall and extended her hand toward Grace.

"Probably not a good idea," Grace said as she shook her head. She bit her bottom lip and smiled. "But I bet you're full of bad ideas."

"One or two," Chris said with a grin.

She began to feel slightly uncomfortable as Grace Gallagher's eyes held hers. Letting her eyes move down to Grace's inviting cleavage and imagining soft breasts pressing against her, her grin deepened. She'd been telling herself for the last year that even though she didn't have Jill anymore, there were plenty of other fish in the ocean. Unfortunately, she'd never enjoyed fishing all that much. Chris raised her eyes to Grace's again after she saw the blonde's nipples harden beneath her body caressing top.

"You look...hungry," Grace said.

"Starving," Chris managed in a low, husky voice.

"There's a decent little diner not far from here."

"Thanks."

Chris watched appreciatively as Grace sashayed toward the bar and leaned forward to order. A connoisseur of fine asses since she first discovered women, Chris marveled at the way Grace's jeans caressed her butt. She watched as Grace rejoined three other women at a table and pulled an attractive brunette up, wrapping an arm possessively around the woman's waist. Grace leaned down slightly to whisper in the brunette's ear as the familiar seduction act continued. As the couple made their way toward the dance floor, Grace looked in Chris' direction and smiled, as if she knew Chris was watching them. When Grace pressed the brunette's shapely body against hers, Chris shook her head and finished her mug of beer before making her way out the front door of the bar. She drew in a deep, stiff breath of cold air. Grace Gallagher was a beautiful, sexually tempting woman. If it hadn't been for the Barrie case and her father's involvement, Chris felt relatively sure that jeans weren't the only things that would have been rubbing against the blonde's perfect ass that night. She saw the red neon sign over a small building on the corner of the next block and decided to give it a try to stop the growling of her stomach.

Chris rubbed her hands together to warm them when she entered the diner. It wasn't crowded and she spotted a booth near the back that would let her keep an eye on the door as well as the front counter. The little diner didn't look much bigger than the old Airstream trailer her father had owned when Chris was a kid.

"What can I getcha?" an older woman wearing a Pepto pink uniform covered by a white apron asked.

Chris picked up the paper menu which was held up between the salt and pepper shakers and a napkin holder. "Hot roast beef sandwich and a cup of coffee, black."

"Be right up."

Chris was halfway through the tender beef smothered with gravy when the door to the diner swung open. The cold air that blew in was accompanied by talking and laughter. Chris saw Grace and her friends wave at the waitress behind the counter and move to a table in the middle of the small room. Grace removed her coat and placed it on the back of a chair. She smiled when she noticed Chris sitting in the back booth. Chris winked and went back to her dinner. She drank two or three refills of her coffee and leaned back in the corner of the booth to give the food a chance to begin digesting. She was making a terrible mistake by staring at Grace Gallagher and she knew it. The way the woman's body moved fascinated Chris. No doubt about it, she needed to find someone to replace Jill. In the beginning she hadn't minded being alone. But when she began carrying on a conversation with the pigeons that camped out on the window sills of her apartment, she knew she'd been alone too damn long.

The chairs around the table where the four women were seated made a loud scraping noise as they rose to leave. Grace said something to the other women with her, one of whom leaned over slightly to look at Chris briefly. Grace kissed each of the women lightly on the cheek and watched as they left before picking up her coat and walking to Chris' table.

"Mind if I join you, Detective Shaw?" Grace asked.

"I still can't talk about the case."

"We'll think of something."

"Then have a seat."

"Did you enjoy your meal?"

"Very much."

"I eat here quite often. The price is right and the food is generally decent."

"Don't cook at home, huh?" Chris asked.

Grace smiled. "My mother taught me many useful things. One of them was how to order from a menu. Judging from your accent and the way you dress, I'm guessing you're not from around here."

"Damn, I thought I hid my accent pretty well," Chris said.

"What brought you to New York?"

"An overactive libido."

"What happened?"

"Same old story." Chris shrugged. "Girl meets girl. They hit it off and have sex like wild monkeys for six years. Then girl meets someone more interesting and flies off into the wild blue yonder with her."

"I take it you followed her here."

"She's a flight attendant and was transferred here to service overseas flights. She met a pilot who needed personal servicing. Must've been that spiffy uniform." Chris shrugged again as she sipped her coffee. "Come to think of it, I may have been in uniform the first time I met her."

"She broke your heart?"

"She kicked it around some, but mostly she wounded my

pride. Enough about me. What's your story."

"I don't have a story."

"Everyone has a story, babe."

"Are you flirting with me, Detective Shaw?" Grace asked playfully.

"Could be," Chris said. "What made you decide to be a lawyer?"

"It lets me be a pain in the ass, especially where the police are concerned, and get away with it."

"Did I forget to mention that I hate lawyers," Chris said with a laugh while trying not to think about Grace's ass. "So how come you and your friends decided to drop in here tonight? Pretty sure it wasn't my sparklin' personality."

"One of my friends is getting married next week and we decided to have a girls' night out. The DJ at the club plays a God-awful heavy metal set every evening. We usually take a food break then." Grace glanced at the clock on the wall. "Set's almost over."

Chris paid her bill and escorted Grace through the blustery night toward the bar. When they reached the front door Chris stopped.

"This is where I leave the wagon train, Counselor," she said. She thought she saw a flicker of disappointment in Grace's blue eyes. Or perhaps she imagined it.

"You're not coming in?" Grace asked. "I promise I won't tell anyone."

"But then you wouldn't respect me in the morning."

"What kind of woman do you think I am?" Grace asked, obviously insulted by Chris' implication.

Chris stuck her hands into her pant pockets, stepped closer, and leaned forward to whisper in Grace's ear. "You don't really want to know the answer to that." An instant later Chris was jogging across the broad street toward her car.

DESPITE HER LACK of company over the weekend, Chris felt amazingly relaxed and refreshed Monday morning. A good breakfast at a hole-in-the-wall bistro near her apartment made Chris ready to tackle whatever the day might bring by the time she arrived at work. It was unusual for Carmen to beat Chris to work and when she threw her coat over her chair Carmen looked up from her paperwork momentarily.

"Mornin'." Chris smiled. "Looks like a great day."

"Captain Savage wants to see us."

"About what?"

"Probably this." Carmen frowned, handing a newspaper across

the desk.

Chris didn't like the look on Carmen's face as she took the paper, afraid to let her eyes record what was written on it.

"Shit," Chris breathed under her breath, her mood darkening.

Carl Janus had committed suicide by taking an overdose of sleeping pills. Apparently Doctor Blankenship hadn't found everything Carl had squirreled away.

"Did you notice the approximate time of death?" Carmen asked.

Chris looked at her and back at the paper. Between eleven and two. "The same as Elaine's," she said.

Carmen leaned back in her chair and rubbed her eyes. "Went out in style. Washed it down with champagne in front of her portrait in the living room."

According to the report the body had been found by Ted Warner when he went to administer Janus's two o'clock medication.

"How the hell did he get into the living room?" Chris asked. "The man could barely move."

"Read on," Carmen said as she got up and walked toward the restroom.

Warner admitted he and Janus shared a glass of champagne in the room before going to bed. Warner left Carl alone and fell asleep. Robert Blankenship was called to the apartment by Warner. The doctor speculated that Carl Janus had hidden the pills in the pocket of his dressing gown.

Chris dropped the newspaper on her desk. It didn't seem like more than a hunch on her part, but Chris suspected that Elaine, or at least Janus's love for her, had given him the strength to carry out his suicide plan and she felt enormous sadness.

Chris met Carmen as she came out of the bathroom. "Let's see what Savage wants."

Chris and Carmen took the steps to the second floor and were admitted to Captain Lennie Savage's office by his secretary. Savage had been promoted to captain the previous year and had been fair but tough with his detectives.

"Tell me what you got on the Barrie case," Savage said, avoiding the usual greetings.

Carmen and Chris recounted what they knew as the captain's eyebrows knitted and unknitted themselves. He was a habitual blinker and it sometimes proved distracting.

"That it?" he asked at the end of their report.

"So far," Chris said.

"Well, it seems our mayor was a huge Barrie fan, and now, with the death of Janus, who, by the way, was a close personal friend of the mayor's, we need to intensify our efforts. Or rather you two do. What do you plan to do next?"

"We're goin' to re-interview a few people," Chris said, sitting up straighter. "We still have to go through the surveillance tapes from the Montclair and Carmen has an idea that's worth pursuin'."

"I don't want you pursuing anything. I want you breathing down its fucking goddamn neck. I want a report every day."

Chapter Sixteen

CHRIS SAT ALONE in her apartment, eating leftover frozen pizza and washing it down with a cold beer while listening to the sounds of her neighbors celebrating the arrival of yet another year in the relentless grand march of time. She wished she was celebrating the beginning of another year as she usually did, making love. Now thoughts of what she no longer had filled her with melancholy.

Chris sat in the dark and stared at the lights outside her apartment window. When had everything changed? Probably after she met Jill. She loved being with Jill. When had she become nothing more than another stopover in Jill's globe-trotting adventures? Why hadn't she seen it coming? The signs had all probably been there and she failed to pay attention.

The ring of the apartment phone jarred Chris from her dark thoughts. "Shaw," she said, watching a rocket sail into the black sky and explode into a multi-colored display.

"Happy New Year!" a woman's voice said. Chris could hear the sounds of partying in the background.

"Happy New Year to you, too. Who the hell is this?"

"I'm crushed that you've forgotten me so soon. I hoped I'd made a better impression than that."

"Grace?"

"My parents are throwing a party and my presence was requested. I wanted to wish you a happy New Year. You do know that you left me seriously frustrated and disappointed the last time I saw you."

"That's my specialty. Disappointin' beautiful women."

"It's just as well. I had to be in court early the next morning anyway."

"You don't have to explain anything to me. Enjoy the party. Maybe this year will be better for everyone."

"Perhaps. Goodbye, Detective."

"Yeah, take care." Chris noted that Grace hadn't said good night. It was goodbye, a word that could only be interpreted one way. She smiled as she hung up the phone. Gradually her thoughts drifted back to Carl Janus and Elaine Barrie. Two people deeply in love, yet separated by a physical barrier that kept their bodies apart. She couldn't imagine lying in bed next to someone she loved, unable to touch her. What was it Dr. Blankenship had said? She pulled out her notes and read through what the doctor had told her about Carl's disease. In the grand scheme of things, it was a minor point, but Chris hadn't been able to shake it.

THE DAY AFTER New Year's Chris leaned back in her desk chair and punched a number into her cell, waiting for someone to answer.

"Artie, Chris Shaw. Great, great. Yeah, Happy New Year to you too. Listen, were you able to identify the father of Elaine Barrie's baby?"

"The test results came in yesterday and I was just going over them."

"And the winner is?"

Arthur hesitated and Chris could hear pages flipping. "Do you need a slide rule or what, Artie?"

"Just double checking, Tex. Keep your chaps on." A few minutes later, Featherstone cleared his throat. "Carl Janus is the best match. Ninety-five percent probability based on the samples we had."

"Thanks, Artie," Chris said. She gently lowered the receiver into its cradle and rubbed her forehead with her thumb and index fingers. Had Elaine known, or suspected she was pregnant? Had she suspected who the father was? Was that why she was now dead? There had to be something Chris was missing. She looked up a phone number and dialed. After a brief conversation she cleared folders and reports off her desk. She had to find the answers to her questions.

She took her weapon from a desk drawer and replaced it with the files. The clock on the precinct wall showed she had thirty minutes to reach her destination. That was cutting it close. She caught the front door of the precinct as two uniformed officers entered and jogged to her car. The drive to Dr. Clifford Purcell's office would take about twenty minutes, if traffic cooperated. It crossed her mind to try Carmen's cell to see how things were going with the family counselor, but she dismissed it. She could bring her partner up to speed when she returned to work. It was still cold outside, but at least it had stopped snowing. The forecast for the next few days called for cold, but clear skies although the weather map showed a storm system moving through the Midwest and headed in their direction.

She signaled and pulled into the parking garage attached to the building in which Dr. Purcell's office was located. She went to the garage elevator and pushed the button for the fifteenth floor. When the elevator door slid open, she walked down a long corridor until she reached the last office. She pushed the door open and stepped inside. The rather plain interior surprised Chris as she stepped up to the receptionist's counter. An older woman with gray hair pushed the glass barrier over the counter aside and smiled.

"Do you have an appointment?" the woman asked.

Chris pulled out her badge and showed it to the woman. "I called a little while ago and need to see Dr. Purcell. It's official police business regardin' one of his patients."

The woman frowned as she looked at the badge. "Just a moment. I'll see if he's free now."

After the woman disappeared through a door behind the reception counter, Chris wandered around the comfortable-looking waiting room and looked through a small stack of magazines. She turned around when she heard the door open and close.

"Dr. Purcell can see you now, Detective. Through the door to your left."

"Thanks."

Chris opened the door into another, smaller hallway. An older man with salt-and-pepper hair and a close-cropped beard stepped out of one of the rooms and smiled, offering his hand.

"Dr. Purcell?" Chris asked. When he nodded, she took his hand and said, "Detective Christine Shaw, NYPD, Midtown Precinct. I appreciate you takin' time to speak to me."

"I understand you have some questions about Elaine," Purcell said as he sat in the chair behind his desk.

"How long have you been her personal physician?"

Purcell stared at the ceiling and closed one eye. "I first treated her when I think she was around twenty-one or two. The flu, as I recall."

"Did she just pick your name out of a phone book?"

"No. I don't get many of those any more. She was referred to me by a friend, Della Summers. I believe they worked together."

"I find it amazin' that you've remained her doctor for all these years, Dr. Purcell."

"You mean you can't believe she stayed with a low-rent guy like me," Purcell said with a smile. "I thought it was rather unusual myself, but the truth is there really isn't much difference between one general practitioner and another except the cost of the rent for their office space."

"Were you Carl Janus's doctor as well?"

"I treated him a few times for minor complaints, but not for anything serious until the ALS was diagnosed. Then I referred him to a specialist."

"I'm a little surprised you haven't pulled the doctor-patient privilege card."

"It probably sounds a little ghoulish or something, Detective, but considering the situation, I'm not very worried that Elaine will sue me. If something I tell you helps find the person who killed her, I'm willing to risk it. She was a wonderful woman."

Chris wiggled around a little uncomfortably before asking her next question. "Did she have her pregnancy confirmed by your office?"

"Yes. We ran a urine analysis to confirm it. The ever-popular 'rabbit test'. Then we sent it off to the lab."

"Did she say who the father was?"

Purcell frowned and leaned forward on his elbows. "She and Carl had been trying to have a child since he was first diagnosed with ALS," Purcell said. "Their chances were diminishing significantly, so she was anxious about the results. I assumed Carl was the father. I felt a little sorry for her though since the likelihood of Carl surviving until she delivered was remote at best."

"What if the result had been negative?"

Purnell leaned back in his chair. "If you don't mind me asking, Detective, what does whether or not she was pregnant have to do with her murder?"

"Maybe nothin', or it could have been because she was pregnant and someone didn't want that to get out. When did you give her the test result?"

"Elaine and Carl had already made arrangements for a sort of final solution. Carl had me harvest his sperm in case they weren't able to reproduce normally. Considering his condition, I was both shocked and delighted that using the sperm wouldn't be necessary, unless, of course, Elaine decided to have more children in the future. She wanted children so badly. She called them Carl's gift."

Purcell flipped through his desk calendar and read the notations he'd written in each box.

"Ah, here it is. We ran the test on December twentieth. She hoped to know by Christmas to surprise Carl if there was good news, but the lab was backed up and in a rare gesture of generosity they gave their employees a three-day holiday. In other words, they were closed. My family and I left the day before Christmas for a holiday at our cabin in New Hampshire and only returned last night. So, officially, I haven't given anyone the test results yet. However, from the way she was behaving when she was here, I think she already knew," Purnell finished with a smile.

"She never had a chance to tell Carl," Chris mumbled. She brought her head up quickly. "Thanks for your cooperation, Dr. Purcell. You've been very helpful." Chris stood and reached across the desk to shake the doctor's hand.

"Let me know if there's anything else I can help you with."

"I will."

CHRIS MADE HER way up the steps of the building that had once been the home of Carl and Elaine Janus and pressed the doorbell. She wasn't sure anyone would be in the now empty apartment overlooking Central Park. She waited a few minutes before pressing the button once again. The last tremulous baritone chime was fading away when the door finally opened. Ted Warner, now dressed in faded jeans and a battered Marine Corps sweatshirt, looked strangely out of place.

"What can I do for you, Detective?" he asked, his voice subdued.

"I'm surprised you're here," Chris said.

"I don't have anything to celebrate. I'm sure you understand."

"I do and don't mean to disturb you. I needed to clear up somethin'," Chris said. "May I come in?"

Ted stepped away from the door and waved her in with a flourish of his arm. "Nothing to hide now, I suppose. I'm packing up some of Carl's personal belongings. He left a few things to a sister in Indiana. Didn't even know he had one."

Ted seemed sluggish, or at least resigned to performing his final service to his former employer, as he trudged up the main staircase toward the second floor. Chris shrugged off her coat and laid it across the carved railing before following him.

"What are your plans now, Ted?" she asked.

"The nursing agency has a couple of possible placements for me, but it'll be hard to adjust. I was with Carl over two years."

Chris followed Ted into the bedroom and watched as he went through the dresser drawers.

"What was it like livin' with the Januses?"

"It wasn't difficult at all until recently. Carl and Mrs. J began to argue more. She was really pissed because he seemed to be giving up." Ted shook his head and wiped his hand over his face. He sucked in a deep breath and blew it out through his mouth. "She really loved him, ya know. She learned all the physical rehab exercises he needed to keep his strength up and his muscles as active as possible. She learned how to prepare his meals so he wouldn't choke. She did everything anybody could have done to make his life easier."

"Witnesses have told us she slept with other men."

"That's a goddamn lie!" Ted said in a raised voice.

"She was still a woman, Ted. Beautiful, in her prime, and saddled with a husband who was growin' more and more helpless every day. No one would blame her if she played around a little," Chris said with a shrug.

Ted moved to the settee at the foot of the bed and sat down heavily. He looked up at Chris and said, "See this bed? Top of the line water bed. It relieves stress on the joints. It's put together so when one person moves anyone else in the bed will never feel a thing." He stood up. "Come in here," he motioned as he moved into the room next to the bedroom. "See that tub? Oversized with twice the number of jets to relax just about every muscle in the body. Mrs. J had it installed."

"What's your point?"

Ted smiled. "ALS doesn't attack everything. Carl could still *feel*. His body could still react. They were always very playful."

Elaine entered the master bedroom and went to Carl's side of the bed. She lifted the open manuscript from his lap and carefully pulled his glasses off.

"Trying to sneak up on me, woman?" Carl asked.

"You looked so peaceful, darling. I didn't mean to wake you." She leaned down and kissed him tenderly.

"That was worth waking up for," he said with a smile.

"I can do better," she said in a breathy voice. She sat on the edge of the bed and leaned closer, gazing into his eyes.

"Talk's cheap, baby."

"Shut up." She laughed lightly as she brought her lips to his once again.

Carl managed to bring his left arm up and bury it in Elaine's chestnut hair as the kiss deepened. He moaned slightly as her tongue slid slowly into his mouth, completing the connection between them.

She felt a change in his breathing and gently ended their kiss. She leaned her forehead against his and said, "Have I ever told you what a fabulous kisser you are?"

"You think so?"

"I know so, stud," she said with a chuckle. "How about a nice, warm, relaxing soak? It'll make you forget all your problems."

"Promises, promises."

"And I always keep my promises." Elaine stood and went into the bathroom.

Carl heard the water running, filling the tub and smiled.

Elaine tapped on the door on the opposite side of the large bathroom. A moment later Ted opened the door leading into his room.

"Yes, ma'am," he said.

"Could you please prepare Carl for a bath while I change?"

"Certainly," Ted said with a nod.

Elaine blew a kiss at her husband as she disappeared into their dressing room. "Don't start without me," she ordered with a grin.

The water running in the tub turned off and Ted stepped into the bedroom, drying his hands. "Ready, Mr. J?" he asked as he turned back the bedcover and unbuttoned Carl's shirt.

"I'm sorry to be such a bother, Ted."

"No bother at all, sir."

Elaine returned wearing a thick, fluffy terry cloth robe and pulling her hair from under the collar. Ted lifted Carl from the bed and carried him into the bathroom. He carefully sat Carl on a seat attached to the large tub.

"We can handle it from here, Ted," Elaine said. "Thank you."

"Let me know when you're ready to return to the bedroom," Ted said as he walked through and closed the door to his room.

"I can't tell you exactly what went on in the bathroom after I left, but I know in my mind it was something pretty hot."

"You mean they had sex," Chris said.

"I *mean* they made love, Detective. Like I said, Carl's disease didn't affect everything. I'd seen books on sensual massage and touching techniques on the nightstand on Mrs. J's side of the bed. Sometimes, to me, the way they looked at one another or touched was almost enough to make me blush. I'm not saying it was down-and-dirty monkey sex like when they were younger and Carl was healthy, but they found a way to make one another happy."

"When was the last time you helped Carl into the tub?"

Ted shrugged. "Maybe a week before Mrs. J died. Something happened and Carl began to choke. I heard him coughing and Mrs. J called for me. When I came in she was tying the belt around her robe and was dripping wet, like she'd just gotten out of the tub. By the time I got Carl settled down and back in bed he was exhausted. Kept apologizing to his wife."

"Was she upset?"

"Only worried about him. ALS messes with the ability to swallow and I think Carl might have gulped down a little water the wrong way. The coughing was hard on his lungs and he was having some trouble breathing. I put the Bi-PAP on him just in case there was a problem during the night. He hated that thing."

"What is it?"

"An apparatus he wore over his face to help him breath. Said it made him feel too restricted. Pretty much had to sleep on his back all night, but he was breathing better by morning."

"Did you turn him durin' the night?"

Ted smiled and shook his head. "I went in to check on him

once. He woke up and shook his head. Mrs. J was curled up asleep against him with her arm over his abdomen and he was stroking her hair with his good hand. He was smiling and breathing fine so I left them alone." He rubbed his face with both hands. "I can't imagine being loved that much. Man!"

"You said they had been arguin'. Do you know what about?"

"Not really. Carl couldn't project his voice much anymore. I could only pick up bits and pieces of what she said."

"Such as?"

Ted seemed to contemplate whether or not to repeat part of a private conversation.

"Nothin' you tell me can hurt either one of them now, Ted."

"I know. I know. Will it help you find whoever killed them?"

"Carl committed suicide."

"Technically, but whoever killed Mrs. J took away his reason to live."

"What did Mrs. Janus say?"

"She said she wasn't going to pretend to be a whore any longer to make him feel better."

"Any idea what she meant by that?"

"Not a clue."

"Her personal physician told me Elaine was pregnant when she died," Chris said softly. "The ME confirmed Carl was the father."

A tear fell onto Ted's cheek and he nodded. "He...he would have been happy to know that."

"Elaine may not have known herself."

"She'd have been a great mom. Well, they're all together now." Ted took a deep breath and blew it out slowly. "Happy fuckin' New Year."

Chapter Seventeen

CHRIS BRAKED PERIODICALLY to avoid running over a worker dashing across the busy street to catch the subway home, wishing she had the time to stop and issue jaywalking citations. Two-thousand-and-eleven had limped out on a shitty note and two-thousand-and-twelve, barely twenty-four hours old, wasn't starting out much better. Somehow Chris wasn't surprised by the ringing cell phone in her inside jacket pocket. She jerked it out of her pocket and flipped it open. "Shaw."

"I'm watching the world's greatest hotel surveillance videos," Carmen's voice announced with a chuckle. "I think we might have a winner."

"Who?"

"Malcolm Gallagher."

"Gallagher?"

"He told us he didn't go to the Montclair with Barrie the night she died, but I'm watching him walk arm-in-arm into the hotel lobby with her in living black-and-white. Time stamp reads eleven-thirty-three. That gives us opportunity, partner. And guess whose fingerprints were found in the living room of the suite, according to the lab report sitting on my desk?"

"Have him picked up for questionin' as soon as possible. Do we have anything else we haven't matched from the scene?"

"Some as-yet-unidentified hair fibers from the bedroom and living room. I'd be willing to bet at least one or two will match him. Lab's still working on that black smudge from the body."

"I'm not far from the precinct. Where are you?"

"Already at the precinct."

"Call the DA's office. They might want to send someone over for the questionin'. Let's not do anything to screw this up."

ASSISTANT DISTRICT ATTORNEY Sheila Morgan walked into the squad room. She seemed a little out of sorts as she poured a cup of coffee and pulled a chair up to join Chris and Carmen. She was dressed casually in slacks and a bulky cable knit sweater that highlighted her hair and brought out the green in her hazel eyes.

"What do you have?" she asked as she pushed sandy brown hair behind her ears.

"We have Malcolm Gallagher in with his attorney right now,"

Carmen answered. "He lawyered up the moment he was brought in for more questioning about the Barrie murder and he's sweating like a pig when it's twenty-five degrees outside."

"Evidence?"

"He argued with the deceased the night she died. The argument was heard by at least two witnesses. He lied about accompanying the victim to the Montclair and his prints were found in the suite. We already have the murder weapon. All that together gives us motive, means, and opportunity," Carmen summarized.

"Any prints on the murder weapon?" Sheila asked.

"Wiped clean."

"Anyone know what the argument was about?"

"No," Chris admitted.

"So all you really have in the way of evidence is a video surveillance clip of Gallagher going into a place he had every right to be and a set of prints in the victim's suite? A place he had probably been to many times. You picked him up on that shitty evidence?"

"He lied about being in the suite the night Barrie was killed," Carmen argued. "If he had the right to be there why lie about it?"

"I don't care what your crystal ball tells you, Detective Sandoval. I have to have something the grand jury can believe."

"Housekeepin' at the Montclair cleaned the penthouse every day," Chris said. "That included vacuumin' and dustin'. Forensics gave us a match on his fingerprints in the livin' and bedrooms of the suite. If we can get a hair sample they can probably match that as well. And I'd be willin' to bet a month's pay he's got scratches somewhere on his body. If the apartment had been cleaned that day accordin' to housekeepin' records, the only way his prints could have been there was if he was there that night."

"Or maybe the maid did a shitty job of cleaning," Sheila said. "Or maybe she lied."

"The surveillance video shows him enterin' with Barrie and accompanyin' her onto the penthouse elevator. He lied about not bein' there and acted a little strange the last time we questioned him."

"In a city with a couple of million certifiable whackos, you're working on one guy who *acted* kind of strange one time. Fabulous," Sheila said, rolling her eyes.

Chris was well into her second cup of coffee when Grace Gallagher stepped out of the interrogation room and signaled the three women to join her and her client. Her clear blue eyes met Chris' for a moment before she shifted back into attorney mode.

"It's good to see you again, Sheila," Grace said with a smile, not offering the same greeting to Shaw and Sandoval.

"Does your client wish to make a voluntary statement?" Sheila responded with a glance at Malcolm Gallagher. He sat at the table in the interrogation room, expressionless, with his intertwined fingers on the table in front of him. Sandoval was right about the sweating.

"From what I've seen, most of your evidence is purely circumstantial at best," Grace answered as she pulled out a chair next to her father and sat down.

"I send people to prison every day on circumstantial evidence, Grace. If we had a video camera at the scene of every crime it would be nice, but until then..." Sheila stopped and shrugged.

"What if my client were to admit that he was in the suite that night, but that Ms. Barrie was alive when he left?"

"Why did he lie to the police about being there in the first place? The deceased was his client. He had a vested interest in her business dealings."

"Since he was there, he was afraid of exactly what's happening now."

"Would Mr. Gallagher be willing to give us a hair sample?"

"Of course. But if you're planning to drag that DNA crap into court, I can produce a dozen experts to dispute it."

"Sounds like you're assuming we'll be able to make a match."

"Since my client is willing to admit to having been in the apartment several times, including the night of December twenty-sixth, I'd be shocked if you didn't."

"The victim's head was crushed with a fireplace poker," Chris interrupted.

Gallagher's head snapped up and a look Chris couldn't identify twisted his features. He looked as if he might be sick as he squeezed his intertwined fingers together so tightly they turned white.

"Perhaps, but not by my client," Grace said calmly. "Or while he was present."

"Did Mr. Gallagher engage in sexual activities with Miss Barrie that night?" Chris asked.

"Of course not," Grace said, glaring at the detective.

"That's ludicrous!" Malcolm said forcefully. "Elaine was my client and my friend!"

"She slept with other men, why not you?" Chris pressed. "But even if you did, it must have been pretty lousy sex, since there wasn't any semen found in the victim," she added.

"One would suppose that you have heard of condoms, Detective Shaw. Or do you personally prefer riskier sex?" Grace asked pointedly. "After all, if Miss Barrie had slept with other men it would have been foolish of my client not to protect himself to prevent transferring anything to his wife."

"Is he now admittin' he slept with her?" Chris asked.

"My response was purely theoretical," Grace answered.

"Would Mr. Gallagher care to revise his previous version of what happened that evening?" Sheila broke in.

"He's willing to make a statement, but I will advise him not to answer any questions I feel are inappropriate or irrelevant to your investigation."

Gallagher sat passively during the exchange between his daughter and Morgan. Chris leaned against the wall opposite Gallagher and could barely bring herself to look at the man she now believed might have murdered Elaine Barrie nor the woman she had fantasized about making love with less than a week before. Carmen sat at one end of the table arranging the microphone for the tape recorder. She pushed the record button and nodded at Sheila Morgan.

"This is New York County Assistant District Attorney Sheila Morgan. This statement is being voluntarily given by Malcolm Gallagher, business manager for the deceased, Elaine Barrie. It is January second, two-thousand-and-twelve and the time is nine twenty-two p.m. Present in the room are Mr. Gallagher, his attorney, Grace Gallagher, Detectives Christine Shaw and Carmen Sandoval of the Midtown Precinct and myself. You may begin any time you're ready, Mr. Gallagher," Sheila recited for the microphone.

Gallagher cleared his throat and glanced at Grace before speaking. "I met with Elaine in her dressing room at the Lerner after her last performance on December twenty-sixth. The performance ended at about ten-thirty that evening. Elaine and I talked in her dressing room while she changed. It's true we did have a few heated words at that time and our voices may have been loud enough to be overheard by others. We were arguing about an offer she received to screen test for a motion picture. She refused the offer, as usual. I believed the refusal was at least in part due to Carl's influence. He had been adamant about her staying on the stage and not being lured away by people he thought would corrupt her," Gallagher recited calmly.

"The Carl you are referring to was the victim's husband, Carl Janus?" Sheila interrupted as a point of clarification.

"Yes," Gallagher answered. "I understood that Elaine was under a great deal of pressure recently because of Carl's illness, but I thought she needed to keep her options open for, you know, the future."

"You mean after Mr. Janus passed away?" Sheila asked.

"Yes. My understanding was that Carl most likely wouldn't survive his illness more than another year. But Elaine couldn't seem to think that far ahead or didn't want to. Anyway, she became irrational, which wasn't like her. But as I said, she was under quite a strain, emotionally."

"Were you aware of the relationships Miss Barrie had with Damon Hunter, Alex Webb, and Kent Devine?" Carmen asked.

Gallagher nodded. "Yes, and I'm afraid our disagreement lapsed into that. I didn't mean for it to happen, I swear. But I was already pretty steamed. I warned her that if she continued sleeping around the way she was, I might not be able to keep a lid on it. A thing like that, even the rumor of it, could have destroyed her career. But she only laughed."

"It could have destroyed your commission as well," Sheila observed.

"I wasn't worried about that. A fabulous talent was going to be flushed after years of hard work."

"What did she have to say about these liaisons?"

"That they weren't any of my business. We were in the middle of that discussion when we were interrupted by Del. Della Summers. By the time Del left, Elaine and I had both calmed down and that was about it. I walked her out of the theater. Outside she asked me to accompany her to her suite at the Montclair."

"Did she say why?"

"Not then."

"Was anyone else in the dressing room when you were arguing with Miss Barrie?"

"Todd, my son, may have been. I don't remember."

"But you remember everything else clearly," Carmen said.

"I was upset. Backstage can be chaotic after a performance."

"In your initial statement you said you didn't go to Miss Barrie's suite. The hotel video tapes confirm you lied about that. Is there anything else you lied about?" Chris asked without looking at Gallagher.

"I'm telling the truth now. She asked me to accompany her to the suite."

"What time did you arrive at her suite?"

"I'm not sure. Eleven or eleven-thirty."

"Do you have a key card to the penthouse at the Montclair?"

"No."

"Was your son with you?" Chris asked.

"No. He left the theater before Elaine and I did. Said something about meeting a friend for a drink before he went home."

"What time was that?"

"Again I don't know. I didn't look at a clock. Probably before eleven or thereabouts," Malcolm sighed.

"What happened when you arrived at the suite?"

"Elaine changed and called Carl. She told me she might consider a screen test in the future, but not now."

"What time did you leave Miss Barrie's suite?" Sheila asked.

"I don't know the exact time, but it must have been around midnight because I was home between one and one-thirty."

"Did anyone see you leave the Montclair?"

Gallagher glanced at Grace before answering. She nodded and he continued.

"I walked out the main entrance," Gallagher explained. "I don't know if anyone saw me, but I swear to God that Elaine was alive when I left her suite. Surely the video captured me leaving."

"As a matter of fact, it did. And since I trust the video more than I do you at the moment, you were in the suite a little over an hour. How long did it take her to change clothes and talk to her husband?" Chris asked.

"Not long," Malcolm answered. "A few minutes, maybe ten or fifteen."

"So it took her another forty-five minutes to say she might agree to a screen test in the future?" Chris asked. "Was she stutterin'? What else did you discuss?"

Gallagher looked at her momentarily before answering. "Nothing."

"Will your wife corroborate what time you arrived home?"

"You're not going to drag her into this, are you? She doesn't know anything."

"We'll do what we can, Mr. Gallagher, but can't make any promises," Sheila said.

"It might have been after one-thirty by the time I got home. I called Laura to tell her I was on my way home. She might know what time that was."

"Did you call from the suite?"

"No. From my car. She asked me to stop at an all-night market to pick up something on my way home."

"Was your wife upset about you being late?"

"She's used to it," Gallagher answered with a shrug. "In my business most of my clients don't work normal business hours."

"Is there anything else you'd like to add at this time?"

"I tried to call my son before I drove home. There was a business issue we needed to discuss the following day, but he didn't pick up. I left a message."

"That it?" Sheila asked, looking at Chris and Carmen.

Gallagher leaned toward Sheila. The look on his face was

serious. "I did not kill Elaine Barrie."

"That's an interestin' story, Mr. Gallagher," Chris said as she pushed away from the wall.

"It's the truth," Gallagher said.

"It's a load of bullshit!" Chris said in a raised voice and slammed her hand on the table. Malcolm jumped and shook his head.

"The first time I interviewed you, you said your argument with Elaine was over a recording contract. That makes lie number two."

"What difference does it make? It was an argument over business."

Chris leaned down close to Gallagher's ear and hissed, "I don't like it when people lie to me. One lie always leads to another."

"That's enough, Detective," Grace said. "It's a small point."

Chris ignored her and brought her mouth closer to Gallagher again. "Didn't Elaine tell you she was pregnant?"

Gallagher slowly shook his head and buried it in his hands, but Chris saw what might have been a tear drop fall to the tabletop.

"Didn't she tell you—" Chris started to repeat her question.

"Yes!" Gallagher answered, snapping his head up to glare at Chris. "She told me that night." Chris glanced at Grace and saw the surprise in her eyes.

That statement stopped Chris' questioning for a heartbeat. "You stood to lose everything, didn't you? Were you the father?"

"No and no."

"Didn't you have an affair with Elaine?"

"No, of course not."

"But you wanted to, didn't you? After all she was a beautiful woman."

"Yes, but we weren't having an affair," Malcolm said weakly. "I wouldn't do that to my wife."

"Didn't it piss you off?" Chris hammered. "Weren't you angry that Elaine let herself get knocked up by some young stud? She was going to ruin everything. In fact, you were so angry you decided to get rid of the baby by killing its mother," Chris stated.

"That's absurd!" Gallagher said loudly as he stood to face Chris.

"That's enough," Grace said, her voice hard as steel. She pulled her father back down to his seat.

But Chris was on a roll. Gallagher knew more than he was saying. She was certain of it. "Did your wife think you were sleepin' with Elaine?"

"Of course not. I love my wife."

"But she's not quite as desirable as Elaine Barrie, is she?"

"Mrs. Gallagher has nothing to do with this investigation,"

Grace tried.

"Did you speak to her after you got home that night?" Chris went on, ignoring Grace.

Gallagher paused for a moment. "She...she was asleep when I got home. I didn't wake her."

"So she can't corroborate what time you arrived home after Elaine and her baby were dead?"

"Elaine was alive when I left the hotel," Gallagher insisted.

"Didn't you want to tell her about Elaine's pregnancy? That's pretty excitin' news. Was it because you knew Elaine was already dead?"

"No, no, no. You're twisting everything around. I did not kill Elaine. Grace, please."

Grace stood up and slipped her overcoat on. "This interview is over, Sheila. Either arrest my client or we're out of here." When Sheila waved her hand dismissively at Grace, she said, "Let's go, Dad."

As Grace Gallagher escorted her father out of the interrogation room, Chris pulled out a chair and straddled it, resting her arms on the back of the chair.

"You believe him, Sheila?" she asked.

"What's not to believe? He admits he was in the suite that night, but it doesn't prove much. He had a legitimate reason for going there," the ADA said with a shrug.

"Guess we'll have to question the wife, even though I'm sure Gallagher and his attorney are racin' home right now to prep her," Chris said, blowing out a puff of air. "I think there's still somethin' he's not tellin' us."

"He's probably still trying to protect Barrie's reputation. The royalties from her recordings are still worth a tidy amount and he gets all or a part of it now that she's dead and has no living relatives," Sheila said. "What was that about Barrie being pregnant?"

"Artie confirmed it during the autopsy."

Sheila shrugged. "Maybe the father wasn't thrilled about it."

Chris looked up at Sheila. "Based on the DNA, Carl Janus was the father." She cleared her throat. "He *would* have been thrilled."

"You got any other hot prospects in the suspect category?" Sheila asked. She stood up and looked at her wristwatch. "It's just a gut feeling, but I'm not sure Malcolm Gallagher is your guy. You better find another viable suspect soon because this case is getting colder every day."

CARMEN RELUCTANTLY TOOK the next day off to accompany Mercedes to meetings with Frankie's probation officer and a family counselor. Chris killed most of the morning going through the growing stack of files, reports, and interview statements relating to the Barrie case. Periodically, she jotted down a note on a legal pad. She was trying to leave her mind open to even the remotest possibilities they could track down. She flipped a page on the legal pad on her desk and wrote a series of questions. If they eliminated Gallagher they would need to re-interview several persons.

Bored with going over the same information time and time again, Chris grabbed her jacket from the back of her chair and unlocked her desk drawer to remove her Beretta. She never could stand sitting around. She pulled an address from a file and strode toward the main doors of the precinct.

Less than an hour later and despite the midday traffic, Chris swung the Trans-Am into the long, slightly uphill drive of a stately home on Long Island and let out a low whistle as the estate came into view, shining white against the clear blue sky. She noticed the drive was pavement, not asphalt. A pristine blanket of snow covered the yard and lay gracefully on the branches of nearby trees yet not a flake adhered to the drive, leading Chris to believe it was probably heated. Must be nice, she thought. Further deductions followed. Malcolm Gallagher was either an extremely successful business manager or in hock up to his eyeballs. Grace and Todd Gallagher had grown up wallowing in the lap of luxury. Probably spoiled beyond belief and accustomed to the idea there was nothing daddy's money couldn't buy.

Chris pulled her vehicle into a widened area of the driveway that would allow her to back up easily and exited the car. She straightened her blazer and wiggled her pant legs around until they fell across the tops of her shoes in a way that satisfied her. She walked slowly up the front steps of the house and leaned in to press the doorbell. The sound of melodic chimes echoing through the interior sang of affluence without seeming gaudy. Chris turned and surveyed the property which overlooked a nearby village. It was picturesque. She smiled and rocked back and forth on the balls of her feet. She'd never been anywhere she could describe as picturesque before. The word itself conjured up New England villages and hamlets she'd only seen in travel magazines at her dentist's office.

The front door opened and Chris turned at the sound, smiling at an older woman dressed in a blue and gray uniform topped by a starched white apron.

"May I help you?" the woman said softly.

Chris removed her shield and identification from her belt and held it up for the woman to see. "I'm here to see Mrs. Laura

Gallagher," she said. "Is she home?"

"Please, come in, officer."

Chris stepped inside as she tucked her ID holder back into the waist of her slacks.

"I'll let Mrs. Gallagher know you're here," the maid said. She used her hand to motion Chris into a room off the main entry.

Chris took the time while she waited to take in the entryway. It opened up into a large area that led to a wide staircase several feet from the front door. Tables on either side of the entryway held pieces of sculpture, figures of men and women dancing. Their arms, even those of the men, seemed artfully graceful and Chris expected them to step off into a dance any moment. She moved into the room the maid had indicated and walked around the perimeter to take in the furniture and accessories. Pictures hung on one wall seemed to chronicle the growth of Grace and her younger brother from infancy to adulthood. A second wall was dedicated to Malcolm and included photos of him with many of his clients and well-known celebrities from the world of the theater. Mrs. Gallagher had a wall to herself. Pictures of her wedding to Malcolm, with her children, and several of her walking down the catwalk during fashion events when she was apparently much younger. Chris could see the fierce determination in her eyes. Laura Gallagher had been a beautiful woman.

"How may I help you?" a strong voice behind Chris asked.

Chris turned and looked at the woman behind her. Laura Gallagher was still a striking woman. She had slipped gracefully into her early fifties and was impeccably dressed in a midnight blue floor length skirt and a yellow long-sleeve blouse that was gathered at her wrists. Her dark hair was fashioned into a French braid that seemed to encircle her head and matched her dark brown eyes. "Mrs. Gallagher?" Chris asked.

"Yes."

"I'm Detective Christine Shaw, NYPD, Midtown Precinct. I'd like to ask you a few questions, if that's all right."

A tight smile crossed Laura's face. "And what if I said it wasn't all right?"

"Then I'd have to take you to my precinct for questioning," Chris answered.

"Well, then get on with whatever you're here for," Laura said, sounding slightly annoyed.

"I'm investigating the murder of Elaine Barrie and have just a few preliminary questions."

"I don't know anything about that unfortunate event. I don't see how I can possibly help you." Laura walked to a settee and lowered her body gracefully onto its edge.

"Did you know Miss Barrie?"

"Of course. She and her husband were guests in our home many times. She was a lovely woman."

"Can you tell me what time your husband arrived home on the evening of December twenty-sixth or the morning of December twenty-seventh?"

"He called some time after midnight to let me know he was on his way home from the theater."

"Do you know why he was at the theater that night?"

"I assumed he had business to discuss with Elaine."

"How long does it generally take to drive from the city to your home?"

"Forty, forty-five minutes. It depends on the traffic. But you should know that. Didn't you just drive here from the city?"

"Yes. It took me about fifty minutes, but I didn't know exactly where I was going," Chris answered.

"There's an all-night market in the village and I asked Malcolm to stop there on his way home and pick up a carton of milk for breakfast the next morning."

"What's the name of the market?"

"Cheshire's. I believe it's just off Main."

"Did you speak to your husband when he got home?"

"Actually I fell asleep on the sofa in the den. But he was here when I woke up around three and went to bed."

"So you can't really say what time he arrived. Is that correct?"

"Yes."

"Is it possible he arrived home later than you thought? Say two in the morning?"

"Anything is possible, but he should have been here between one and one-thirty. He was home when the police called to notify him of Elaine's death. The phone awakened us."

"Mr. Gallagher stated he went to Miss Barrie's suite at the Montclair. Were you aware of that?"

"He didn't mention it."

"Have you ever suspected he might be having an affair?"

Laura looked down at her hands before answering. She took a deep breath and said, "He did once, early in our marriage."

Chris was surprised by the candidness of Laura's answer, but pressed on with her next question. "Did you ever have reason to believe he might have been sexually involved with Miss Barrie?"

Laura smiled. "Once a man cheats, Detective, he can't be trusted again, but, no, I never suspected Malcolm of having an affair with Elaine. Frankly, he can't afford it financially. My attorney has made sure of that."

"Did you know Miss Barrie was pregnant at the time of her death?"

Chris saw something flicker through Laura's eyes. "No, I didn't," she answered after a brief pause. And then in a voice that seemed to reek with insincerity, she said, "Pity." While she awaited Chris' next question Laura stared down at her hands, twisting them around nervously.

Chris glanced at Laura's hands, catching a glimpse of medium-length, French-tipped fingernails. Laura closed her eyes and then raised her head, slowly opening her eyes to stare at Chris calmly. "Is there anything else, Detective?"

Chris smiled. "No, ma'am. Not at the moment, but I'd appreciate it if you remained available in case I should have any other questions in the future."

THE CELL PHONE in Chris' pocket vibrated. She flipped it open while still staring at the autopsy report in front of her. "Shaw," she mumbled. Her eyebrows knitted together as she listened to the caller. She gathered everything on her desk haphazardly and dumped it into a desk drawer, locking it before she ran from the precinct toward her car. She buckled her seat belt and peeled out of the parking garage, barely missing a patrol car that had just entered. She slapped the flashing red police light onto the dash as she sped through the streets and around cars toward Spanish Harlem. Her heart stayed in her throat until she slid the Trans-Am to a stop and jumped out the second the ignition died. She sprinted past the yellow police line and down the sidewalk toward Carmen's building. She came close to striking a uniformed officer who tried to stop her before jerking her badge from her pocket and scribbling her name on the clipboard he shoved into her hand. Two ambulances were backed up near the entrance to the building. She pounded up the stairs to the third floor two at a time and found herself out of breath as she stared in the door to the Sandoval apartment. Quickly surveying the living room, she saw a team of paramedics working feverously over someone on the floor, but she couldn't see who it was. As she took a step into the room, a strong hand grabbed her arm. When she looked up she saw Sam Hernandez, another detective with Midtown Precinct.

"Let 'em work, Shaw," he said quietly.

"What the fuck happened?" she asked angrily as she jerked her arm away from his grasp.

"Looks like a burglary gone real bad right now."

"Carmen..."

"Banged up some and took a pretty good lick to the head.

Probably needs a few stitches. She wounded the one in here and took out another one. Her gun was discharged three times from what we can tell."

Breath caught in Chris' throat as she slumped back against the wall. She looked up quickly and asked, "Mercedes?"

"Only a little shaken up. A few bruises."

"Where are they?"

"Kitchen. A paramedic is checking Carmen out."

Chris stepped away from the wall and looked over the paramedic's shoulder at the young man on the floor. She frowned as she spun around, coming nose-to-nose with Hernandez. "I wanna see the one Carmen took out."

Chris and Hernandez skirted the edge of the living room and moved down the narrow hall leading to the back of the apartment. The body of a young Latino male lay just inside one of the bedrooms. Chris knelt down to look more closely at the body.

"Recognize him?" Hernandez asked.

Chris nodded and said, "I've seen him around. You got an ID?"

"His wallet had a driver's license issued to Ricardo Aguilar. Address here in Spanish Harlem."

"Better get some units to start turnin' over garbage cans lookin' for any acquaintances. And put out an APB for Frankie Sandoval. I saw him hangin' with this guy and the other one last week."

A sound coming from the living room caught Chris' ear as she stood. She strode rapidly toward the sound and looked down at the face of the young man being strapped to the gurney. "He gonna make it?" she asked.

"Not if we don't get him outta here pronto," the paramedic said in a clipped voice without looking at Chris.

She stepped out of the way and watched the gurney disappear from the apartment. She took a deep breath and turned toward the kitchen, hesitating a moment before pushing the door open. Carmen's bandaged head jerked up when she saw Chris, tears welling up in her eyes. Chris crossed the small room quickly and wrapped her arms around Carmen as she buried her face into Chris' shoulder. Chris glanced across the table and saw a stunned-looking Mercedes wringing the life out of a white handkerchief.

"It'll be all right, Carmen," Chris whispered softly. "Are you and Mercedes okay?"

"I...I have a splitting headache," Carmen answered as she sniffed.

"You did good, partner. Can you tell me what happened?"

Carmen slid onto the kitchen chair and wiped her eyes with

the back of her hand as Chris knelt down in front of her.

"I took Mama to the meeting with the family counselor this afternoon and afterward dropped her off in front of the building before I went to park the car. When I got to the apartment maybe fifteen minutes later, those two were inside. One of them was hitting Mama, so I drew my weapon and identified myself. Oh, Chris, they're both so young."

"You did what you had to do, Carmen. Were there only two of them?"

"I thought so. I ordered the one guy to release Mama, but he didn't. Then I spotted the second one coming out of the bedroom holding Papa's pistol Mama keeps in the nightstand next to her bed. Everything went pretty fast after that. He raised the pistol toward me and I fired. I guess it scared the one holding Mama because he shoved her away and came at me. I fired again, but don't remember anything after that. Something hit me on the head from behind."

Chris looked over the table at Mercedes. The older woman's eyes were closed, rosary beads dangling from her fingers, her mouth moving silently as she rocked back and forth. Chris walked around the table and rested her hand on Mercedes' shoulder. She leaned down and asked gently, "Did you see the third person, Mercedes? Can you identify him?"

Mercedes shook her head slightly and looked up at Chris. There was something in her eyes that said she knew more than she was prepared to reveal. Chris turned her attention to the paramedic examining Carmen and asked, "Is she okay?"

"Should be, but she could have a concussion. Probably needs a few stitches, too."

The kitchen door swung open as Ruben rushed inside, breathing heavily. "Carmen," he said as he moved quickly to her and took her in his arms. "Are you okay? Who did this to you, baby?"

"I have a headache," Carmen repeated. "What are you doing here, Ruben?"

"I heard the address when dispatch sent an ambulance out." Ruben looked at the paramedic working on Carmen's head. "You taking her in, Marco?" he asked.

The mustachioed man nodded. "She needs a few stitches. Might have a concussion."

Ruben turned his attention to Chris. "You have to find who did this, Shaw."

Chris' eyes met Ruben's and she nodded. "I will. I promise. But right now she needs to get to the hospital."

"But—" Carmen started.

"That's the only deal on the table, Carmen. Don't make me pull rank on you," Chris said firmly. "Ruben will be with you. I'll take Mercedes and we'll meet you there."

CHRIS MADE SURE Mercedes was securely buckled into the passenger seat of the Trans-Am before she closed the door and walked around the back of her vehicle. She slid behind the wheel, glancing across the seat at Carmen's mother, trying to decide how to ask her about her suspicions. She turned the key in the ignition, shifted into drive, and looked over her shoulder before swinging into the flow of traffic. She was less than two miles from the hospital, but wasn't in a hurry, confident Ruben would make sure Carmen was taken care of.

Chris took a deep breath and said, "Frankie was there, wasn't he, Mercedes?"

The older woman looked out the passenger window and didn't speak.

"He was the third person Carmen didn't see and the one who hit her. But you saw him, didn't you?"

Even though Mercedes refused to look at her and began shaking her head slowly, Chris knew in her gut she was right. Frankie Sandoval had attacked his own sister.

Finally unable to control her anger and frustration, Chris hit the steering wheel with the heel of her hand. "Come on, goddammit, Mercedes! I saw Frankie with those two thugs last week. We've put out an all-points bulletin for him already! Help me find him and maybe he won't get himself killed when we do."

Mercedes looked at Chris and tears fell from her eyes. "You have to help him, Christina. He with bad people now. I pray every day, but my prayers are not answered."

"Where would he go, Mercedes?"

"I don' know."

"Do you know the wounded man?"

"His name is Carlos Medina. He go to school with Frankie."

As Chris pulled her car into a parking spot near the emergency room, Mercedes touched her arm as she opened the door. "Don' tell Carmen about Frankie, please."

"She'll find out sooner or later."

"She hurting enough now. I tell her," the older woman promised quietly.

By the time Chris and Mercedes arrived Ruben was holding Carmen's hand while a doctor worked on the laceration on her head. Chris stood by the door, allowing Mercedes to go to her daughter. It would be difficult for Mercedes to reconcile in her mind the idea that her daughter could have been killed by Frankie. When the doctor finished stitching the wound on Carmen's head, Chris followed him out of the room.

"She gonna be okay, doc?"

"Should be fine in a few days. Her CAT scan came back negative for a concussion."

"Well, I guess that hard head came in handy for somethin' then."

"She'll need a day or two of rest and the stitches can come out in a week. I'll be releasing her in about an hour."

"Thanks, doc," Chris said as she shook his hand and re-entered the room. Ruben and Mercedes were helping Carmen sit up on the examining table.

"This has been a real fun evening," Carmen frowned.

"The doc said you'd be fine after a day or two of rest," Ruben said.

"I'll be fine once I get outta here. It's just a bump on the head," Carmen protested.

"You stay home tomorrow, Carmenita," Mercedes said firmly. Looking at Chris she said, "Christina have things to do without you."

"Yeah," Chris said, picking up on what Mercedes didn't say. "We have some stuff to put together about what happened at your apartment that you can't help with."

"Let Shaw take care of it, Carmen," Ruben said softly. "She's got your back."

For the first time, Chris saw Ruben differently. Maybe he wasn't the total asshole she thought he was after all.

"It was a clean shoot, Chris," Carmen said glaring at her.

"I know it was, but you know the review board has to check it out anyway. It's no big deal, Carmen. I'll take care of it, but expect to see your cheerful, smiling face back at work when you feel up to it."

"Fuck that shit," Carmen mumbled. "You just find the son of a bitch who hit me and kick his fucking ass."

With a glance at Mercedes, Chris nodded. "No sweat, partner. I will."

Chapter Eighteen

CHRIS SPENT THE better part of the week following the attack on Carmen and Mercedes searching through the files on the Elaine Barrie case. She also spent a considerable amount of time pestering Sam Hernandez about why he hadn't located Frankie Sandoval yet. Every cockroach in the city had a favorite place to hide and most of Frankie's had been checked and re-checked. Near the end of the week Chris took some time to lend Carmen moral support when she was called to answer questions from Captain Savage and Internal Affairs about the necessity of discharging her weapon, which resulted in the death of Ricardo Aguilar. It didn't take long for the report to come down that the shooting was justified and Chris breathed a sigh of relief. Sometimes, even when you know you did nothing wrong, things don't go the way you hope. Chris was glad Carmen would be returning to regular work at the beginning of the next week.

"You okay?" Chris asked when Carmen arrived for work on Monday morning.

"Yeah. The headache finally went away," Carmen answered as she picked up a stack of messages on her desk. "Anything new I need to know about on the Barrie case?"

"Nothin' of importance. Savage has been all over me because the case is growin' cold. Still waitin' on a few lab reports." Chris stared at her partner. "I thought they shaved part of your head to stitch up your head."

"They did. Pretty good hairpiece, huh? Took me an hour this morning to mix it with my real hair."

"Can't even tell it's there." Chris smiled. "If this doesn't work out for you, you can always take up hair dressin'."

Carmen snorted before looking at Chris again. "I talked to Mama last night," she said. "About Frankie."

"And?"

"I don't think she'll testify against him, Chris."

"He could have killed you."

"But he didn't."

"We'll have to convince her he's dangerous."

"Good luck with that," Carmen mumbled. She seemed agitated as she read through the stack of messages.

"You seem a little antsy, Carmen. What's up?"

"Just anxious to get back to work." She read a message and

held it up. "Haggarty, the security guy at the Montclair, wants to see us. Doesn't say what about, but it has to be the Barrie case."

Chris stood up and grabbed her jacket. She unlocked the drawer in her desk and shoved her weapon into her shoulder holster.

CHRIS STEERED THE Trans-Am over what was becoming a familiar route as she and Carmen returned to the Montclair. When they entered the lobby, Rayburn was standing behind the main desk and Chris nearly laughed at the pale expression on his face when he saw them. She waved at him as they waited for the elevator.

"What's up?" Chris asked as she and Carmen walked into the security office.

Haggarty smiled and limped toward them, shaking hands with both detectives. "One of my men reported that he ran a vagrant out of the main stairwell the night of December twenty-sixth. He felt sorry for her, it being around Christmas and all, so he didn't file a report. Just sent her on her way. I only found out about it because they ran her out again last night."

"What time was that?" Carmen asked.

"He says he found her under the stairs on the fifteenth floor between one-thirty and two. Not sure how she got that far up without someone seeing her or how long she'd been there. She had her stuff parked behind a dumpster outside a side door."

"You got a name?"

"Skeeter's all anyone knows. She's smaller than most mosquitoes I've seen. That's why she's hard to spot. Not much taller than that beat up grocery cart she pushes around."

"We'll keep an eye out for her," Chris said.

"She usually has an old can of mace on her, so watch out," Haggarty smirked. "She got me once."

"Anyone know where she hangs out?"

"Those homeless types can cover a pretty big area, but from what I've seen, she's no spring chicken. I'd guess she stays around this area somewhere so she's close to the big hotels. Probably only comes here when the shelters are full and the temperatures drop fairly low. If she's not in a shelter or here, you might check some of the other hotels in the area, especially ones that hold banquet events. Pretty good dumpster diving after those."

"Keep an eye out for her." Chris handed him a business card with her personal cell number on it.

"She'll turn up," Haggarty said. "I hear a cold front is supposed to come through in the next night or two."

CHRIS ISSUED AN APB for the woman known as Skeeter, but she managed to elude patrol cars during the day. Chris and Carmen staked out the area around the Montclair for the next two nights, hoping the cold temperatures and wind would drive Skeeter into her favorite hiding place. Surprisingly, with nothing waiting for her at home, Chris was enjoying their stake-out. Mercedes packed homemade soup and bread for Carmen to eat in the car, but there was always more than enough for Chris as well. Along with two thermoses of coffee, it was almost like camping out. Chris decided to give the stake-out a week. After that she would turn it over to patrol and hope for the best. They received a couple of calls from soup kitchens, but the woman slipped away before they arrived.

"Where the hell could she be hiding?" Carmen asked for no apparent reason on their third night.

"I don't know, but I hope she hasn't turned into a Popsicle in an alley somewhere," Chris said.

"We got thousands of people living on the streets in the city. Who can live like that?"

"Guess they're doin' what they have to. Sort of like campin' except in a concrete campground."

"You camp?"

"Used to all the time back home, especially during deer season."

"You shot at Bambi?"

"We don't regard them as a cartoon character, Carmen. More like meat on the table."

"That's why we got grocery stores."

"Deer are free and grocery stores don't stock venison."

"You gotta buy a damn license. How much does that cost?"

"Used to be about a hundred-and-fifty."

"I can buy a whole lotta cow for that and I don't have to worry about cutting it up."

"Good point. I haven't been huntin' in years. Not since I was a kid and my old man used to let me skip school when the season opened."

"You know everything about my family. How come you never talk about yours?"

Chris shrugged. "Nothin' much to tell."

"Got any brothers and sisters?"

"Why the sudden need to know about my family?" Chris asked, shrugging her shoulders deeper into her coat.

"Because I'm freezing my ass off and if I doze off I might freeze to death. Come on, Chris."

Chris gazed out the side window of her vehicle. Finally she took a deep breath and said, "My mother's dead. Committed suicide when I was around twelve."

"I'm sorry," Carmen said. "That's tough."

"I found her body when I came home from school. Took one too many pills. My old man still lives on the ranch I grew up on, but I haven't talked to him in years." Chris laughed harshly. "I couldn't wait to get old enough to leave."

"Do you know why she did it?"

"He drove her to it. He broke her spirit. Might as well have put a gun in her hand. She was creative and artistic, not cut out for the ranch. Guess she just couldn't take the isolation and dirt any more. I have a sister, Gloria, but haven't talked to her in a while either." She chuckled to herself. "When I left, I *really* left."

Before Carmen could ask more questions, their radio squawked. "This is dispatch. A patrol car reports an individual matching subject's description entering an alleyway behind St. Luke's."

Chris started the engine and pressed her mike button. "Roger, Dispatch. We'll investigate. Have patrol meet us in front of the church. No lights, no siren." With a quick glance into her rearview mirror, Chris pulled away from the curb and accelerated away from the Montclair. Ten minutes later she swung to the curb across the street from the old church a few blocks away. She stepped out of her vehicle and walked to the driver's window of the patrol car.

"Which alleyway did the subject enter?"

"To the left of the main entrance," the officer responded.

"Take the front and right side. We'll take the alley."

"Roger."

Chris and Carmen darted across the street silently and carefully entered the alleyway. Halfway down Chris shined her flashlight behind the church's dumpster and spotted a grocery cart loaded down with various items. Across the alleyway, three steps led to a side door of the church. Chris drew her weapon and started toward the steps.

"What you doing, Chris? You'll scare the shit out of her," Carmen hissed. "We just want to talk to her."

"For all I know she found a throwaway somewhere," Chris said. "Besides, this might not be her." Chris took the steps and stopped to peek into a small side window. She shined the flashlight beam around, but saw nothing. She reached out and turned the doorknob. It was unlocked. She pressed her mike button. "Patrol, we're enterin' a side door. Cover the front and back and wait for my signal before you enter."

Chris swung the door open and entered in a crouched position, aiming her weapon to the right while Carmen covered her left. St. Luke's was a relatively small church with a single center aisle between rows of pews. They checked the area behind the altar before starting down the main aisle. They ran a flashlight beam down each row as they progressed slowly. A fourth of the way down the aisle, Chris heard a rustling sound from Carmen's side. She brought her flashlight around in time to catch a wizened face pop up aiming an object in her hand at Carmen. Chris jumped in front of Carmen and wrapped her arms around her, turning so that whatever it was struck her back. She felt something wet hit her neck and run down her shirt. She caught the discernible scent of mace as it coated her back. She heard the sound of feet shuffling and was able to release Carmen in time to semi-tackle the fleeing figure, knocking the can from her hand.

"Get off me," a strong voice said before it began to cough. "I'm chokin'."

Chris managed to pull her handcuffs from the case on her belt and attach them to the woman's wrist and a metal bar at the base of the closest pew. She stood up quickly and tore her jacket off, tossing it away from her. "Well, that was fun," she muttered. She looked down at the woman handcuffed to the pew. "You Skeeter?" she asked.

"I didn't do nothin'. I was mindin' my own bidness."

"We just need to talk to you. You're not in trouble," Chris said between coughs. She extended a hand to help Carmen up. "You okay?"

"Yeah, just need a change of clothes," Carmen said with a nod.

"We got her," she said into her mike. "Can you transport the subject back to the precinct?"

"No problem."

Chris released the handcuffs and turned Skeeter over to a patrol officer. He made a face when he started to escort her to his car. "Mace?"

"Just a touch," Chris laughed.

"What about my stuff?" Skeeter whined.

"It's safe," Carmen said. "I'll leave a note for the priest to look after it until you return."

"My car's gonna smell like this crap for a week," Chris grumbled as they walked back to the Trans-Am.

"Next time, use a car from the garage," Carmen chuckled. "Hey, you left your coat inside."

"Consider it my donation to charity," Chris said as she shivered against a cold breeze.

AFTER A QUICK, hot shower and a change of clothes, Chris ruffled her hair with her hand and went up a flight of stairs to the squad room. Carmen wasn't far behind.

"You got copies of the pictures taken at the memorial for Barrie?" Chris asked after Carmen sat down.

"You betcha," Carmen answered, pulling out a stack of pictures from her bottom desk drawer. "Think they'll do any good?"

"Can't hurt. Just take the ones of legit suspects, women too," Chris answered with a shrug. "Where's Skeeter?"

"I asked a female officer to find her a change of clothes and show her to the showers. She smelled bad enough before the mace got on her. Maybe I won't need another shower when I get home then." Carmen stuck her tongue out and shook her head in disgust.

Fifteen minutes later the patrol officer assigned to clean Skeeter up wandered into the squad room. She stopped next to Carmen's desk. "She's ready," the female officer said, her face a picture of distaste. "Just let me say it's a privilege to protect and serve, ma'am."

"That's the LAPD motto, officer. Ours is 'Faithful Until Death'."

"That works too, since I thought I'd die from the smell and I'm not talking about the mace." The officer turned and walked away.

Chris and Carmen both started laughing and it felt good after the tragic events they had been dealing with for the last two or three weeks. Chris grabbed an interview form and started toward the interrogation room. Carmen followed with a handful of pictures.

Chris was shocked when she entered the room and saw Skeeter. With her hair washed and combed she turned out to be much younger than Chris originally thought, probably in her thirties. The orange overalls she was wearing swallowed her and the sleeves and pant legs were rolled up. Chris pulled out a chair and turned it around to straddle it, resting her hands on the back section.

"You hungry, Skeeter?" she asked. "Thirsty?"

"Some," the woman said.

"When was the last time you ate?" Carmen asked.

"They put on a real good buffet over at the Milford a couple of nights ago. The Swedish meatballs were to die for," she said with wide eyes and a toothless laugh.

"Well, we can't do that good, but I can send out for a Big Mac," Chris offered.

"Hows about a double cheeseburger? I like those. And a chocolate malt. Haven't had one in a while." Skeeter grinned and Chris wished she wouldn't, mentally reminding herself to give her dentist a call for a check-up.

"Sure thing," Chris said as she handed a ten to Carmen, who left and returned a few minutes later.

"We understand you sometimes camp out at the Montclair, Skeeter," Carmen said as she sat down.

"Been known to. There's a real small space under the steps. Fits me just right." She leaned forward and said, "Sometimes they let me stay the whole night and even bring me a cup of coffee in the morning."

Chris couldn't resist a smile as she shook her head. It was a pretty good bet Rayburn wasn't aware of his staff's generosity.

"There's some nice people there if you give 'em a chance," Skeeter volunteered. "It's a shame guests leave all that good room service in the halls to go to waste though. Good snackin'."

"So were you at the Montclair the night of December twenty-sixth?" Chris asked.

"Mighta been. I'd have to check my social calendar," Skeeter answered with a cackle.

"What were you doin' in the hotel that night?"

"Mostly S and S." Skeeter saw the question on Chris' face. "Snackin' and snoozin'."

Carmen looked at Chris and grinned.

"A woman was killed in the penthouse that night," Chris said.

"Well, I didn't do it!"

"No, no, we know you didn't," Chris said to calm the woman down. "But you might have seen somethin' that could help us catch who did. Maybe someone you saw in the hallway or the stairwell around the time of the crime."

"I don't know about that. That was a while back, ya know."

"A little over three weeks," Carmen reminded Skeeter. "We have some pictures and want you to look at them to see if there's anyone you recognize. Think you can do that?"

"Maybe after I get somethin' to eat." Skeeter leaned closer to Carmen. "To tell you the truth, I'm powerful hungry."

They were saved by the desk officer delivering a familiar white bag with the smell of a hamburger and fries wafting from it. He also set a large, frosted cup on the table in front of Carmen, who grabbed it before Skeeter could. As Carmen lifted the lid from the cup Skeeter's eyes darted back and forth between Carmen and the cup. After she saw drool practically falling from Skeeter's mouth, Carmen slid the cup and bag toward her. Chris had been hungry before, but she had never seen food disappear so quickly. Following the last bite and a resounding belch Skeeter settled back in her chair to savor the remainder of the chocolate malt at a more leisurely pace.

"Don't s'pose you got a smoke on ya," Skeeter said. "That

would make for a perfect endin' to the meal, know what I mean?"

"Sorry," Chris said.

Skeeter shrugged. "Can't have everthing, I guess."

Carmen placed a set of pictures on the table in front of Skeeter in three rows of four pictures. Carmen and Chris were certain Galway and Levinson were not suspects, but they would serve as a test for Skeeter. She continued to suck at the straw in her malt, her cheeks caving in and almost meeting in the middle as she examined the pictures. She pulled out the photo of Della Summers and Marissa Parilli and laid it to the side. Then she discarded Galway and Levinson, followed by Ted Warner and Robert Blankenship.

"These are nice-lookin' fellas," she said, "'cept for this one." She pointed to Malcolm Gallagher and made a face. "Wouldn't mind stayin' warm with these three though," she giggled. She shrugged and put the pictures of Alex Webb, Damon Hunter, and Kent Devine aside. She picked up Malcolm's picture and seemed to study it. Finally she placed it back on the table and tapped it with her index finger. "This one looks the most like a guy I seen that night while I was checkin' out the room service trays in the hallways," she said with a nod as if trying to convince herself. "Ya see, I always start on the top floor and work my way down—" Skeeter started to explain.

"You're certain you saw this man," Chris said, placing her finger on Malcolm Gallagher's picture, "at the Montclair on December twenty-sixth?"

"No, not him. The young fella behind him. The one gettin' in the car."

Chris slid her finger to the man in the background. "This man?"

"Yepper doodle." She leaned closer to the picture. "He's kinda cute, too. I never forget a good-lookin' man. He had on that same nice pair of gloves. I'da killed to have 'em."

"What floor did you see him on?"

"Top floor. He was gettin' on the elevator."

"On the nineteenth floor?"

"If that's the top one."

"What time was that?"

Skeeter pursed her lips together and looked at her wrists. "Damn. Musta left my Rolex back at my place." She glared at Chris. "How the hell would I know? It was kinda late though, I think."

"But you saw his face clearly?"

"Nuthin' wrong with my eyesight."

"Did you notice what floor the elevator went to after he got on?"

"Nope. But since he got on at the top floor, I reckon he was goin' down, don't you? I skedaddled out of there in case he tol' someone I was up there."

"Did you see anything else?"

Skeeter shook her head. "I went back to fifteen." She paused and scratched at her head. "Come to think of it, I was woke up a little later by somebody tromping down the steps, but didn't see nuthin' but a pair of shoes."

"How long do you think that was after you saw the man on the elevator?"

Skeeter shrugged. "Maybe an hour or two. I was sleepin'."

Chris picked the photos. "Do we have Todd Gallagher's prints?" she asked Carmen.

"Yeah."

"Can I go now?" Skeeter asked. "I gotta check on my stuff."

"As long as we know where you are," Chris said.

THE NEXT MORNING Chris and Carmen stopped at the receptionist's desk at Malcolm Gallagher's agency, looking for Todd. Chris paced around the small waiting area, anxious to question the young man again. Finally the receptionist reported that Todd Gallagher was not at work that day and Chris requested to see Malcolm Gallagher. He was also unavailable and Chris left a message for Todd to contact her as soon as possible.

After lunch Chris rested her chin on her fist and stared at the forensic report on the desk in front of her. She was half asleep when Carmen tossed a wad of paper across the desk to get her attention.

"Looks like we got a visitor," Carmen said as Chris tossed the paper back.

Chris turned around and saw Grace Gallagher striding purposefully toward Captain Savage's office, followed by Todd. She didn't look happy. Chris took a deep breath and returned to the paperwork in front of her. A tap on her shoulder about thirty minutes later broke her train of thought and she looked up to see Sheila Morgan standing over her.

"Now what?" Sheila asked. "Savage called and asked me to come over."

"Todd Gallagher's here with his attorney," Chris said.

"I assume you have some questions for him."

"Yep. A witness placed him at the Montclair the night of December twenty-sixth."

They watched as Captain Savage escorted Grace and Todd to an interview room. Chris opened her desk drawer and took out a bottle of aspirin. She popped three tablets into her mouth and washed them down with a mouthful of lukewarm water from the water fountain. "You ready?" she asked over her shoulder.

Carmen nodded and together they walked to the interrogation room. As soon as they entered Grace stood. She offered a hand to Chris and then Carmen. "This seems to be becoming a tedious habit, Detectives," she said.

"It must save a fortune havin' your own attorney in the family," Chris commented.

"My father will receive my bill. I don't work gratis," Grace shot back. "We understand you have some questions for my brother."

"One or two," Chris grinned as she looked at the tall, well-dressed strawberry-blonde with electric blue eyes. She pulled out a chair and sat down while Carmen prepared the recorder. "You don't have any objections to having this interview recorded, do you?" Chris asked.

"Will we be provided with a transcript?" Grace asked in return.

"Certainly. Based on a statement by a witness who was at the Montclair on December twenty-sixth, we have a few questions Mr. Gallagher might be able to answer that will help our investigation. We may have more later."

Carmen nodded that the equipment was working and ready. Chris said, "My name is Christine Shaw, homicide detective with the NYPD, workin' out of the Midtown Precinct. This interview is with Mr. Todd Gallagher, a person of interest in the death of Elaine Barrie which occurred on December twenty-sixth. Also present are Mr. Gallagher's attorney, Grace Gallagher, Assistant District Attorney Sheila Morgan, and Detective Carmen Sandoval, also of the Midtown Precinct. Please state your name and address for the record," she said, nodding at Gallagher.

"Todd Gallagher, 5734 Lexington Avenue, New York City."

"Where were you on the night of December twenty-sixth, Mr. Gallagher?"

Todd cleared his throat and loosened his tie. "I attended a performance of Elaine Barrie's show. It ended about ten-thirty. My father, Malcolm Gallagher, and I spoke with Miss Barrie for a few minutes afterward. I stopped in at O'Malley's Pub on Lex for a couple of drinks, then went home and went to bed…unfortunately alone."

"Did anyone see you at O'Malley's?"

"I suppose, but they were relatively busy since it was the day after Christmas."

"An eye witness has identified you as the man they saw at the hotel the night of the twenty-sixth."

"Who is this mystery witness?" Grace asked.

"Does it matter?"

"She's mistaken. I had no reason to be at the Montclair that night or any other night," Todd volunteered.

Chris raised an eyebrow and looked at Carmen before she continued. "Wasn't Miss Barrie one of your agency's clients?"

"I don't handle clients directly. My father does that. I manage their financial accounts."

"Your father said he called you that night, but you didn't pick up."

"I always turn my cell off when I go home. I got his message the next day. I don't remember what he wanted now, but I'm sure we talked about whatever it was when I arrived at work."

"Please take off your jacket and shirt," Chris said.

"For what purpose?" Grace demanded.

"The victim fought for her life, and that of her unborn child," Chris said pointedly, looking at Grace. "It's probable she scratched her attacker."

"Don't do it, Todd," Grace advised.

"Got somethin' to hide?" Chris quipped.

"Goading won't do you any good," Grace said.

"It was worth a try. I can get a warrant," Chris replied.

"Then get one if you think you can. Is there anything else?"

Chris returned her attention to Todd. "Did you speak to your mother that night?"

"My mother? I might have."

"Your phone records show that you called her about nine on December twenty-sixth. Was that before the show ended?"

"At intermission between acts."

"Why did you call her?"

"Is that really relevant?" Grace asked.

Chris shrugged. "Maybe."

"I call my mother almost every evening," Todd said.

"Kinda old to be checkin' in with your mama, aren't you?" Chris said with a smirk.

Todd ignored the question and Chris turned her eyes toward Grace. "You call your mama every night, Counselor?"

"Irrelevant and none of your business," Grace responded.

Chris ran her finger down the phone record in front of her. "I don't see a phone call to your mama the three nights before the twenty-sixth or the three or four nights after either. But I do see you called her three times the night of the twenty-sixth. So you don't really call her every night, do you, Mr. Gallagher?"

"It's the holidays. I was with her some of those nights so there was no need to call."

"What was so important that you needed to call her three times on the twenty-sixth? Once around nine, again about eleven-thirty, and finally the last time about an hour later?"

"I forgot to tell her something."

"The third call only lasted a few seconds. Barely long enough to grunt."

"Is there a point to these questions?" Grace interrupted.

"Just curious," Chris answered with a smile. "Your father said he called you around twelve-thirty, but you didn't pick up."

"Must've just missed him," Todd said with a shrug.

"Are we about finished here?" Grace asked.

"Would your client agree to a line-up?"

"What do you think, Detective?"

Chris turned her attention back to Todd. "How long does it take to drive from your parents' house on Long Island to mid-city?"

Todd shrugged again.

"Your mama said about forty-five minutes. That sound about right?"

"Depends on the traffic, I guess."

"Could be an hour one way then?"

"Possibly. So what?"

"Just thinkin'," Chris said. She looked at Carmen and shrugged. "Keep yourself available, Mr. Gallagher, in case we have further questions." As Todd stood to pull on his overcoat, Chris asked, "By the way, what made you think our witness was a woman?"

Todd paused, frowning slightly as he buttoned his coat. "Lucky guess," he finally said.

He followed Grace out of the room. Chris smiled to herself as she watched the attorney walk away. Grace looked damn good. The only thing better looking than the tall blonde with her clothes on would be the blonde with her clothes off. Yeah, Carmen was right. Chris definitely needed a new woman, but Grace Gallagher probably wasn't the one.

Chris plopped down in her desk chair and picked up the phone. She opened a file and thumbed through it until she found what she was looking for. She and Carmen would have to make a trip to O'Malley's Pub on Lexington to check out Todd's whereabouts after the show on the twenty-sixth. Fabulous! Another long night. Hopefully, everything else she had requested would be at the precinct by the following afternoon. She hadn't shared her suspicions with Carmen yet, but the tingly feeling in her stomach usually meant she was very close to the end of her hunt.

Chapter Nineteen

IT WAS AFTER six that evening when Chris trudged up the stairs to her apartment. She'd stopped on the way home to pick up Chinese take-out, hoping a full stomach would make her feel better. She shouldered open the door of her apartment and set the four white cartons of take-out on the kitchen counter. She needed to get comfortable before settling in for the evening. She could veg out on the couch and fall asleep with a full stomach. She had just pulled on an old, faded pair of jeans, pulling the zipper up and leaving the top unbuttoned, when there was a knock at her door. She tossed her bra into the bathroom hamper and tugged a t-shirt over her head. Barefooted, she half-heartedly made her way to the door and peeked through the security peephole. She took a deep breath and opened the door. Grace Gallagher marched into the apartment and spun around to face Chris.

"You seem to be developing an unhealthy fascination with my family, Detective Shaw," Grace started. "The only member you haven't hauled in for questioning yet is me."

"Where were you on the night of December twenty-sixth?" Chris asked with a grin.

"Entertaining a guest."

"An overnight guest?"

"None of your business." A pale pink blush covered Grace's cheeks as Chris grinned at her.

"Will he, or she, be willin' to give a statement verifyin' that?"

"Of course."

"Will he, or she, tell me it was a memorable evenin'?"

"What! How dare you."

"Consider yourself questioned," Chris said as she grabbed Grace's arm to lead her toward the door. "Interview over."

Grace jerked her arm away and glared at Chris.

"Look, Counselor, all I want is to eat my dinner in peace and get an uninterrupted night's sleep," Chris said. "How the hell did you get my address anyway?"

"I have my sources."

"Well, now you can toddle off to your condo."

"How do you know I live in a condo?"

"I've got a couple of sources myself."

"You know, you kind of left me hanging in the wind that night outside the bar," Grace said. She brought her hand up and lightly traced Chris' lips with her fingertip. "I'm not accustomed to being left like that." She bit her bottom lip. "I didn't like it."

When Grace stepped closer Chris grabbed her and pinned her against the door of the apartment with her body as she kissed her hungrily. Grace responded just as eagerly and let her hands roam under Chris' t-shirt. Chris groaned at the feel of Grace's hands on her breasts. This is so wrong, she thought, but it feels so good. She kissed along the side of Grace's face and whispered, "You should go before this gets out of hand."

"In case you aren't paying attention, it already has," Grace said as her tongue traced Chris' ear. She pushed her hands past the waist of Chris' loose jeans and squeezed her ass. "I like commando," she breathed.

They groped and kissed their way to Chris' bedroom, leaving a trail of clothing along the way. Chris pulled her t-shirt over her head as Grace slipped off her skirt and underwear. She pulled Grace onto the bed and rolled her onto her back before wrapping her arms tightly around the blonde's hips and lifting them to meet her lips. She let her tongue and lips convey her need as she lavished Grace's wetness with attention. Her body began to gyrate wildly in Chris' arms as she struggled to escape the intensity of the pleasure coursing through her. She screamed Chris' name as her tongue plunged inside, drawing the orgasm from within her and drinking up the proof of her pleasure. When there was nothing left to take, Chris lowered her lover's hips back to the bed, resting her head on Grace's abdomen.

"Oh, my God," Grace gasped, her hands covering her eyes. "Oh, my God."

"I don't think God had anything to do with it, baby," Chris panted as she crawled up Grace's body and brought her into a long, lingering kiss, probing her mouth with her tongue.

"I like the taste of me on your mouth," Grace whispered.

"It's even better...hotter...from the source," Chris rasped.

Making love with Grace Gallagher was a mistake and Chris knew it, but at that moment she didn't give a damn as she prepared for round two.

BY NINE O'CLOCK they were sitting cross-legged in the middle of Chris' bed eating from white take-out cartons. Chris had pulled on a navy blue Dallas Police Academy sweatshirt and given Grace a matching gray one. Grace used chopsticks, but Chris, who preferred not to fight or play with her food, used a fork. Periodically, Grace would extend a bite of food toward her with the chopsticks.

"I don't know how you do that," Chris said, shaking her head.

"It's a gift, darlin'." Grace smiled.

"This stuff didn't stay hot very long," Chris said as she chewed.

"Maybe we should have eaten before we came into the bedroom."

"Uh-uh. I like my dessert first."

"Really?" Grace asked with a grin.

"That way in case my meal is interrupted by a nuclear attack or a Martian invasion, I've already had the best part."

"You're awful, Chris." Grace laughed, shoving her slightly.

"That's not what you said half an hour ago."

Grace poked around in the container in her hand. "We both know this was a mistake, but when I'm around you it's extremely difficult to concentrate."

Chris was preparing to stand up when the phone next to the bed rang. She reached across Grace and grabbed it. "Shaw," she answered.

"It's Hernandez," a rough voice replied.

"What's up, Sam?"

"We got a location on Frankie Sandoval. Thought you might want to be here when it goes down."

Chris grabbed a pen and notepad. "Where?"

"An SRO over on West 101st. We'll wait for you. He ain't going nowhere."

"I'll be there in half an hour, maybe less," Chris said as she hung up. She walked quickly into the bathroom and turned on the shower. A few minutes later she came out tucking her shirt in. She slung her shoulder holster across her back and checked the ammunition in her Beretta.

"Please be careful," Grace said when she saw the weapon and shivered involuntarily.

"You bet," Chris said as she headed for the apartment door. "Lock up when you leave, will ya?" She didn't wait for a reply as she shut the door behind her.

CHRIS RAN TO her car and jumped in, closing the door as she pulled out of the parking lot. Even with late traffic, she made it to Sam Hernandez's location in forty-five minutes. She parked down the block and joined him and a team of uniforms. She tightened the straps on the sides of her Kevlar vest and leaned against the brick of the old hotel that had been converted into a single room occupancy building, probably sometime in the sixties.

"You know he's in there for sure?" she asked as she drew her service weapon.

"Showed his picture to the idiot manager who said he'd been up there for the last two days. The place belongs to his girlfriend."

"What's the plan?"

"I thought you and I would wake him up and have the uniforms cover the exits. I know you're anxious to have a word or two with him...privately," Hernandez said with a grin.

Hernandez sent the uniformed officers to various locations around the building as he and Chris walked inside the building.

"The girlfriend lives on the fourth floor, but as far as we can tell she's not there," Hernandez said as Chris pulled open the front door.

The inside of the building smelled like most old, uncared for buildings Chris had been in. The hallways were littered with trash and no amount of paint could have helped the looks of the place. The building reeked of a combination of urine, spoiled food, and marijuana. Hernandez motioned to an officer to keep an eye on the front desk clerk. Chris and Hernandez climbed the stairs quietly before reaching the fourth floor landing. Chris glanced at Hernandez who stood on the other side of the hallway. As she looked down the hallway, there were twelve apartment doors. Hernandez pointed to a door halfway down the hall. Chris stayed close to the wall as she approached the door he had indicated. She could hear music and adrenaline pumped through her body as she stood across from the apartment. It was wrong for her to be there because the suspect they were after was her partner's brother, but she didn't give two shits in the wind about department regulations at that moment.

She motioned Hernandez to the wall next to the apartment and took a deep breath. Finally, keeping an eye on the door, she nodded to the other detective and counted one...two...three before she slammed her foot into the door with every ounce of anger-driven power she had, counting on the age of the building to help her. The door flew open allowing her to enter the small main room quickly, aiming her weapon at a man lying on the couch. Hernandez entered the room low immediately behind her and trained his weapon on the man as well. Chris made sure Hernandez was covering the first man before she moved swiftly down a short hallway toward the bedrooms. Halfway down, a bedroom door opened and Frankie Sandoval stepped out, shirtless and rubbing his face. Before he had time to react she slammed him against the wall and shoved her revolver under his chin.

"Anyone else here?" she hissed.

"N...No," he rasped.

"In the livin' room. Now!" she ordered, glancing into the

bedroom and seeing no one else.

"What the fuck are you..." Frankie started.

Chris brought her hand up rapidly and backhanded him, knocking him off balance. As he righted himself, she saw anger flare in his eyes as he looked at the weapon in her hand, a trickle of blood running from his lip. He glanced quickly at Hernandez and frowned.

"What the fuck you want, Shaw?" Frankie said as he spit blood from his mouth.

Chris looked at him coldly, her eyes narrowed. "You're under arrest for the attempted murder of Mercedes and Carmen Sandoval."

"I don't know what the fuck you're talkin' about!" Frankie shouted as he took a step toward her.

Chris backhanded him again. She seethed with anger as she twisted his arm behind his back and closed the handcuff around his wrist. "Your friend almost killed your mother and you could have killed your sister. If Hernandez wasn't with me, I'd fuck you up *real* bad, Frankie." She cuffed his other wrist and clicked it shut before shoving him toward Hernandez.

Fifteen minutes later Chris stepped back onto the sidewalk with Frankie in custody and turned him over to a patrol unit for transport back to the precinct. She leaned back against her car, working hard at calming her nerves and quieting her hands. Hernandez walked up and stood next to her. "Thanks for calling me," she said quietly.

"You gonna be the one who books him?" he asked as he lit a cigarette and inhaled deeply.

Chris nodded silently, walked to the driver's side of her car, and fell exhausted into the seat. She rolled the window down to let the cold air flow into the car to clear her mind as she drove toward Midtown Precinct.

Chris held on to Frankie's arm as she led him, handcuffed, into the precinct and shoved him roughly against the front counter. Frankie straightened his body and leaned closer to her.

"You gonna be real sorry you done that, *puta*," he rasped.

"Well, I'm all kinds of shook up about that, Francisco," Chris retorted.

"I be outta here before you finish the stinkin' paperwork," he said as Chris signed the form transferring Francisco Enrique Sandoval, Jr. from her custody.

CHRIS WAS SURPRISED to find Grace still in her bed and softly snoring when she dragged into her apartment. She smiled as she stripped out of her clothes and joined her under a down comforter as quietly as possible. It had been a long time since anyone had been there to welcome her home, even if she was unconscious. Grace rolled toward Chris, resting her arm across Chris' chest. Chris kissed her forehead softly and drew her closer. Seconds later Grace's breathing returned to the soft, deep breaths of sleep. Although she believed the coffee at the precinct and her troubled thoughts about making love with Grace would keep her up the rest of the night, the warmth of the soft body snuggled against her was relaxing and she drifted off, surprised when the sound of the alarm next to the bed worked its way into her consciousness.

She rubbed her face and blinked to clear her eyes. Grace was no longer lying next to her and she sat up. Snow was falling steadily outside her bedroom window as she swung her legs from under the comforter. When she made her way into the kitchen, the light on the coffeemaker signaled her that a fresh brew awaited her. A note was propped against it.

Chris was dressed and beginning a second cup as Grace came through the door of the apartment carrying two large bags of groceries. She set the bags on the counter and said, "It's really beginning to come down out there. I borrowed your key in case you were still asleep."

Chris took a second cup from an overhead cabinet and filled it. Grace kissed her briefly with cool lips before warming them with coffee. Half an hour later they were half-dressed, sitting on the bed wolfing down bagels topped generously with cream cheese.

Chris swallowed a mouthful and washed it down with her now lukewarm coffee. "Might have to consider makin' this the dinin' room," she said, glancing around her bedroom. She couldn't stop looking at the blonde. Even with her hair in serious disarray and her lips slightly swollen from making love, Grace Gallagher was magnificent, possibly the only woman Chris had been with who was as sexually aggressive in bed as she was. Grace was a lady with a delicious touch of wantonness, unafraid to take what she wanted. Chris felt comfortable with her and the blonde gave as good as she got both verbally and sexually. She made no demands and wasn't clingy. Unlike other women Chris had been with, Grace didn't seem to want or need permanence once they had made love. She took it for what it was. Two adults getting what their bodies craved with no attachments. "So, are we just fuck buddies now or what, Grace?" she asked, almost afraid to hear the response.

Grace chewed on her bagel and seemed deep in thought. "I don't know, Chris. What do you want it to be? An occasional tension reliever between cases?"

Chris swallowed and opened her mouth to respond, but was interrupted by banging on the apartment door. "Now what?" she muttered. She looked through the security peephole and rested her forehead against the door. "Great," she said, unlocking the door.

For the second time in less than twenty-four hours, an irate woman stomped into her apartment. Carmen shoved past Chris roughly, dropped a couple of large suitcases inside the door, and marched into the kitchen. She grabbed a mug and filled it with coffee before picking up a bagel. Grace leaned against the bedroom door, wearing Chris' old sweatshirt that barely covered her pubic area, holding a half-eaten bagel, and a coffee mug.

"Really?" Carmen asked, tossing her head in Grace's direction. "What the fuck is she doing here?"

"She brought breakfast," Chris answered with a shrug.

"You trying to get fired?" Carmen shifted her attention to Grace. "What's your story, Counselor? Looking for a refuge from the weather?"

Grace took a bite of her bagel and chewed it thoughtfully. Finally she said, "No. Actually I enjoyed fucking Chris so much last night I thought I'd stick around and give it another shot, just to make sure she wasn't a one-hit wonder."

Carmen spit coffee on the counter trying to suppress a guffaw at the unexpected response. When she was finally able to swallow she slapped the counter several times with her hand. She jabbed an index finger in Grace's direction and nodded. "I think I could like you."

Carmen turned her attention to Chris. "I see you found Frankie. You also know, of course, that he's already back on the street."

"I figured," Chris said.

"Mama posted bail and brought him home. I couldn't stay there looking at his smart-ass smirk."

"You can stay here. I have an extra room."

"Might be a little crowded," Carmen said, glancing at Grace.

"I'm just visiting," Grace said. She turned to look at Chris. "Chris knows where I live."

"And it looks like she's already got your number, too," Carmen said.

Grace finished her mug of coffee and strolled back into the bedroom, closing the door behind her.

"Are you out of your ever-lovin', cotton-pickin', deep fried mind?" Carmen half-whispered forcefully.

"Opportunity knocked and I answered," Chris said. "It was just one of those things. Nothin' more."

Carmen jerked her thumb toward the bedroom. "She know that?"

"Yeah."

The bedroom door opened and Grace re-entered the front room. She looked around to make sure she had everything. She went to the front door and said, "Later, and hopefully not in your precinct interrogation room again."

"Can't promise anything," Chris said.

Without another word Grace kissed Chris deeply before she left the apartment, quietly closing the door.

"Need help movin' your stuff?" Chris asked as she licked the taste of Grace's lips from her mouth and carried her mug to the kitchen sink.

"I only got a couple of bags of clothes. That's about it."

"Does Ruben know?"

"I'll call him later."

"I'm sure he'll be delighted to know you're livin' with me instead of him."

Carmen snorted. "His mama has six kids and they're all living with her. Here I just gotta put up with you and don't have to worry about whether the toilet seat is up or down." She glanced at the door. "And maybe an occasional visit from the lawyer."

"Last night was it," Chris muttered. "We need to get to the precinct."

Chapter Twenty

CHRIS HELD THE front door of O'Malley's open for Carmen. They found seats at the bar and waited for the bartender to wander their way. It was after midnight and about the time Todd Gallagher would have been there December twenty-sixth, if he had, in fact, been there at all. A rough-looking man in his forties stopped in front of them. "What can I get you?" he asked.

"Information," Chris said, flashing her badge and ID. She placed Todd's photo on the bar and asked, "Ever seen this guy in here?"

"Just about every night. Todd's a regular," the bartender answered in a deep bass voice. "What'd he do, forget to feed the meter?"

Chris ignored him. "Was he here the night of December twenty-sixth?"

"That was weeks ago."

"Really?" Chris said, sarcastically. "Who knew? Was he here or not?"

"Does he usually sit at the bar or at a table?" Carmen interrupted.

"Usually a table. The girls like him because he's a good tipper."

"Do you remember who was waitressin' that night?" Chris asked.

"Let me check the work schedule. Good tips between Christmas and New Year's." He turned and examined a handwritten sheet of paper tacked to the wall behind the bar. "Looks like Anna and Olivia worked that night."

"Either of them working tonight?" Carmen asked.

"Anna's here now. Olivia is off." He looked around the crowded bar then yelled, "Anna!"

A cherubic-looking woman in her early twenties bounced up to the bar. She rattled off a list of orders to the bartender. Short ringlets of blonde hair encircled her face and rosy cheeks. The bartender nodded to Chris and Carmen. "These ladies need to ask you a few questions." He turned away to fill her orders as she smiled at Chris. Anna was relatively short and Chris had to look down at her, unavoidably staring at the woman's ample cleavage.

"What can I do for you tall, dark, and handsome?" Anna asked.

"Do you know this man?" Chris asked after she cleared her throat.

Anna took the photo and leaned into the light. "It's Todd," she answered.

"Was he in here the night of December twenty-sixth?"

"Probably. He stops in just about every night on his way home for a drink or two. He's fond of a shot of tequila with a beer chaser."

"The twenty-sixth," Carmen repeated as she held out her badge. "It's important."

Anna's eyes widened and she grabbed three order pads from the short apron around her waist and began thumbing through them. "I usually serve him. Great tipper." She looked at every ticket in her order books. "Either he wasn't in that night or Olivia served him. I'm sure I would have written it down. It's how I total up my tips each night."

"Has he been in tonight?" Chris asked.

"I haven't seen him in a couple of days. He might be out of town or something."

The bartender pushed a tray full of drinks across the bar.

"That all?" Anna asked. "I've got a bunch of thirsty folks waiting on these drinks."

"Thanks for your cooperation," Chris said with a smile as her eyes took in another appreciative look at the waitress' cleavage. Carmen grabbed her by the arm and pulled her toward the door.

"You got enough woman problems without adding any new ones," Carmen said as they stepped out of the bar, dodging couples on their way inside. "That one's barely at the legal limit."

"You can never have too many woman problems, Carmen," Chris said. "Makes life interestin', you know."

"Let's call it a night on that happy note and start fresh tomorrow."

"Looks like we might have to have another chat with Todd Gallagher since he seems to have misplaced his alibi."

"You planning to call him in or drop in?"

"Neither yet," Chris said. "Maybe we should take another look around the Montclair tomorrow."

"For what?

"Something I saw on the lab reports."

CHRIS AWAKENED BEFORE daybreak the next morning and flopped around on the bed. The birds weren't even awake yet and she finally gave up. The piddly-ass facts they had in the Barrie case had floated around in her mind all night, occasionally mingling with flashes of intense blue eyes and soft blonde tresses. Chris swung her legs off the bed and dressed, hopefully being quiet enough to not disturb Carmen. She smiled as she slipped her feet into her shoes, wondering if Ruben knew Carmen was a world-class snorer. She scribbled a note and left it on the kitchen counter, along with a spare key, before leaving the apartment.

After making a fresh pot of coffee Chris sat down at her desk at the precinct and thumbed through the files she and Carmen had put together concerning the Barrie case, idly running her fingers through her hair over and over again. What had they missed? No matter which way she looked, the little pieces all seemed to point to Malcolm Gallagher. And yet there weren't enough pieces to seal the deal. She leaned back in her chair and tilted her head back, lost in thought. A loud splat made her lower her head to see Carmen standing in front of her desk with a stupid grin on her face.

"What?" Chris asked.

"Lose your hairbrush or going for the punk look?"

"What the hell are you talkin' about?"

"Your hair is sticking up all over your head, Shaw."

"That's what happens when I spend too much time thinkin'," she said as she tried to smash her hair back in place. "Better?"

"My cousin's a beautician. I can get you a deal on a haircut."

"Figures," Chris muttered as she closed the file in front of her.

"Since you left me all alone at the apartment I started thinking about the hotel videos," Carmen said.

"What about 'em?" Chris yawned. "They confirm the times Gallagher finally admitted he arrived and left," she groaned as she leaned back and stretched her long body.

"Feel better?"

"You bet."

"You got the rest of the phone records we requested?" When Chris nodded, Carmen said, "Let's take those and the videos into a room and go over them one more time."

"Okay," Chris said as she stood. "Any idea what we're lookin' for?"

"A murderer," Carmen said. "I hope."

Chris spread out the telephone records while Carmen slid a CD into the computer in a small conference room and fast forwarded to the time Malcolm Gallagher and Elaine Barrie entered the elevator to the penthouse. She paused it and said, "Since we first examined the videos we've gotten an interview with Skeeter and another one from Todd."

"And I interviewed Laura Gallagher and we re-interviewed Malcolm," Chris added.

"After we confirmed Malcolm's story we never really checked

the video any further. Didn't Todd call his mother about the same time Barrie and Malcolm went to the penthouse?" Carmen asked.

Chris scanned the pages. "Still can't rule out Malcolm," she said. She followed her finger down the pages. "Okay, here's a call from Todd to Laura, but it's around nine, which he said was during intermission."

Carmen picked up Todd's file and took her notebook from her jacket pocket. "It might have been intermission, but in our first interview Todd said he met Malcolm at the theater between nine-forty-five and ten. If he called his mother, it wasn't from the theater. How long did the call last?"

"Record says about fifteen minutes," Chris said. "He made a second call about... Wait a minute. What time did Malcolm and Elaine enter the hotel?"

"Eleven-fifteen, according to the time stamp."

"Todd placed a second call, to a different number, around eleven-thirty." Chris looked at the number for a moment. "The number he called is listed as Laura Gallagher's cell number. The nine o'clock call was to her home phone. Why didn't he just call the home phone again?"

"Was there a call to the home phone right before that?"

"No," Chris answered with a frown.

"He must have known she wouldn't be there to answer it. Maybe she told him she was going out for some reason," Carmen speculated.

"What time did Malcolm leave the hotel?"

"Time stamp is twelve-ten."

"He still had plenty of time to kill Barrie before he left the hotel. For all we know she was dead by twelve-ten. It falls within the time of death range Artie gave us."

"Any phone calls around twelve-thirty?"

"Another call from Todd to his mother that lasted way less than a minute."

"Also to the cell number?"

"Yep. Run the video from the time Malcolm and Elaine entered the elevator until Malcolm leaves the hotel. Keep an eye out for anyone getting on the main elevators, especially anyone going to the Nineteenth Floor." Chris shuffled through the folders in front of her and pulled one out. "Sure wish Skeeter could have been more specific than 'kinda late' about the time she claims to have seen Todd."

"That could be anytime," Carmen said as she watched the video. "On the streets anything after dark is kinda late when you're looking for a place to sleep." Suddenly Carmen stopped the video. "Write this time down," she said. "Eleven-thirty." She backed the picture up and played it back frame by frame.

"Can you enlarge it?" Chris asked.

"A little, but then the pixels get distorted."

The two women watched as a man entered the elevator and stood facing the back wall until the door closed.

"He had to know there was a surveillance camera," Chris said. "What floor does he go to?"

Carmen advanced the picture and enlarged the area above the elevator. Chris squinted until the illuminated numbers stopped. "Eighteen. Close enough" she said with a smile.

"Whoever that was might have stepped out on eighteen and taken the stairs up one flight and that's when Skeeter saw him," Carmen speculated. "Too bad she didn't have a Timex on her."

Chris grabbed the folder containing lab reports and thumbed through it. She turned from page to page impatiently.

"What are you looking for?" Carmen asked.

"Artie said there was a smudge on the victim's upper arm." She followed her finger down the lab findings. "Here it is. The lab identified it as some kind of industrial grease." Chris left the room and returned a few minutes later with another folder.

"What's that?"

"When I got to the hotel the night the body was found I checked the area between the elevator and the penthouse. I pushed open the stairwell door and a few minutes later noticed something black and sticky on my glove. So I changed into a clean one and sent it to the lab to see if it's the same substance. Since it matches the smudge on on the victim's body, then..."

"Whoever opened that door also touched Barrie and may be the killer," Carmen finished.

"Or an accomplice at the very least." Chris stood up. "Let's check out that elevator," she said crisply as she strode toward the entrance of the precinct. She had already turned the key in the ignition when Carmen joined her. A light snow had begun to fall again. The rear end of the Tran-Am fishtailed as Chris accelerated away from the curb.

CHRIS FOUND A parking space in the garage that ran under the Montclair Hotel and pulled in. She didn't seem to be in a hurry as she entered the lobby and walked directly to the main desk. A pleasant looking older woman greeted her, her expression changing quickly as Chris flashed her badge.

"You have a ladder or step-stool I can borrow?" Chris asked.

The woman nodded and disappeared into a room behind the desk. She reappeared a moment later with a short step-stool and handed it to Chris.

"Are there maintenance closets on every floor?" Chris asked before she left the desk.

"Only on the even-numbered floors," the woman answered.

"Thanks," Chris said before walking to the bank of elevators and stepping inside. She pushed the button for Sixteen and set the step-ladder down.

"What are you doing?" Carmen asked.

"Just checkin' out a hunch. The guy on the video wasn't carrying anything I could see. If he used the elevator shaft to access the penthouse, how'd he get up there?" When the elevator stopped on Sixteen she flipped the maintenance switch putting the elevator temporarily out of service. They walked down the hall until they located a maintenance closet. Chris picked the lock and opened the door. She flipped the light on and saw an aluminum ladder hanging on a hook on the far wall. She turned the light off, closed the door, and returned to the elevator.

"Now what?" Carmen asked.

"One more stop," Chris said as she pressed the button for Eighteen.

Once again she flipped the maintenance switch of the elevator and made her way to the maintenance closet. She held her breath as she opened the door and turned on the light. She clapped her hands together and said over her shoulder, "No freakin' ladder."

"So, what does that mean?" Carmen asked.

"Someone could have used the ladder from here to get on top of the elevator."

"Wouldn't anyone notice an elevator was out of service?"

"It was after midnight and there are four public elevators. That leaves three others for hotel guests to use and there's only one call button. Most people use whichever one opens first. Let's check the tops of the elevators. If someone got on top of the one closest to the penthouse elevator that might be the way they reached the twentieth floor."

They stepped back on the elevator and Chris punched the button for Nineteen. When it stopped, she took it off-line for the third time. She opened the folded stool and stepped onto the top rung. "Catch me if this doesn't work," she said.

Chris heard Carmen laugh as she pressed her hands against the ceiling until she found the access tile and pushed it up and over. Straightening up, she poked her head into the opening and looked around.

"See anything?" Carmen called.

"No ladder, but the main elevators and the private elevator are all in the same shaft. Someone might be able to access the private elevator by climbin' up the service ladder to get on top of it. Only problem would be gettin' on top of this one."

"See if you can reach the service ladder."

"Do I look like a member of Cirque de Soleil?"

"Where's your sense of adventure?"

"It'll be splattered all over the floor at the bottom of this shaft if I slip," Chris groused. "Guess there's only one way to find out," she said, expelling a breath before she braced her arms on the edge of the opening and bounced slightly on the balls of her feet to hoist her body onto the top of the elevator car.

"We could just call the guys from forensics and let them check it out," Carmen said belatedly.

"I'm up here now. Hand me a pair of damn gloves," Chris said, dropping her hand back into the elevator car and wiggling her fingers. "Might want to call them to check for prints in the main elevators even though Skeeter said the guy was wearing gloves."

"Where do you think the maintenance ladder is?" Carmen asked.

Chris shivered slightly as she stood and pulled on the blue latex gloves, then shuffled slowly to the edge of the elevator car and looked down into the nothingness below her. "Best guess, it was dropped to the bottom of the elevator shaft."

"And no one heard it when it hit?"

"This shaft probably goes down into the basement sub-level. Call Haggarty and get his guys to check it out." Chris swallowed back a slight feeling of vertigo and reached over the open space to grab the maintenance ladder bolted to the shaft wall. She wrapped her arms around the ladder and laced her fingers together.

"Did I forget to mention I have this slight fear of heights?" Chris called out as she hugged the metal ladder. "Especially ones that disappear into a fuckin' black hole."

Carmen chuckled. "I have confidence in you, Shaw."

At the top of the ladder Chris grabbed the last rung and leaned over to reach a thick metal strut on the side of the private elevator. She stepped across the open space to the private elevator and felt a shiver run up her body. She pulled her body over the metal railing that ran around the top of the car and served as a cushion to prevent it from striking the top of the shaft. As soon as her legs were over the top she was able to pull off the access panel and look into the vacant elevator. She finally rotated her body and looked down at Carmen who was now standing on the stool, watching her.

"Well?" Carmen called out. "Could someone do it or not?"

"I just did," Chris called back. "From here I can drop down

into the penthouse elevator and no one would know. Whoever it was would have to be at least as tall as I am though. It was a stretch for me." Chris looked down at Carmen. "What do you think?"

"I think if someone did all that advanced preparation it would be the definition of serious premeditation. Come back down and I'll get someone over here to check for prints."

"I'll meet you on nineteen," Chris said before she dropped into the private elevator. She pulled open the door into the stairwell and descended one floor.

"Time to do a little theorizin' and try to prove it when we get back to the precinct," Chris said when she entered the public elevator.

"What are you looking for?" Carmen asked.

"Even if the elevators are the way the killer got to the penthouse, we still got jack for evidence and nothin' more than a theory. We need to come up with somethin'. Elaine Barrie sure as shit didn't smack herself on the head. Someone's responsible and the sooner I can find him, the sooner we can move on. This case is beginnin' to piss me off."

Chris felt like a woman possessed as she pulled her car into the police garage and got out. "I'll meet you in the conference room," she said over her shoulder and smiled. "We're close."

Chris found a large white board and four dry erase markers in various colors. When Carmen joined her back in the conference room, she laughed.

"Talk about old school," she said.

"Newer don't always mean better," Chris shot back as she drew columns on the white board.

"Print out a picture of the guy entering the public elevator after Malcolm and Barrie went to the penthouse," Chris said. As soon as the sheet slid out of the printer she grabbed it and taped it to one side of the board. "This is the killer, or at least one of them," she said. "I'd bet money on it." At the top of the board she taped a picture of Elaine. Below it she placed pictures of Malcolm, Todd, and Laura Gallagher. She highlighted the phone records and attached them below each picture. She stood back and looked at the display. "Call the toll authority," she said. "Get the license plate numbers of any vehicles owned or leased by any member of the Gallagher family. Have the toll authority check their cameras in the booths from Long Island into the city, comin' and goin', between nine p.m. on December twenty-sixth and three a.m. on December twenty-seventh. Then cross your fingers."

"If any of their vehicles make frequent trips into the city they'd have an express pass to avoid the booths," Carmen said.

"I know, but it's worth a shot."

"They quick scan express passes. I'll see if any that night matches the Gallagher vehicles. Who am I looking for?"

"A killer."

Chapter Twenty-one

THREE HOURS LATER Chris gazed at the snippets of information hanging from the board. "I think I know who did it," she said.

Carmen, who was dozing at the conference table, snapped her head up and yawned.

"What?"

Chris turned to face her partner and grinned. "I think I know who killed Elaine Barrie," she repeated.

"Can you prove it?"

"Everything is pretty circumstantial. Hopefully someone will confess."

"Morgan will never go for it."

Chris stepped to the left side of the white board and tapped the first picture. "We know Todd was at the theater that night, at least for a while. His alibi afterward didn't pan out. He called his mother around nine, then again at eleven-thirty, right after Malcolm and Elaine entered the hotel."

She stepped to the second picture. "We know Malcolm not only saw Elaine, but accompanied her to the suite at the Montclair. He left a little after midnight and the video doesn't show him returnin' later. I think we can rule him out as a suspect, even though I think he knows or suspects somethin'."

Chris pointed back to the picture of Todd Gallagher. "I think Todd is the unidentified person enterin' the public elevator a few minutes after Malcolm and Elaine took the private elevator to the penthouse. I think he either killed Elaine or was workin' with another person who did."

Chris pointed to the picture of Laura Gallagher and took a deep breath. "I think she is our killer," she said. "But all of our evidence is circumstantial and we don't have an established motive."

"So what's the circumstantial evidence?" Carmen asked.

Chris moved back to the phone records below each photograph. "It's pretty convoluted," she said. "Okay. Todd called his mother around nine from wherever he was. They talked approximately fifteen minutes about somethin'. Accordin' to the phone records that call bounced off two microwave towers, one in Midtown and the other on Long Island. He made a second call around eleven-thirty that bounced off the same two towers. I think

Todd was callin' his mother to let her know his father had accompanied Elaine to her suite at the Montclair."

"So what? According to Malcolm it was a business meeting."

"And Elaine told him she was pregnant. Anyway, Malcolm leaves a little after twelve and calls his wife. Only according to the phone records *that* call only bounced off the Midtown tower. It should have bounced off the Long Island tower as well, but didn't. That means Laura Gallagher was already in Midtown." Chris pointed at a picture of Laura Gallagher. "We'll need to check the list of plate numbers recorded goin' through the express lane around eleven-forty-five to see if any of the vehicles are registered to Malcolm."

"Could have been coming into the city for anything," Carmen said.

"At eleven-forty-five at night? Why didn't she tell her husband and why would she ask him to stop and pick up milk when she was already out?"

Carmen shrugged. "Maybe she was meeting someone for a drink or something."

"I think she was meetin' Todd. Skeeter swears she saw him in the hotel corridor even if she didn't know the time. I think she saw him when he entered the public elevator while Malcolm was in Elaine's suite."

"You're doing a lot of thinking without much proving," Carmen sighed.

Chris sat down heavily at the table and rubbed her face. "I know. I need someone to break and confess."

"We've interviewed all of them before. Who do you think is the weakest link? What's the motive? Not to mention that your girlfriend will be thrilled."

Chris whipped her head around. "She's not my girlfriend dammit! We need to re-interview all of them, starting with Todd. We need a warrant to search his apartment and office."

"For what?"

"Gloves and anything he was wearin' that night. Whoever was on that elevator might have touched something with grease on it that will match the smudge on Elaine's body and the grease I picked up from the door to the stairwell."

CHRIS UNLOCKED THE door of her apartment and stripped off her overcoat and blazer. She would have a few hours alone before Carmen returned from a last minute date with Ruben. Hell, maybe Carmen would stay with him for the night. She began unbuttoning her Oxford shirt as she made her way into the bedroom. She slipped into the pair of comfortable, well-worn jeans, pulled on a lightweight sweater, and padded into the kitchen in her stocking feet. She heated a mug of coffee in her microwave and plopped down on the sofa. She was exhausted and didn't know how long she had been dozing when her cell phone buzzed. She flipped it open and mumbled, "Shaw."

"Hey! Open the door. My hands are full," Grace announced.

"Give me a minute."

Chris took her coffee mug into the kitchen before she went to the door. Grace was juggling several food containers as she stepped inside. She made her way to the counter between the front room and kitchen and set them down carefully. Satisfied they wouldn't fall, she turned and wrapped her arms around Chris' neck, pulling her into a long, fevered kiss. When the kiss finally ended, Grace said, "I haven't heard from you and thought I'd drop by."

"Been busy," Chris said as she opened a container and picked up a piece of barbecued pork, shoving it into her mouth. She nodded as she chewed, "Not bad for New York barbecue."

"There's enough for Sandoval too." She saw the frown on Chris' face. "Is something wrong, Chris?" she asked.

"No. Why?"

Grace shrugged. "You seem a little distracted."

"Just tired."

Grace ran her hands around Chris' waist. "Maybe I can find a way to cheer you up," she whispered as her hands wandered.

"You shouldn't be here," Chris said. She took Grace by the arms and stepped away. "It's an ethical violation."

"That didn't seem to bother you before."

"I could lose my fuckin' job if anyone found out I was seein' you."

"Are you afraid I'll blackmail you or something?"

Chris knew the expression on her face revealed what she was thinking.

"I don't believe it," Grace laughed. "You *do* think that."

"I don't know what you'd do if my investigation pointed to someone in your family."

"Does it?"

"You know damn well I can't discuss the specifics of the case with you."

"Can we at least have dinner before I leave?"

"You bought it." Chris shrugged.

Grace pulled two dishes from the cabinet next to the sink. "I don't understand you, Chris," she said.

"I'm not very complicated. If it weren't for this case we probably would never have met anyway."

"Do you wish we'd never met?"

"I didn't say that. Jesus Christ! Don't turn everything I say around to bite me in the ass."

Grace narrowed her eyes for a moment and took a deep breath. "I'm not going to let you provoke me into a fight, Chris. It's obvious you don't want my company right now. Are you having second thoughts about our relationship?"

"We don't *have* a relationship. Just because I slept with you doesn't mean I want to marry you." Chris regretted her words the moment she said them. They were cruel and hurtful, but she couldn't get them back.

Grace looked as if she'd just been slapped and sucked in a harsh breath. She grabbed her purse and slung it over her shoulder. "Enjoy your dinner," she said as she walked to the front door and opened it. She left as Chris stared at the tall blonde's back.

TODD GALLAGHER SAT down across the table from Chris. "I'm not answering any questions until my attorney arrives," he said as he leaned back heavily in his chair.

"I already figured that," Chris said. She hadn't been able to convince Sheila to get a search warrant for Todd's apartment, but decided to bring him in for questioning again anyway. "I'm sure she'll be here soon. You want some coffee while we wait?"

"Sure, why not?"

Chris left the room and stepped into the room next to it.

"How long do you think it'll take to break him?" Carmen asked.

"Hopefully not too long," Chris answered. "Depends on how much objectin' his lawyer does. I gather you had a pleasant stay at Ruben's last night."

Carmen's cell beeped and she flipped it open. "Hang on," she said. She looked at Chris and said, "His attorney's here."

Chris watched as Todd stood and began pacing around the small room. The white board sat against the back wall, turned to hide the paperwork taped to it. "Tell the desk officer to send her back," she said. "Did you get the item I asked for?"

The door to the interrogation room opened and Grace stepped inside. Chris took a pair of black leather gloves from Carmen, inhaled a deep breath and let it out slowly. She left the room she had been watching them from and poured a cup of coffee, carrying it to the interrogation room.

"Sorry for the delay, Mr. Gallagher. Had to make a fresh pot," she said when she set the cup in front of him. "How about you, Counselor?" she asked, deliberately avoiding Grace's eyes.

"No, thank you," Grace answered coolly. "Can we get on with this, please?"

"Sure," Chris said as she sat down. She tossed the gloves on the table and stared at Todd long enough to make him fidget before she spoke again. She turned her attention to Grace and their eyes finally met for a moment. "I just have one or two questions about phone calls your brother made the night of December twenty-sixth." Chris cleared her throat and pulled out a copy of Todd's cell phone record. "You already told me you called your mother a couple of times that night."

"Yes, I did."

"But actually you called her three times within a relatively short period of time. The first time was around nine and lasted about fifteen minutes." Chris stood up and turned the white board around to show a map of the Midtown and Long Island area. "Your call bounced off a couple of towers," she said, pointing at the map. "One here in Midtown and the other on Long Island."

"So what?" Grace asked, sounding bored or perhaps annoyed.

Ignoring her Chris continued, "Apparently that was a call from your cell to your parents' home phone."

"I repeat, so what?"

"Well, I find it a little odd that he called his mother again two and a half hours later. That call was a cell-to-cell call and only lasted a couple of minutes. Coincidentally, it was also about the time Elaine Barrie went to her suite across the street at the Montclair, accompanied by your father. That call bounced off the same two towers."

"I forgot to—" Todd started.

"You don't have to explain anything," Grace said to shut him up.

"And then," Chris continued, her voice slightly louder, "you called your mama a third time, also cell-to-cell, but that call only bounced off the microwave tower in Midtown. That call lasted only a few seconds and at almost the same time the hotel cameras showed your father leaving the penthouse elevator." Chris picked up a remote and pointed at the television against the wall. They watched as Malcolm left the hotel and the elevator door closed. Chris paused the video. "Notice the time stamp at the bottom of the frame. This is almost exactly the same time the last call was made to your mother's cell phone. Quite a coincidence." Chris sat down and let Todd think for a moment. "Did you know your father tried to call your mother after he left the hotel?" When Todd glared at her, Chris said, "He tried to reach her at their home number, but there was no answer. So he called her cell. Bingo! Coincidence number two. That call also bounced off only the Midtown tower."

"How the hell would I know that? I wasn't there!"

"Calm down, Todd," Grace cautioned.

"I think you were there," Chris said. "In fact, I think that third call was a signal to your mother that it was safe for her to go up to the penthouse."

"That's ridiculous!" Todd was sweating and breathing heavily as he stood up.

"Sit *down*, Mr. Gallagher," Chris said. "In what I'm sure is coincidence number three, the license number for a car registered to Malcolm Gallagher was recorded passing through an express lane from Long Island into Mid-Town at eleven. The same vehicle made the return trip at one-thirty. This is your last chance to come clean, Todd." Chris raised her eyes to look at Grace.

Grace frowned. "This is nothing more than supposition," she said without conviction. "You haven't shown us a single piece of evidence a jury would believe. Everything you've said so far proves nothing. My client's mother could have been driving into the city for anything. The phone calls were simply, as you've admitted, coincidences."

Chris picked up the gloves and tapped them on the palm of her hand. She stared at Todd and leaned forward slightly. "It's two counts of premeditated murder, Todd," she said softly.

Todd's head snapped up. "I didn't kill anyone!"

"But you were there, weren't you?" She tapped the gloves against her hand again. "These gloves prove it and that makes you an accomplice. As an accomplice you can face the same charges."

Todd was becoming agitated and began rubbing his face with his hands.

"If you tell the truth now, Todd, the DA might be willing to make a deal. Take the death penalty off the table," Chris continued.

"Where did you get those gloves?" Todd asked as he reached out to grab them. Chris managed to jerk them away.

"Does it matter where I got them?"

"Don't say anything, Todd," Grace ordered.

Todd ran his hands through his hair and lowered his head, covering it with his arms. "It was her own damn fault," he muttered.

"Whose fault?" Chris asked.

"Todd —" Grace started.

"It's over, Grace. It's over," Todd said, shaking his head as tears ran down his face. "I heard Elaine and Dad talking. He was glad she was pregnant and said he'd be there for her. He would take care of everything," Todd said.

"You assumed he was the father of Elaine's baby?" Chris asked.

Todd nodded. "As soon as he left I called my mother. Then I let her in through the stairwell door."

"Was the penthouse door unlocked?" Chris asked.

Grace placed her hand on Todd's shoulder. "Don't answer any more questions, Todd."

Todd shrugged off his sister's hand. "I thought she was only going to confront Elaine. But she just...just lost it."

"Go on," Chris urged.

"I'd like a few minutes alone with my client," Grace tried.

"Elaine came out of the bathroom in her robe and found us. She was pretty calm until Mom slapped her and accused her of having an affair with Dad. Mom called her a whore. Elaine got pissed and told us to get out. She threatened to call security. She admitted she was pregnant, but said Dad wasn't the father. Mom got this funny look on her face when Elaine said she was pregnant. I don't think she heard anything else after that. Next thing I knew Mom grabbed the poker next to the bedroom fireplace and took a swing. She missed and Elaine ran toward the front room. They wrestled and Elaine scratched her on the arm. Mom let her go and Elaine tried to get away, but Mom finally hit her with the poker. She just stood there, breathing hard and staring down at Elaine's body."

"Then what happened?"

"I was freaking out and left. I ran down the stairwell and out a side door."

"Where was your mother?"

"Still in the penthouse, I guess."

"Where did you go after you left the hotel?"

"I just walked around. I didn't know what to do. I swear to God I didn't know she would kill Elaine." Todd slumped back into his chair.

"You're lyin', Todd," Chris said flatly.

"He's confessed to being an accomplice," Grace said. "What more do you want?"

"You grabbed Elaine when she tried to get away, right Todd?"

He shook his head. "No, no, no!"

"There were bruises on Elaine's upper arms where she was held. I've met your mother and don't think she's strong enough to hold a strugglin', younger woman and hit them with the poker. Smudges of grease from the elevator shaft were on her arm. I think Elaine got away from your mother. You grabbed her and shoved her against the wall. Then when she was stunned *you* hit her with the poker. Isn't that the way it went down, Todd?"

"She made me do it!"

"Who?"

"My mother!"

"Malcolm wasn't the baby's father," Chris said. "A paternity test proved it. You murdered Elaine Barrie for something she didn't do." She looked at Grace then stood up and walked around the table to stand behind Todd. She took her handcuffs from the case on her belt. "Stand up," she said. "Todd Gallagher, you're under arrest for the murder of Elaine Barrie and her unborn child," she began as the handcuff encircled his wrist. "You have the right to remain silent. Anything you say can and will be used against you. Do you understand?"

"We're aware of his rights, Detective," Grace said.

The door of the room opened and Carmen stuck her head inside. Chris took a deep breath and said, "Contact the police on Long Island. Tell them we'll be there in about an hour to execute a warrant for the arrest of Laura Gallagher for murder. Would you take Mr. Gallagher to bookin' for me? I'll be there in a few minutes to sign the paperwork."

Grace patted her brother on the shoulder as Carmen gripped his upper arm. "I'll talk to you after I finish here, Todd," she said. She cleared her throat and glanced briefly at Chris. Chris opened her mouth to say something, but closed it again, trapping the words in her throat. There didn't seem to be anything she could say that could make Grace feel better. Sorry seemed like a lie because she wasn't sorry for doing her job.

Grace's voice came unexpectedly out of the darkness, causing Chris to jump involuntarily.

"You knew yesterday when I came to your apartment, didn't you?"

Chris nodded as she fiddled with papers on the table. "I suspected it."

Grace picked up the leather gloves lying on the table. "Are these even Todd's?"

"I never said they were. I had no way of knowin' what he would think."

"Is that all you have to say?"

Chris' eyes came up, futilely trying to probe the dim light to meet Grace's. "It's the best I can do right now."

Chapter Twenty-two

CHRIS, FOLLOWED BY a patrol car, negotiated the road toward the Gallagher home on Long Island. Despite her protests, Captain Savage allowed Grace to accompany them for the arrest of Laura Gallagher. Grace had elected to ride in the patrol car and Chris had been relieved.

"Officers from the Sheriff's Department will meet us at the house," Carmen stated.

"Hopefully we won't need them," Chris said as she glanced in the side mirror of the Trans-Am and signaled to change lanes.

"At least it's finally over and we can move on to our pile of other cases now." Carmen cleared her throat and hesitated before saying, "Sorry about Grace."

"Nothin' to be sorry about," Chris responded tersely.

"I just thought–"

Chris looked across the seat at her partner. "It's over. Got it?"

Carmen nodded and turned her attention to the vehicles flashing by as Chris accelerated.

Chris slowed as she approached the drive to the Gallagher home and pulled alongside a Sheriff's Department vehicle. Her car was still rocking slightly when she and Carmen stepped out and walked to the back. Chris opened the trunk and began pulling on her bulletproof vest. "Tell her to stay in the patrol car until we come out," she said while she checked the ammunition in her Beretta. She watched as Carmen instructed Grace to remain in the patrol car. Grace pushed Carmen away and began walking toward the house, but Chris grabbed her by the arm and pulled her back to the car.

"You interfere with this arrest and I'll personally arrest you for obstruction," Chris said.

"I'm her attorney. I have a right to be here," Grace spat.

"Not until we have her in custody. Then you can do whatever the hell you want. Clear?"

Grace stomped back to the patrol car and leaned against its side, pouting like a child who was being punished. Chris led the others toward the front door. She took a position on one side of the door while Carmen took the other side. Sheriff's deputies moved to the back and sides of the home to await Chris' signal. Once she was satisfied Laura Gallagher couldn't escape, Chris pounded on the front door. "Laura Gallagher! Police!" she shouted. "We have a warrant for your arrest! Open the door!"

There was no response from inside the house and Chris repeated her demand. Receiving no answer the second time, she reached out and turned the door knob. Satisfied the door was locked she motioned for an officer to bring the battering ram. As the officer moved quickly forward, there was a gunshot from inside the house. Chris pressed the button on her mic and said loudly, "Go, go, go!"

The front door splintered as the ram struck it. Chris pushed it aside and entered the foyer, her pistol held in front of her. She swung it quickly from side to side. She directed Carmen to the left while she covered the right as other officers came in behind them. They searched the downstairs rooms until they joined a second group coming from the rear of the large house. Chris looked at Carmen and pointed up. Halfway up the wide staircase they heard raised voices and moved as quickly as possible. Chris pressed her body against the wall next to an open door and peeked briefly into the room. Malcolm Gallagher was sprawled on the floor and Laura paced back and forth in front of his body, still holding a pistol in her hand. She was running her hand through her hair and apparently talking to herself.

Chris made sure everyone with her was out of the line of fire before she and Carmen stepped into the room with their weapons trained on Laura. "Put the gun down," Chris ordered in a firm voice.

Laura looked up and then pointed to Malcolm's body. "Malcolm's hurt," she said, her voice quivering.

"Put the weapon down and we'll get someone to take care of him," Chris said, taking a step closer. "Do it now, Laura."

"I...I warned him," Laura stammered. "I didn't want to hurt him."

"You didn't want to hurt Elaine either, did you?"

"I told Malcolm I didn't mean to. I only wanted to talk to her, but she wouldn't listen."

Chris kept an eye on Laura's hand holding the gun, but thought she looked older, smaller. She hadn't taken the time to apply her usual make-up or run a brush through her hair. Laura's eyes ran around the room and she looked lost until she finally seemed to notice the two detectives in the room with her. Chris watched Laura Gallagher stand up a little straighter and struggle to project an air of dignity and confidence.

Chris readjusted her grip on her weapon and stated, "Laura Gallagher. You're under arrest for the murder of Elaine Barrie." Casting a quick glance at Malcolm's body, she added, "And for the murder or attempted murder of Malcolm Gallagher. Place the gun on the floor."

Carmen kept her weapon trained on Laura Gallagher, ready to move, when Grace suddenly appeared in the bedroom door. Chris couldn't take her eyes off Laura, but ordered in a voice calmer than she felt, "Get her out of here!"

"My parents are in here. As their attorney I need to be here," Grace hissed.

Carmen held her weapon in one hand as she tried to push Grace away. Laura raised her revolver and looked confused as another officer reached in and pulled Grace out of danger.

"Let me get someone in here to check Malcolm," Chris said, trying to draw Laura's attention back to her. "He needs medical attention, Laura," Chris said. Moisture on her hand was making it more difficult to grip her weapon and she needed to put an end to their minor stand-off.

"That whore was having an affair with my husband and got what she deserved," Laura snapped. She pointed toward Malcolm, jabbing the barrel of the gun in his direction. "I wasn't going through that humiliation again, but he didn't listen. There are limits to my forgiveness," Laura said.

"Go through what again, Laura?" Chris asked.

Laura Gallagher's eyes were steely when she looked at Chris. "I raised one bastard because he wouldn't keep it in his pants. That was enough," she spat. Laura shook her head and started to pace again. "She never belonged. My best friend had the same perfect, sparkling deep blue eyes," Laura continued. "And such beautiful blonde hair." Laura's face twisted into something ugly Chris couldn't identify. Her hand trembled slightly as she pointed at Malcolm's body. "He couldn't resist and then brought their bastard love-child home, expecting me to raise it," Laura spat. Then she laughed. "I thought I could do it until she grew up to look just like her whore of a mother, reminding me every damn day of my husband's dirty little indiscretion," she said bitterly, jabbing the barrel of her gun toward Malcolm.

Chris had slowly inched forward to within a few feet of Laura Gallagher and seized the opportunity to disarm her. She grabbed the wrist of the hand holding the gun and wrapped her other arm around Laura's waist, lifting her off the ground and onto the floor. "Carmen!" she called out as she held Laura's arm away from her.

Carmen quickly twisted the gun from Laura's hand, allowing Chris to roll the older woman onto her stomach and cuff her. "Check him," she said, nodding at Malcolm.

Carmen knelt down next to him and pressed her fingers against his throat. "Weak pulse," she said. "Get a paramedic up here!"

Chris pulled Laura up from the floor and handed her off to a uniformed officer who had come into the room, instructing him to read the woman her rights. Then she moved next to Carmen to assist her with Malcolm. Carmen leaned down closer to the floor and looked as Chris partially rolled Malcolm onto his side. "Looks like a shoulder wound," Carmen said. "But he's lost a bucket of blood."

After Malcolm was taken away by ambulance and Laura was secured in the back of a patrol car, Chris left the room. She found Grace leaning against the wall of the wide hallway. Tears hovered at the edges of Grace's eyes. Chris touched her lightly on the arm and asked, "Are you all right?"

"Don't touch me," Grace said as she started to push her way past Chris. Chris grabbed her by the arm to stop her, but Grace jerked away. "I can't talk to you right now," she said as she strode to the stairs.

Chris watched her walk away. Her investigation had destroyed Grace's family just as surely as Laura Gallagher had destroyed Elaine Barrie's family. Chris shook her head thinking about how far the fingers of betrayal had reached. Carmen joined her and asked, "What was all that about?"

GRACE PUSHED THE door to Malcolm's hospital room open and stepped inside. Her appearance was a little disheveled and she ran her fingers through her hair as she stood next to the bed and stared down at Malcolm. The doctor had told her his wound wasn't too serious and he would probably be released in the next day or two after they made sure his blood levels were stable. She touched his arm lightly.

His eyelids fluttered open and took a moment to focus on the person standing over him. "Gracie?" he asked, attempting a smile.

"We need to talk," Grace said through clenched teeth.

"I'm exhausted," he mumbled.

"Tell me about my real mother. Not the woman pretending to be my mother all these years."

"What the hell are you talking about?" Malcolm wiggled around on his bed, obviously uncomfortable.

"I was *there*. I heard her tell the police she wasn't my mother."

"She's lying."

"Did you have an affair with her best friend?"

"You don't understand," he said as he moved around.

"You're damn right. Are you even my father?"

"Of course I am, and Laura is your mother. Her name is on the birth certificate. I was there when you were delivered, for Christ's sake."

"Bullshit!"

"Try to understand, Gracie. Laura and I were told she couldn't have children."

"So you thought you'd solve the problem by fucking her best friend?"

"It wasn't like that," Malcolm said, raising his voice. "Katherine knew we wanted children. She agreed to be artificially inseminated and turn the baby over to us as soon as it was born. But I *never* slept with her. There were unexpected and tragic complications not even her doctor anticipated and she died."

"Mother knew about the arrangement?"

"Of course she did. She and Katherine cooked up the whole idea. When Katherine went into labor she checked into the hospital as Laura Gallagher. I was with her."

"That's not what she's saying now."

"Well, it's the truth. She never got over her guilt about Katherine's death."

"What about Todd?"

Malcolm shook his head. "Laura's idiot doctor was wrong and she became pregnant with Todd a couple of years after you were born. Something happened to her after that, mentally. She blamed me because Katherine became pregnant with you and died."

"She murdered Elaine because she was pregnant and got Todd to help her do it." Grace turned and stared out the room's window. "What was my mother's name?"

"Katherine Hagen. She was Laura's best friend when I met her." Malcolm's eyes scanned Grace's profile. "You look like her in so many ways."

"Where is she buried?"

"Her parents arranged to have her flown home."

"Where!" Grace demanded.

"Some small place in Texas," Malcolm snapped. "I don't remember the damn name. It's been too many years."

"Did they know about me? About your arrangement?"

"No. Katherine's parents were told she died in surgery. It wasn't a total lie," Malcolm mumbled. As Grace wheeled around, obviously leaving, he asked, "Where are you going?"

"I don't know yet."

CHRIS TRIED TO contact Grace several times by phone throughout the week and even stopped by her condo, all without success. She was certain Grace was suffering. Malcolm Gallagher hired Edgar Hamilton to defend his wife and son. Hamilton had a reputation for handling complex criminal cases and would certainly earn his exorbitant fee this time. However, Laura ignored his advice and confessed to murdering Elaine Barrie and her unborn baby in a fit of jealous rage. It was obvious to everyone that Laura Gallagher would need a psychiatric evaluation. Malcolm would probably be blamed for driving his wife to kill. Chris and Carmen had both been amazed at the curtain of lies that surrounded the Gallagher family and were certain Laura was taking the blame to spare Todd.

"We should celebrate," Carmen said. "We closed a tough case."

"Don't feel much like celebratin'," Chris said, picking up a file from her desk and packing it away. Later the DA's office would need it to present their case to a jury.

"Well, I do. A couple of drinks will make you feel better. Besides, you owe me."

"For what?"

"For putting up with that down-home folksy way you talk all these years."

"At least I don't snore. Sounds like a damn buzz-saw."

"I don't snore," Carmen said with a smile. "I breathe deeply."

Chris pushed away from her desk and stood up. "Okay. Just one drink."

"One drink," Carmen nodded.

The bar was a few blocks from the precinct and had been a hang-out for off-duty police officers for as long as anyone could remember. Callahan's was run by a retired police officer and there was something about the semi-dark bar with its shiny dark mahogany walls that seemed to envelope its patrons in a cocoon of warmth and safety. The juke box was never loud enough to drown out conversations and no one felt the need to face the door. They all knew Jake Callahan had at least one weapon behind the bar.

Oddly enough Chris felt better after only one drink and contemplated a second, but decided she could have that at home and not have to worry about driving afterward.

"I've been thinkin' about takin' some time off," Chris said as she absently twirled the ice in her glass.

"And do what?" Carmen asked as she finished her drink.

"Dunno yet," Chris said with a shrug. "Maybe just drive until I run out of pavement."

"Drive east and you can do that in a couple of hours." Carmen laughed.

"How're things with Ruben?"

"Like you care," Carmen snorted.

"If he makes you happy that's all that counts, right?"

Carmen tore a strip from her napkin and rolled it between her fingers. "Ruben satisfies me, but I don't know if I'm ready for a forever commitment."

"You're still young, Carmen. Someone will ring your bell one of these days." Chris shrugged.

"Grace Gallagher does it for you, doesn't she?"

"She could, but since I helped destroy her family, I'm not seein' much of a future with her."

"Have you heard from her?"

"Nope," Chris said as she exhaled and slid out of the booth, stopping to drop a twenty on the table.

Chris held the front door to the bar open and stepped outside, taking a deep breath. "You know, if I ever left here I might actually miss the smell of exhaust fumes and the sound of horns honkin'," she said with a smile.

The headlights of a car along the curb across the street flipped on as the two women strolled leisurely down the sidewalk, talking and laughing. The driver whipped the car into a U-turn as soon as there was an opening in traffic along the busy street and gunned the engine, accelerating toward them.

Chris noticed the shadows of their bodies lengthening and turned to look over her shoulder. She reached into her jacket and drew her Beretta, shoving Carmen away as the vehicle bore down on them. Automatic gunfire erupted from the passenger side of the car. Chris felt the impact on her body as she returned fire as rapidly as she could squeeze the trigger. She saw the vehicle suddenly turn, jump the curb, and smash into the brick front of a building half a block away. Carmen trained her weapon on the vehicle as Chris speed-loaded more rounds, ignoring the pain in her right side and thigh. The doors opened and two armed men stumbled out.

"Frankie! No!" Carmen's voice yelled. "Drop it!"

Chris paused for an instant as she heard the sound of sirens rapidly approaching. In that instant she saw Carmen hesitate as Frankie Sandoval raised the automatic weapon in his hand in his sister's direction. Suddenly all sound vanished as Frankie pulled the trigger. Carmen returned fire, muzzle flashes punctuating the night. Chris dropped to her knees and squeezed off three rounds. She couldn't let Carmen be responsible for her brother's death.

"No!!" she screamed when she saw Carmen's body jerk. A blossom of red bloomed on her chest and she pitched forward. Chris forced her body up and limped toward Carmen. Jake Callahan rolled Carmen onto her back to feel for a pulse. "Carmen!" Chris said as she pushed Jake away and fell next to her partner. She blinked to clear her clouded vision as tears streamed down her face. "Carmen, please."

Chris pulled her partner's limp body into her arms and rocked back and forth, ignoring the piercing squeal of vehicles stopping nearby. Hands tried to pull her away.

"She's hurt," Chris said. "Do something!"

There was a scuffle behind her as she held Carmen tightly. Two uniformed officers and a paramedic struggled to hold Ruben Montanez away from the scene. He collapsed onto the curb and dropped his head into his hands.

"Shaw," a man's voice said softly. "Shaw, let us take care of you."

"I'm okay," Chris said hoarsely before she was overcome by emotion. She felt cold and sick as she stroked Carmen's slack face and brushed her hair back. She grasped the man's arm. "Take care of Carmen."

"We will. Just relax, Shaw," the paramedic said. "Everything's okay now. We gotcha."

Chris felt her arms being pried from Carmen's body as she was lowered to the pavement. She shivered from the cold as her clothing was cut away from the wounds in her side and leg.

Chapter Twenty-three

CHRIS STOOD AT attention. She fought the pain in her side to stand erectly. Most of her weight was balanced on her left leg, a cane keeping her right leg steady. The bandage on her right side pulled uncomfortably on the bruised skin surrounding the spot a bullet had pierced her body. The shiny front brim of her uniform hat was pulled low enough on her forehead to hide the emotions that filled her eyes and revealed the unrelenting pain and sorrow she felt over Carmen's death. Beneath the brim of her dress hat, Chris could still scan the rows of fellow police officers gathered to honor a fallen comrade as well as the friends and relatives who had known Carmen Sandoval since her birth.

Against her doctor's orders Chris had demanded she be released in time to attend her partner's funeral and signed a hospital release form that she was leaving against medical advice. It had taken her nearly an hour to dress. She slid a black band over the center of her badge before joining the other detectives in her squad as they formed an honor guard at the church where Carmen's funeral would be held.

"What are you doing here, Shaw?" Captain Savage asked when he saw her.

"Honorin' my partner, sir," she said as she adjusted her hat.

"You look like you're ready to keel over. Go home. No one will know."

"I'll know," Chris said as her eyes met his.

"I don't want to lose another detective."

"You won't," Chris said.

Savage leaned forward slightly. "The squad is walking behind the hearse, Shaw. Personally, I don't think you're up to that."

"I can make it," Chris said stubbornly. "I owe it to Carmen. She was my friend."

"Keep an eye on her," Savage said, pointing at the officer next to Chris.

"Oh, for fuck's sake," Chris said under her breath.

"What was that, Detective Shaw?" Savage asked.

"Nothin', sir," Chris replied.

The Midtown Precinct Detective Squad entered the church in single file and took seats across the aisle from Carmen's family. Chris removed her hat and rested it on her lap. Savage was probably right. Her leg would hurt like a bitch before the funeral procession made it to the cemetery. She closed her eyes and lowered her head. Maybe she wanted to suffer. She should have reacted more quickly. She should have pumped her whole clip into Frankie's body before he could get off a shot. She should have known the little shit was unstable enough to do something stupid. But shoot his own sister? She hadn't seen that coming. She should have. Chris turned her head and leaned forward far enough to see Mercedes on the opposite side of the aisle. Friends and relatives had their arms around her shoulders in an attempt to comfort her. Chris knew that even though they might be sad, those around Mercedes would never know the depth of her grief. In one moment, one burst of gunfire, she had lost both of her children. She would never bounce the grandchildren she dreamed of on her knees. Three families had been torn apart or destroyed during the Barrie case. The price had been too high.

When the long mass ended, Chris used the back of the pew in front of her to pull her body upright. Mercedes, aunts and uncles and cousins followed the casket and priest down the red carpeted aisle. The detectives fell in behind the family. Outside, Chris pulled her hat on and made her way, one step at a time, down the stone stairs that led to the sidewalk. Carmen's rose-tinted casket slid quietly into the back of the hearse as the family entered vehicles for the final drive. Chris took her place in line and waited until the procession was ready to leave. Captain Savage had escorted Mercedes to her limousine and helped her inside. They spoke for a moment before he stood and looked toward the detectives assembled behind the family car. He raised his hand and motioned to Chris to join him.

"Sir," Chris said as she reached the vehicle.

"Mrs. Sandoval has requested that you join her for the ride to the cemetery," Savage said.

"I can walk," Chris said, shaking her head.

Savage leaned closer and placed a hand on Chris' shoulder. "It's her request, Shaw. I didn't suggest it."

A hand covered by a black leather glove protruded from the back seat of the vehicle. "Christina? Please. For Carmenita."

Chris felt warm tears flow down her cheeks as she took the hand. As soon as she was in the vehicle, Savage closed the back door and patted the roof. Before the car pulled away from the curb, Chris dissolved into tears and let Mercedes pull her close to comfort her. When the car finally stopped, Captain Savage opened the back door and helped Mercedes exit. She waited for Chris and took her arm for the final walk to Carmen's burial site.

TEN DAYS LATER Chris sat on the sofa in the front room of her apartment, watching heavy flakes drift past the window. She had been jolted awake early when an angel with laughing brown eyes and hair the color of burnished copper drifted through her dream. Her face had dissolved into a mixture of blood and tears. The backfire of a vehicle on the street below startled her and her breathing quickened. She was wrapped in a heavy quilt that had once belonged to her grandmother. She couldn't remember the last time she'd been warm. Her soul felt empty. She hadn't spoken to anyone since Carmen's funeral. Anonymous people knocked on the apartment door, but she ignored them. The telephone rang, but she didn't have the energy to answer it. She'd unplugged the answering machine and hadn't charged her cell. She hadn't checked her mail or email. She felt safe with only her thoughts for now. If she could just sit and let her mind remain unoccupied for a while, she would figure out what to do. She was sure she should be doing something. She closed her eyes and dozed, praying there wouldn't be any more nightmares.

A warm hand on her shoulder brought her out of the first nightmare-free sleep she'd had in over a week. Her eyebrows knitted into a frown at being awakened and she slapped at the hand.

"Wake up, Chris," a familiar voice said.

"Go away and leave me alone," Chris mumbled.

"When was the last time you ate?"

She shrugged, but the movement sent a searing pain through her side and she gasped.

"Where are your pain meds?" the voice asked.

"Bedroom."

She felt the vibration of footsteps walking away on the wooden floor. Who the hell was in her apartment? She was sure she'd locked the door. She forced her eyelids open a slit and felt for her Beretta. When her fingers found the cold metal under the sofa cushion she curled her fingers around the comforting object and pulled it against her chest.

"Planning to shoot me, Detective?" the voice asked.

"Carmen?" Chris asked, her voice hoarse. She felt her weapon began to slide out of her hand and tried to grip it more tightly. "I'm sorry, Carmen. I'm so sorry."

"It's all right, Chris," Grace said softly. "Let me have the gun so you can take this pill."

A small tablet replaced the security blanket of her gun, followed by a cool glass of water.

"What are you doin' here?" Chris asked as she forced her body farther up on the sofa, grabbing her side as she tried to sit up straighter. She popped the tablet in her mouth and washed it down. She pushed her body to a standing position and hobbled through the front room. She made her way into the bathroom that adjoined her bedroom, closed the door, and leaned against the sink. She was hurting inside and out and needed to be alone. She ran cold water in the sink and splashed it over her face. She stared at the gaunt face staring back at her from the medicine cabinet mirror and wondered how many pounds she'd lost. Her eyes looked vacant, as if her soul had leaked out.

She dreaded the beginning of the next week. She would be returning to work on a limited basis, mostly desk duty, and wasn't sure she would be able to stand the sympathetic looks in the eyes of her fellow detectives. Would they blame her for Carmen's death? She needed to go back to work so she could stop thinking so damn much. All it did was keep her in a perpetually foul mood. She forced a deep breath to calm her mind.

Chris pressed a towel against her face and made a half-hearted attempt to make her hair do something other than stick out in various directions. When she left the bathroom she would have to face Grace. She had to come up with a reason to make Grace leave and not return. Not seeing Grace again would probably be for the best. Chris needed to forget what had happened between them and try to re-establish a semi-normal life. She cleared her throat and slung open the bathroom door.

"Why're you here?" Chris snapped when she saw Grace leaning casually against the counter that separated the kitchen from the front room.

"The coffee's fresh," Grace said, ignoring Chris' question. She sipped carefully at the hot liquid before sliding a second cup toward Chris. "I needed to know you were all right. No one's seen you since the funeral."

"I'm fine, so get out. I don't want you here."

"Don't push me away, Chris. We need to talk."

"Nothin' to talk about." Chris took a deep breath and winced, grabbing her side. "In case you haven't noticed, I'm not in any shape to entertain you privately right now."

"I don't go to bed with someone just for the hell of it," Grace retorted. "It...it has to mean something."

"All it meant was we both had a good time and we walked away satisfied. That's all it was. Why can't you just accept that and leave me alone? All I'll do is hurt you."

"I don't believe that."

"I destroyed your fuckin' family!"

"They did that to themselves," Grace said forcefully. She set her cup down and moved closer to Chris. "That's the problem with lying. It always comes back to bite you in the ass." She reached out and drew a hand across Chris' shoulders. She felt the muscles beneath her hand stiffen as Chris continued to stare at the countertop. She breathed in Grace's scent, felt warmth spread down her back when Grace touched her. She shook her head and couldn't stop her tears from falling to the counter. "Everyone leaves," she muttered, barely loud enough for Grace to hear. "You will too." She wiped her eyes and stared at Grace. "My mother committed suicide. Jill found a better lover. Carmen was murdered. I couldn't stand to lose anyone else I cared about."

Grace smiled and squeezed Chris' shoulder. "You care about me?"

"More than I should," Chris answered.

"Show me how much," Grace whispered as she wiped Chris' tears away with her thumbs.

EARLY MONDAY MORNING Chris drove within the speed limit toward her precinct, possibly for the first time in six years. She nodded to a few colleagues as she entered the squad room, made her way to her desk, and sat down. She unlocked the top drawer, staring at the empty drawer for a moment. She'd already made a decision. There was no sense in delaying the inevitable. She pushed her body out of her chair and headed toward Captain Savage's office. She patted her hand against the front of her jacket and felt the envelope containing her resignation before knocking on his door.

"Good to have you back, Shaw," Captain Savage said when she entered.

Chris pulled the envelope from her pocket. She took her badge from her belt and drew her service weapon from her holster. She didn't look at the captain as she gently laid her weapon and badge on Savage's desk. She tapped the envelope against her fingers before holding it out to Savage.

"This what I think it is?" he asked.

"Probably," she answered.

He held the envelope and looked up at Chris. "You and Sandoval did good work on the Barrie case."

She flinched when she heard Carmen's name and blinked hard. "The price was too high, Cap. I need to get my head screwed on straight again and don't think I can do it here."

"You'll have to testify at the trials," Savage said.

"What trials? They confessed."

"Todd Gallagher's claiming his confession was coerced and Laura Gallagher's pleading diminished capacity. And just to make it interesting, since each implicates the other, they'll have separate trials with separate attorneys. Sheila will be up to her ass in alligators and paperwork."

Chris looked down and smiled. "It'll take the lawyers and judges a couple of years to get it all figured out. I can fly back to testify, if it ever comes to that."

Savage stood up and offered Chris his hand. "All we can do is give it our best shot."

"Somebody should pay and this time the price was too high."

"Oh, by the way, the shooting board cleared you for the Sandoval shooting."

No fuckin' shit, Chris thought angrily.

She left the captain's office and went back to her desk to clear it out for the next poor bastard who'd call it home. She barely had time to pour a cup of coffee and settle behind her desk before her phone rang. "Shaw," she answered.

"Could I tempt you with dinner at my place this evening?" Grace asked, her sultry voice caressing Chris' ear.

"Do you think that's a good idea?"

"It seems the least I can do to repay your efforts on my behalf over the weekend."

"It wasn't an effort." Chris wanted to believe there was something more than physical pleasure between her and Grace, but she knew there wasn't. Aside from the sexual aspect, they had little in common and Chris would never earn enough as a cop to meet Grace's needs. Good, or even great sex would eventually grow old, just as it had with Jill. She'd made a decision about her future and there was no sense in stringing Grace along with the false hope of permanency.

"I'm leavin'," Chris said bluntly. "I'm goin' back to Texas."

There was a pause before Grace responded. "When did you make that decision?"

"A day or two ago."

"What about us?"

"There is no *us*. Why can't you understand that?"

"Can we at least talk about it over dinner tonight?"

Chris could hear the plea in Grace's voice. "I'm sorry, Grace," Chris said in almost a whisper before she hung up.

Chapter Twenty-Four

FIVE MONTHS LATER Chris was running as fast as she could, the hot Texas sun beating down on her as she pursued a suspect who'd decided he didn't want to answer any questions. "Stop! Police!" she yelled as she dodged a woman pushing a baby carriage. She saw her suspect duck into an old warehouse and slowed as she approached the opening he had entered. She pulled her weapon and sucked in a couple of deep breaths. She could feel the scar tissue on her side stretch and brought a hand up to press against it.

"You okay?" her partner, Delbert Bowers huffed when he caught up to her.

Chris grinned and winked at her partner as she motioned him to the right. "Finer than peach fuzz," she said as she crouched slightly and brought her weapon up. "Looks like you ain't been doin' much runnin' while I was gone."

"That exercise crap is for tree huggers and fern fondlers," he groused as he tried to catch his breath. "Besides, that's why I was so damned glad when you decided to come back where you belonged. So you could do the runnin'." When their breathing returned to normal, they ducked into the building, searching for the man they were chasing.

"Come on, Gilbert! This ain't your first dance at the prom," Chris called out as she edged to her left. She didn't think the man was armed, but she'd been out of the Dallas loop for almost seven years so anything was possible. "I only wanna ask you a couple of questions."

She listened for any sound that might give away Gilbert's position. She grinned and stifled a laugh when she heard the distinctive sound of a fart not far away. Shouldn't have eaten them beans for lunch, she thought. She moved farther to the left, staying behind crates stacked near the wall. She shoved her gun into its holster and stepped quietly onto the protruding beam of a wall support. She was rewarded with a glimpse of shiny black hair. Gilbert Hinojosa was a low-level dealer who rarely had more than a misdemeanor stash on him. Generally not a dangerous guy. Chris had dealt with him not long before she followed Jill to New York. He had been a hundred pounds lighter back then. She inched far enough up the support beam to step onto the closest crate and prayed the old wood was still strong enough to support her weight.

She duck-walked across the crate and stood up aiming her weapon at the man squatting in a narrow opening between crates. "End of the road, Gilbert," she said, startling him. She ordered him to his stomach on the cement floor, jumped down and read him his rights as she handcuffed him while Del covered him. It took a little effort to haul him off the floor. "You need to cut back on the tacos, man," she grunted. She took him by the upper arm and escorted him out of the warehouse. She leaned against the side of the building while her partner left to get their car.

When Del returned, Chris opened the back door and guided their prisoner inside. She leaned slightly into the car. "Now that we've put on a show for your homeboys, tell us what you saw the night Manny Jimenez was killed, Gilbert."

"Didn't see nothin'," he muttered.

"That's not what Israel says."

"He's a punk-ass liar. Stupid fuckin' *bendejo*."

"I can agree with that. So where were you when Manny bit the bullet, so to speak?"

"I want my lawyer," Gilbert said.

Chris squinted at Del and said, "Gilbert must have moved up in *la familia* while I've been gone if he can afford a lawyer."

"I get one free."

Chris nodded. "True, but their success rate sucks the big one, buddy."

She closed the door, walked around the car, and plopped into the passenger seat.

It hadn't taken Chris long to feel comfortable again working with the Dallas Homicide Squad. Before she was allowed to officially resume her former job she had to pass a physical, but the only serious road block had been a couple of sessions with the department shrink who wanted to make sure she was psychologically stable after being shot. She hadn't liked that much and all it really did was cause old hurts to resurface. In the end, he proclaimed her fit for duty. She vowed to never let another case suck her in the way the Barrie case had. After Del pulled into the loading area, Chris got out, and escorted Gilbert into booking while Del parked the car.

Chris shoved her prisoner against the booking counter and signed in. "Which room is open?" she asked the desk sergeant.

"Four."

"Tell Bowers where we are when he comes through."

The desk sergeant nodded as Chris took Gilbert by the upper arm to lead him to the interrogation room.

"I ain't gonna tell you nothin', Shaw. You be wasting my time and yours," Gilbert said.

"I got all day, pal," she said. She glanced at his face. "Why you sweatin', man?"

"'Cause it's fuckin' hot in here. I need a drink." He stopped at a water fountain. "Push the button, bitch."

"You had me right up until bitch," Chris said and pushed him forward. "Let's go."

"Hey! I said I needed a drink," Gilbert said loudly. He spun around and lowered his shoulder and rammed it into Chris' right side. She grunted and gasped as she flew backward and slammed into a file cabinet. She shook her head and launched her body into Gilbert's soft abdomen, sending him sprawling onto his back on the floor. She motioned to a nearby uniformed officer to assist her. Together they struggled to lift the overweight man from the floor.

"Take him to four," Chris said. As soon as Gilbert and the officer disappeared down a hallway, Chris pressed her hand against her right side and sat down at the closest desk, drawing a deep breath.

"You all right, Shaw?" Del asked, kneeling next to her.

"Yeah. He just hit me wrong. Give me a minute."

Chris heard the sound of footsteps clicking on the linoleum as she caught her breath.

"What happened?" a woman's voice asked.

"Got caught off guard," Chris answered. "How are ya, Kim?"

"Better than you at the moment," the Dallas County Assistant District Attorney said with a laugh.

Chris looked up at her and grinned. She stuck her hand out and Kim took it and pulled her up.

"Will you make it to my good-bye party my office thinks is a secret?" Kim asked.

"I'll do my damnedest. When we gonna meet your replacement?"

"Maybe at the party." Kim leaned closer and added, "She's just your type, Chris."

"What's my type?"

"Single."

Chris laughed and patted Del on the back. "Let's talk to Gilbert," she said.

As Chris could have predicted, Gilbert was uncooperative. They would have to continue to beat the bushes and harass their snitches. By the time she and Del released Gilbert and left the interrogation room, Chris had developed a pesky headache and despite her efforts to increase her stamina, was physically exhausted.

"I think you should start driving next week," Del said as he plopped heavily behind his desk.

Chris looked across the desks at her partner. Delbert Bowers was a fifty-ish detective who had been more like a father than a partner. He pushed his glasses up as he leaned back. He ran a meaty hand through still thick brown hair that was generously sprinkled with grey. His off-the-rack suits seemed to fit more snugly than Chris remembered.

"Why's that?" she asked.

"Because I've missed that sweet ride of yours," he said with a smile. "Got plans for the weekend?"

"Got a few things to catch up on. Still unpacking." She was seriously considering several drinks.

"Can we knock off a little early?" Del asked. "I promised to take the old lady out to dinner."

"How're things at home?" she asked.

"Better now that the last kid has flown the coop. Now we can actually afford to go out to eat occasionally. Hell, sometimes I even manage to get lucky." He squinted as he watched Chris type a report into the computer.

"Do they make flash cards for that?" Chris asked with a smile.

"Shut the fuck up, Shaw. I was doing it when you was still warm as toast in your mama's womb," Del retorted. "Maybe now that you're back you should go out and have a few drinks, dance a little or pick up a hot woman. Let 'em know the Big C is back in town and open for business again. You don't wanna become socially stunted."

CHRIS STROLLED INTO the Cattle Company Saturday evening and ordered a beer. Since her recovery she had avoided contact with everyone except criminals. It was time she tried to resume the semi-normal life she led before she met Jill. She looked around and estimated she stood a better than even chance of not going home alone. After two or three beers she was relaxed enough to ask a couple of women to dance, but wasn't tempted to ask either of them for more of a time commitment. She returned to the bar and motioned for a refill. While she waited, a red-head with green eyes slid next to her and placed an order as she blatantly examined Chris.

"Somethin' I can do for you?" Chris asked with a grin.

The red-head return the grin. "I don't know, honey. You any good?"

"Depends on what I'm doin'." Chris' smile widened. "Do you have anything special in mind?"

"I always have something in mind, sugar," the woman said, pressing her body closer against Chris to make room for another patron at the bar. Her hand slid over Chris' ass.

Chris chuckled as she swallowed a gulp of her drink. "I know that game," she said as she leaned closer.

"Interested in a match?"

"I never turn down a challenge," Chris said.

"That's the kind of butch I like. Got a name?"

"Chris."

"Chastity. Let's dance," the woman said with a wink.

"Chastity. Seriously?" Chris said with a smile.

"What can I say," Chastity said with a shrug. "My mama had a sense of humor. Guess you'll have to find out for yourself."

Chris laughed. "Like I said, I never turn down a challenge." She took Chastity's hand and strode to the dance floor. The night was looking more promising. Chastity rested her arm across Chris' shoulders and stroked the back of her neck as they relaxed into the dance.

GRACE ENTERED THE Cattle Company accompanied by two other women. She was unfamiliar with the gay and lesbian scene in Dallas, but had met with a few groups since her arrival. They were in the process of showing her what was available socially. They stopped at the bar and ordered before searching out a table. She hadn't been seated more than a few minutes when her eyes caught a familiar face on the dance floor. She couldn't tear her gaze away from Chris Shaw as she led her dance partner around the floor. She hadn't seen the seductive detective in over five months. Her body ached as she watched Chris bring her lips near her companion's ear to whisper something that made the woman smile.

When the next song began, one of the women with Grace led her through the tables toward the dance floor. Grace allowed the woman to hold her closely. She felt a prickle along her neck and when she opened her eyes they met Chris'. Grace couldn't read what she saw on Chris' face. She raised her head slightly to hear what her dance partner was whispering.

CHRIS FROWNED. EVERY movement of Grace's body against her partner's screamed intimacy and every fiber of Chris' body vibrated with unexpected jealousy. She wanted to be the one touching Grace. The thought of the woman now holding Grace in her arms, her lips pressing against the soft skin along her neck was torture. Well, what the hell did she expect? She had destroyed Grace's family. Chris' fear of abandonment let her convince herself it didn't matter. Grace didn't matter. But she knew she was lying to herself. She cared more for the tall blonde than she ever intended to.

Chris followed Chastity to a darkened booth. Apparently emboldened by their dance, Chastity moved closer, her hand traveling up Chris' leg and into her crotch. Chris had missed being touched. She ran her fingertips down Chastity's cheek and felt rather than saw a shadow pass over them. She raised her eyes and met the deep blue eyes of Grace Gallagher. Grace tapped Chastity on the shoulder.

"She owes me a dance," Grace said without looking at the woman.

The red-head slid away as Grace held her hand out. Chris took it and followed Grace toward the dance floor. She took Grace into her arms, holding her tightly and pressing her right hand into Grace's back. She stepped off into a slow two-step, leading Grace through a series of turns until they both were comfortable with the movements. Grace picked up the rhythm quickly and Chris smiled. Grace Gallagher was almost as tall as Chris and their bodies meshed together well. One song flowed into another and gradually Chris' hand drifted into the small of Grace's back. The dance floor wasn't too crowded and Chris maneuvered them into the least crowded section. She closed her eyes and smiled, relishing the feel of Grace in her arms. Grace turned her face into Chris' neck and lightly brushed her fingers under the hair at the base of Chris' neck.

Chris lowered her mouth closer to Grace's ear. "Why are you here?" she asked.

"I got a job here. With the DA's office," Grace whispered back. "I start at the end of the month."

When the music changed to something livelier, Grace took Chris' hand and led her toward a darker, more secluded area near the back of the bar. When they stopped, Chris leaned against the wall and stared at the gorgeous blonde in front of her.

"How are you, Detective?" Grace asked coolly.

"Fully recovered."

Grace tapped her on the forehead. "Here too?"

Chris only stared at her. "I don't know what you mean."

"Yes, you do."

Chris looked down at the floor and shook her head. "Workin' on it," she admitted.

"Just so you don't think I followed you down here and get a big head, Malcolm told me my real mother was buried in Texas. I located my grandparents and learned everything about my mother. By the time I returned to New York you were gone."

"I told you I was leavin'."

"I guess I didn't think it would be so soon."

"I needed some time to get my head on straight. Couldn't do it in New York."

"What did you figure out?"

"That this is where I belonged."

"No one's ever looked at me the way you do," Grace whispered. "I didn't expect to fall in love with you. Give me a chance to show you how much." Grace was temptingly close, her lips barely separated from Chris'.

"What about your date?"

"She's just a friend. She knows the score."

Chris didn't move. She felt frozen in place as she watched Grace's cool blue eyes move over her face. Grace bit gently on her lower lip and the corners of her mouth curled up slightly. "Tell me what's in here," she said as she pressed her hand against Chris' chest.

"I don't want to be alone anymore," Chris finally admitted. She closed her eyes for a moment. "I need you...to feel whole again. I was sure you hated me."

"I can't hate you for what others did, baby."

Chris shook her head. "Jeezus! I can't believe I've fallen for a damn lawyer." She pressed her lips against Grace's, claiming what she had been denying for too long. She deepened their kiss, savoring the heat of Grace's body against hers.

"You drive me out of my mind," Grace breathed when the kiss ended. "I've missed that."

Chris' hands slipped into Grace's hair as she held her. "Who are you, Grace Gallagher?"

Grace laughed. "Whoever you need me to be, baby."

"Just be yourself," Chris said as their lips met again.

Other Quest Titles You Might Enjoy:

Seminal Murder
by Mary Vermillion

When Dr. Grace Everest is murdered in her own sperm bank, Mara Gilgannon attempts to find the killer and to protect a beloved ex who is desperately seeking motherhood. So what if Mara herself has 858 reasons (and counting) never to have children? She didn't let that stop her when she and Grace launched a radio series on artificial insemination. And she won't let anyone stop her from completing the series and discovering the truth about her friend's murder. Not the thief who trashes her office. Not her flamboyant housemate who invites a top suspect to crash with them. Not the 15-year-old who wants Mara to help find her donor dad. And especially not conservative Christian activist Reverend Leo Spires. As he heightens his campaign against the radio station where Mara works and the sperm bank where the murder occurred, Mara discovers a new mystery at the bank itself — an unusually low pregnancy rate for lesbians.

ISBN 978-1-61929-049-5

Hearts, Dead and Alive
by Kate McLachlan

When fifth grade teacher Kimberly Wayland finds a human heart in the middle school dumpster, she has some explaining to do. Like why she was in the dumpster in the first place, and why she didn't tell the police about her gruesome find. But after giving the police a fake alibi, explaining is the last thing Kim wants to do. Instead, with the help of her friends — hot "best friend" Becca, co-worker "lesbian wanna-be" Annie, and lawyer "stickler-for-rules" Lucy — Kim sets out to solve the mystery of the missing heart. Along the way, she unexpectedly solves another mystery, the mystery of her own heart.

ISBN 978-1-61929-017-4

A Very Public Eye
by Lori L. Lake

Greed? Hatred? Retaliation? Or a Cover-up

Winter has not yet set in, but young Eddie Bolton will never see another snowfall in his hometown of Duluth, Minnesota. Someone has diabolically killed him in what should have been a secure juvenile detox ward at the Benton Dowling Center. Leona Reese, a state investigator of fraud and licensing infractions, has been out of commission for three weeks due to surgery. On her first day back on the job, she is faced with the aftermath of the 17-year-old's death and is shocked by the brutality. Working with the local police, Leona discovers far too many people with motives for the killing, but precious little evidence. As she uncovers long-buried secrets, someone else is murdered, and now Leona realizes that she, too, is in danger. In the midst of her own emotional turmoil, is Leona strong enough and smart enough to confront and catch a clever and ruthless murderer?

This is Book 2 in The Very Public Eye Mystery Series that began with *Buyer's Remorse*.

ISBN 978-1-61929-076-1

More Brenda Adcock titles:

The Sea Hawk

Dr. Julia Blanchard, a marine archaeologist, and her team of divers have spent almost eighteen months excavating the remains of a ship found a few miles off the coast of Georgia. Although they learn quite a bit about the nineteenth century sailing vessel, they have found nothing that would reveal the identity of the ship they have nicknamed "The Georgia Peach."

Consumed by the excavation of the mysterious ship, Julia's relationship with her partner, Amy, has deteriorated. When she forgets Amy's birthday and finds her celebrating in the arms of another woman, Julia returns alone to the Peach site. Caught in a violent storm, she finds herself separated from her boat and adrift on the vast Atlantic Ocean.

Her rescue at sea leads her on an unexpected journey into the true identity of the Peach and the captain and crew who called it their home. Her travels take her to the island of Martinique, the eastern Caribbean islands, the Louisiana German Coast and New Orleans at the close of the War of 1812.

How had the Peach come to rest in the waters off the Georgia coast? What had become of her alluring and enigmatic captain, Simone Moreau? Can love conquer everything, even time? On a voyage that lifts her spirits and eventually breaks her heart, Julia discovers the identity of the ship she had been excavating and the fate of its crew. Along the way she also discovers the true meaning of love which can be as boundless and unpredictable as the ocean itself.

ISBN 978-1-935053-10-1

Pipeline

What do you do when the mistakes you made in the past come back to slap you in the face with a vengeance? Joanna Carlisle, a fifty-seven year old photojournalist, has only begun to adjust to retirement on her small ranch outside Kerrville, Texas, when she finds herself unwillingly sucked into an investigation of illegal aliens being smuggled into the United States to fill the ranks of cheap labor needed to increase corporate profits.

Joanna is a woman who has always lived life her way and on her own terms, enjoying a career that had given her everything she thought she ever wanted or needed. An unexpected visit by her former lover, Cate Hammond, and the attempted murder of their son, forces Jo to finally face what she had given up. Although she hasn't seen Cate or their son for fifteen years, she finds that the feelings she had for Cate had only been dormant, but had never died. No matter how much she fights her attraction to Cate, Jo cannot help but wonder whether she had made the right decision when she chose career and independence over love.

Jo comes to understand the true meaning of friendship and love only when her investigation endangers not only her life, but also the lives of the people around her.

ISBN 978-1-932300-64-2

Reiko's Garden

Hatred...like love...knows no boundaries.

How much impact can one person have on a life?

When sixty-five-year old Callie Owen returns to her rural childhood home in Eastern Tennessee to attend the funeral of a woman she hasn't seen in twenty years, she's forced to face the fears, heartache, and turbulent events that scarred both her body and her mind. Drawing strength from Jean, her partner of thirty years, and from their two grown children, Callie stays in the valley longer than she had anticipated and relives the years that changed her life forever.

In 1949, Japanese war bride Reiko Sanders came to Frost Valley, Tennessee with her soldier husband and infant son. Callie Owen was an inquisitive ten-year-old whose curiosity about the stranger drove her to disobey her father for just one peek at the woman who had become the subject of so much speculation. Despite Callie's fears, she soon finds that the exotic-looking woman is kind and caring, and the two forge a tentative, but secret friendship.

When Callie and her five brothers and sisters were left orphaned, Reiko provided emotional support to Callie. The bond between them continued to grow stronger until Callie left Frost Valley as a teenager, emotionally and physically scarred, vowing never to return and never to forgive.

It's not until Callie goes "home" that she allows herself to remember how Reiko influenced her life. Once and for all, can she face the terrible events of her past? Or will they come back to destroy all that she loves?

ISBN 978-1-932300-77-2

Redress of Grievances

In the first of a series of psychological thrillers, Harriett Markham is a defense attorney in Austin, Texas, who lost everything eleven years earlier. She had been an associate with a Dallas firm and involved in an affair with a senior partner, Alexis Dunne. Harriett represented a rape/murder client named Jared Wilkes and got the charges dismissed on a technicality. When Wilkes committed a rape and murder after his release, Harriett was devastated. She resigned and moved to Austin, leaving everything behind, including her lover.

Despite lingering feelings for Alexis, Harriet becomes involved with a sex-offense investigator, Jessie Rains, a woman struggling with secrets of her own. Harriet thinks she might finally be happy, but then Alexis re-enters her life. She refers a case of multiple homicide allegedly committed by Sharon Taggart, a woman with no motive for the crimes. Harriett is creeped out by the brutal murders, but reluctantly agrees to handle the defense.

As Harriett's team prepares for trial, disturbing information comes to light. Sharon denies any involvement in the crimes, but the evidence against her seems overwhelming. Harriett is plunged into a case rife with twisty psychological motives, questionable sanity, and a client with a complex and disturbing life. Is she guilty or not? And will Harriet's legal defense bring about justice — or another Wilkes case?

Recipient of a 2008 award from the Golden Crown Literary Society, the premiere organization for the support and nourishment of quality lesbian literature. Redress of Grievances won in the category of Lesbian Mystery.

ISBN 978-1-932300-86-4

Tunnel Vision

Royce Brodie, a 50-year-old homicide detective in the quiet town of Cedar Springs, a bedroom community 30 miles from Austin, Texas, has spent the last seven years coming to grips with the incident that took the life of her partner and narrowly missed taking her own. The peace and quiet she had been enjoying is shattered by two seemingly unrelated murders in the same week: the first, a John Doe, and the second, a janitor at the local university.

As Brodie and her partner, Curtis Nicholls, begin their investigation, the assignment of a new trainee disrupts Brodie's life. Not only is Maggie Weston Brodie's former lover, but her father had been Brodie's commander at the Austin Police Department and nearly destroyed her career.

As the three detectives try to piece together the scattered evidence to solve the two murders, they become convinced the two murders are related. The discovery of a similar murder committed five years earlier at a small university in upstate New York creates a sense of urgency as they realize they are chasing a serial killer.

The already difficult case becomes even more so when a third victim is found. But the case becomes personal for Brodie when Maggie becomes the killer's next target. Unless Brodie finds a way to save Maggie, she could face losing everything a second time.

ISBN 978-1-935053-19-4-

Soiled Dove

In 1872, sixteen-year-old Loretta Digby fled her home in Indiana to escape an abusive step-father. Rescued from the streets of St. Joseph, Missouri by brothel owner Jack Coulter, she turns to the only work available. By twenty she became a much sought after prostitute catering to St. Jo's most influential men and dreaming of the day she can leave her past behind and start her life anew. Jack is enraged when he discovers his favorite employee's plan to leave. Bloody and beaten, Loretta is rescued by a young prostitute, Amelia Benson, and customer Reverend Cyrus Langford. Working with teacher, Hettie Tobias, who is traveling west for a teaching position in Trinidad, Colorado, Loretta and Amelia leave their former lives behind.

In the foothills of the Sangre de Cristo Mountains outside Trinidad, Clare McIlhenney has been struggling for years to make her father's dream of owning a cattle ranch in the west come true. Working with a few ranch hands and her foreman, Ino Valdez, Clare has slowly built the ranch over the last twenty years while overcoming everything that should have stopped her.

In the spring of 1876 Loretta and her friends arrive in the dusty Colorado town. Her first meeting with Clare McIlhenney is less than inspiring. When Clare is injured, over her strenuous objections, Ino hires Loretta as a temporary cook and housekeeper for the ranch. Over the next few months, Clare struggles with her unwanted attraction to the much younger woman, unable to forget the events of her past that led to the deaths of everyone she had been close to. Determined to never lose anyone else, Clare closed off her emotions and became a distant and disliked stranger to everyone around her.

Will Loretta be able to keep her past a secret and find a new life? Will Clare open herself up to loss yet again and put her own prejudices behind her? In a story of the struggles in a harsh and unforgiving time will the two women find peace at last?

ISBN 978-1-935053-35-4

The Other Mrs. Champion

Sarah Champion, 55, of Massachusetts, was leading the perfect life with Kelley, her partner and wife of twenty-five years. That is, until Kelley was struck down by an unexpected stroke away from home. But Sarah discovers she hadn't known her partner and lover as well as she thought.

Accompanied by Kelley's long-time friend and attorney, Sarah and her children rush to Vancouver, British Columbia to say their goodbyes, only to discover another woman, Pauline, keeping a vigil over Kelley in the hospital. Confronted by the fact that her wife also has a Canadian wife, Sarah struggles to find answers to resolve her emotional and personal turmoil.

Alone and lonely, Sarah turns to the only other person who knew Kelley as well as she did—Pauline Champion. Will the two women be able to forge a friendship despite their simmering animosity? Will their growing attraction eventually become Kelley's final gift to the women she loved?

ISBN 978-1-935053-46-0

OTHER QUEST PUBLICATIONS

About the Author

Originally from the Appalachian region of Eastern Tennessee, Brenda now lives in Central Texas, near Austin. She began writing in junior high school where she wrote an admittedly hokey western serial to entertain her friends. Completing her graduate studies in Eastern European history in 1971, she worked as a graphic artist, a public relations specialist for the military and a display advertising specialist until she finally had to admit that her mother might have been right and earned her teaching certification. For the last almost thirty years she has taught world history and political science. Brenda and her partner of sixteen years, Cheryl, are the parents of four occasionally grown children, as well as five grandchildren. Rounding out their home are three temperamental cats, a Poodle mix, and a Puggle puppy who snores like a freight train. She is looking forward to retirement sometime in the future. She may be contacted at adcockb10@yahoo.com and welcomes all comments.

VISIT US ONLINE AT
www.regalcrest.biz

At the Regal Crest Website You'll Find

- The latest news about forthcoming titles and new releases

- Our complete backlist of romance, mystery, thriller and adventure titles

- Information about your favorite authors

- Current bestsellers

- Media tearsheets to print and take with you when you shop

- Which books are also available as eBooks.

Regal Crest print titles are available from all progressive booksellers including numerous sources online. Our distributors are Bella Distribution and Ingram.

www.ingramcontent.com/pod-product-compliance
Lightning Source LLC
Chambersburg PA
CBHW050530260626
47157CB00004B/1540